He didn't think this investigation would be particularly dangerous, but in his line of work, you just never knew…

Joe said his goodbyes to his father and was pretty sure, as sure as he could be, that his father would fully recover and was in Pete's good hands. This short stay probably brought the family together better than anything else since Joe's mother died. They dropped him off at 3:30 p.m. right across the river in the City of Rensselaer, which now housed the Rensselaer Train Station, a mausoleum, costing over forty million dollars. It was built because they could. No other reason. It sat in the middle of the most needy small city in the State of New York.

Joe gave Tanya, and for the first time for Pete, a hug and a kiss and told them he loved them and would miss them. He took his bag and went through the front door. He turned around, waved, and wondered if he would ever see them again.

In every investigation he'd ever been in, someone had been hurt, or worse. He was lucky that he'd only been shot in the arm in the Mexican Mafia takedown. It could have been much, much worse. Only inches often separated life from death.

Retired Chief Petty Officer Tom Jones was murdered in his apartment complex in Orlando in what appeared to be a "drug deal gone bad." The police won't even do an autopsy on a dead drug dealer. Coast Guard Chief Warrant Officer Joe Traynor is asked by Tom's daughter to look into his death. His investigation ultimately leads to the largest meth case on the southeastern seaboard. In the meantime, the Russian Mafia, unhappy with being ripped off by Julie Chapman's father, seek revenge. Her father's death, once again, comes back to haunt her and her grandmother, Tillie, placing their lives—and Joe's—in danger.

KUDOS for *Can't Sing or Dance*

In *Can't Sing or Dance* by Daniel J. Barrett, Joe Traynor is back, this time trying to solve the murder of a friend and fellow Coastie, who the cops say is a drug dealer. Joe refuses to believe that his old mentor in the Coast Guard is a drug dealer and he is determined to clear the man's name. His investigation, however, uncovers something much more sinister than just "drug deal gone bad," and puts Joe's life, and those of his friends' in danger. *Can't Sing or Dance* is a good sequel to the first one in the series, Conch Town Girl. The author seems to be coming into his own, and his writing is much improved. The pace is much faster than in the first book. This book is a page turner and should hold your interest from beginning to end. ~ *Taylor Jones, Reviewer*

Can't Sing or Dance by Daniel J. Barrett is about a Tom Jones who is a retired Coast Guard officer and not the Tom Jones of Las Vegas fame, thus the title, *Can't Sing or Dance*. When Tom is murdered and the police say he was killing trying to sell drugs, his daughter calls Joe Traynor, now a chief warrant officer in the Coast Guard, to help clear his name. Since Tom was Joe's mentor when he first came into the Coast Guard, Joe is determined to prove that Tom was no drug dealer. But Joe is surprised by the can of worms his investigation uncovers. It takes a whole team of investigators, and some very high tech equipment, in two different states, for Joe to get to the bottom of the situation. The Russian Mafia also comes into play, still trying to exact vengeance on Joe's fiancée and her grandmother for the money Julie's father stole from them some 17 years earlier. So Joe has to come up with a way to get them to back off as well. *Can't Sing or Dance* is the second book in the *Conch Town Girl* series, and I have to admit that I was impressed with the author's improvement. This book is much more in the moment than the last one, much faster paced, and has a lot more action. It still has the home town community feel of the first book, but I found it much more riveting. The book has a ring of truth that tells me the author has either been in the Coast Guard, or did a tremendous amount of research. Either way, he seems to know what he's talking about. ~ *Regan Murphy, Reviewer*

ACKNOWLEDGEMENTS

To those many friends, who served as readers and advisors. Thank you to all. You are all greatly appreciated

Thank you to Black Opal Books for making this book possible. A special thanks to Lauri Wellington, Acquisitions Editor and to Faith for making Can't Sing or Dance the best that it can be. Your dedication and hard work is very much appreciated.

CAN'T SING OR DANCE

Large Print

Daniel J. Barrett

A Black Opal Books Publication

Black Opal Books

BECAUSE SOME STORIES JUST HAVE TO BE TOLD

GENRE: MYSTERY/SUSPENSE/NEW ADULT

This is a work of fiction. Names, places, characters and incidents are either the product of the author's imagination or are used fictitiously, and any resemblance to any actual persons, living or dead, businesses, organizations, events or locales is entirely coincidental.

DEDICATION

My wife Sandy and our children:
Sean, Eileen, and Ryan

CHAPTER 1

Coast Guard Chief Warrant Officer Joe Traynor walked into his office after lunch and was welcomed by the ringing of his phone. "Hello?"

"Hi, Joe. It's Claire Murphy."

"Hey, Claire. How are you?"

"I've got some bad news."

"What is it?"

"My father's dead," she said, her voice breaking. "I just had a phone call from a detective from the Orlando Police Department, Violent Crime Section. The detective's name is Jim Butler and he's stationed at police headquarters on South Hughey Avenue, in downtown. He said my father was involved in a drug deal that had gone bad. He said Dad was a drug dealer and was knifed to death in his apartment. They found a lot of cash—a roll of large bills that reeked of cocaine residue—and a bag of methamphetamine pills in between his mattress and box spring. My father's no drug dealer, Joe, and now he's dead," she sobbed. "That detective wants me to identify the body. Can you come up and go with me, please?"

Joe was stunned. "Slow down, Claire. I barely got the fact that Tom's dead. Where are you now?"

"I'm home" she said. "I didn't know who else to call. I knew you and Tom were close, so you were the first one I thought of. I've got a list of his other friends and I was going to call the rest after I found out what happened. I don't really *know* what happened and I don't know what to ask. I'm sure Brian doesn't either," she said. "Joe, can you help me? Can you come up and talk to the police? Something is wrong. My father wouldn't deal drugs but how do I prove that? Detective Butler was adamant and upset that he even had to deal with me. And that's just not right."

"I'll need permission to go to Orlando from my assignment at Islamorada as head of investigations for south Florida and the Florida Keys," Joe said. "It's about 2:00 p.m. now, and I have to run to a meeting at the Islamorada facility. I'll discuss the situation with Chief Warrant Officer, Jacob Cramer. I'll contact Detective Butler and, if necessary, meet you in Orlando as soon as I get permission from my line of command."

"Thanks, Joe. I really appreciate it. They aren't releasing the body for a while. Orlando's local morgue is backed up as it is. The detective said that with over 2,500 violent crimes a year in Orlando, Dad's death can wait in line. They aren't planning to do an in-depth autopsy for a dead drug dealer."

After Claire had hung up, Joe took a deep breath and called Mark Silva, his best friend and fellow Coastie, still stationed in Fort Lauderdale. Joe had to leave a message on the answering machine. He didn't expect to get Mark at home, and he didn't want to bother him at his office. It was Mark's day to be at the communications station headquarters, COMMSTA, in downtown Miami, for drug enforcement meetings with the feds and local law enforcement officers, up and down the Florida coast. Mark was one of the leaders of the task force.

"Mark, it's Joe," he told the answering machine. "Call me when you get a chance. It's important. Thanks."

Before his meeting with Jacob, Joe told Joan Talbot, his long-time friend and Jacob's administrative assistant, about Tom's death. She was horrified. She'd met Tom a few times after he retired when he'd visited the station with Joe.

"Joan, can you find out what Coast Guard facility is closest to Orlando because I want to be in on the potential investigation into Tom's death, if possible," Joe asked, hoping she could run interference for him on this. "I want to clear it through the chain of command." He was in charge of all investigations for south Florida and the Keys, but not for the northern section above Palm Beach. "I don't want to step on any toes, but I will if I have to."

"I'll look up the information right after the meeting," Joan said.

They had five investigations going on at the present time and Joe was the lead in each case. It would be difficult to add an investigation that was six hours north in Orlando, but if Joe didn't, no one else would.

Tom's death and classification as a drug dealer, if true, would certainly give the Coast Guard a black eye and Joe wanted to fix this situation before they simply closed the file on Tom's murder. Tom had retired from the Coast Guard in his early fifties, only a few years ago, and moved from Cape May to Orlando, to be near his daughter, Claire, and her family.

Joe thought about how to state his case to make it clear about the black eye. Police departments across the country were very reluctant to spend time and attention on investigating the death of a drug dealer. If Joe didn't clear this up fast, the investigation would stall. Tom and his family would be tainted. And so would the Coast Guard. Joe didn't believe Tom had anything to do with drugs. He also wanted to find out who killed him, and why. There had to be a reason. There was *always* a reason. Maybe not a good one, but something to point to the truth.

Joan walked down the hall to Joe's office. "Joe, I got your information for you. We've several command sites up and down the coast that aren't in our jurisdiction. However, all of those commands report directly to our own rear admiral here in Miami and then to the sector captain of the Jackson-ville port. The chief warrant officer at Station Port Canaveral, Frank Cortez, reports directly to Jack-sonville. I called the rear admiral's office and ex-plained the situation. He'll meet with you at 0800 hours tomorrow morning. He'd just heard about the situation and he's not pleased."

"Thanks, Joan."

Joe would probably be given all the time he needed because he was in charge of investigations, with a dual reporting system, first to the rear admi-ral in Miami and a dotted line to the Islamorada Chief Warrant Officer, Jacob Cramer. Joe went home to pack, not knowing how much time he'd need to at least clarify what had happened to Tom and what was needed from the Coast Guard, if any-thing.

Joe called Claire. "Hopefully, I'll be in Orlando no later than 3:00 p.m. tomorrow."

"Joe, don't get a hotel. You can stay with us."

"I wish I could do that, but until further notice, I have to remain neutral and take the investigation, if there's to be one, where it needs to go to find the truth," he said. "I'll call you when I arrive and then we should go directly to Tom's condo, if it isn't still roped off by the police. Then we can go to the police headquarters to meet the detective in charge. Then we'll go to the Medical Examiner's office and identify Tom's body if it's not too late in the day."

"Call me when you're getting close and I'll

5

leave early from the Hollywood Studios office and pick up the kids at daycare," Claire said.

Claire was younger than he was, Joe mused, and had a whole lot more responsibility. He didn't know if he could've handled the responsibility of a family. It was something he needed to discus with his girlfriend, Julie, before long.

Chapter 2

Joe called Julie that night and told her what had happened.

"Joe, I'm so sorry about Tom. Is there anything that I or Tillie can do for you?" Julie asked.

"Not now, but thanks." I'll keep you up to date when I know anything."

Joe left Key Largo at 5:00 a.m. and stopped to have coffee with Tillie, Julie's grandmother, who worked the breakfast shift at the Waffle House in Key Largo. She'd opened the doors every day at 5:00 a.m. for the last forty years. The manager came in right behind her but rarely ever beat her to the door. Joe walked into the Waffle House and received the same greeting from the same people that he'd met as a nineteen year old when he met both Tillie and Julie.

"Hi, Joe. How are you?" said the manager, Phil Nichols, now in his early seventies.

"Been better, Phil. Can I speak to Tillie, quickly? I have to head to Miami for a meeting."

"She's in the back. I'll go get her."

"Thanks. How about a quick coffee and a few cinnamon buns to go?"

"Coming right up."

"Hi, Joe, what's up?" Tillie asked as she came through the kitchen door with a stack of pancakes ready to go. "I saw you from the window overlooking the parking lot. Eat, Joe. You never know when you'll get another chance today. I saw you were all dressed up in your uniform and in a big rush. Where are you headed?"

"I only have a few minutes, Tillie, but let me tell you what's going on." He explained the situation and where he was going. "I'll keep you informed as best I can so you can relay messages to Julie if I can't get hold of her. I don't know the situation yet, but I'm sure it's not going to be pleasant."

"I'm really sorry about Tom, Joe. I know he meant a lot to you. Does Joan know yet? Does Julie?"

"Yes, in both cases. I called Julie late last night and Joan set up the meeting that I'm heading to with the rear admiral. If I'm to clear Tom's name— if that's the case, and I'm not really sure at this point—I'll be spending a lot of time away from Key Largo. If you need anything, please call Joan and she'll take care of it if she can. I'll try to keep in touch with Julie."

"I know you will. Please be careful, Joe. I know how you are now after the last case. I'm also well aware of what you're capable of, after sitting down with Mark as he explained what you had to do back in Albany with the gangbangers."

"I won't be alone, Tillie. I'm picking up Mark when I get the go ahead from the rear admiral. Mark is packed and ready to go as well. I have to meet him up at his Dania Beach office as soon as I can. Wish us luck. We're going to need it."

With that said, he choked down his third pancake in less than five minutes, left ten dollars on the counter, grabbed his bag of cinnamon rolls, and ran out the door.

છ૭છ૭

The District Commander, Rear Admiral, Jake Barnes, had his office at the District 7 headquarters in the Brickell Plaza Building located on South East First Avenue in Miami. It was fifty-eight miles door to door from downtown Key Largo to the federal building in downtown Miami.

Joe had hoped that traffic would be light getting out of the Keys at that early hour and he was right. He went right up Overseas Highway, which was U.S. Route 1 North, to Florida Route 5. He merged onto 821 N, the Florida Turnpike, for seventeen miles toward the Miami International Airport. From there, traffic started picking up on the Don Shula Expressway toward Fl-826 Miami. If he made a wrong turn at that time of day, he was screwed. So, he took Fl-878 E toward South Miami back to US 1. The Dixie Highway, which was also

US 1, dumped him right on I-95 N, taking Exit 1B, bringing him to Brickell Avenue. He drove the one-mile distance right to the Brickell Plaza Federal Building and parked in the Coast Guard lot.

Driving his government car saved a lot of explaining. He flashed his ID and badge and headed to the rear admiral's office. It was 7:30 a.m. He had time to hit the head and maybe get another coffee. He'd eaten some of the rolls in the car so he felt awake enough not to make a fool out of himself in front of the high command. Joe was known for speaking his mind, but he wanted to control it today. He wanted to be placed in charge of any investigation that involved Tom Jones. Hitting the head and washing his face with cold water would set him in the right mood. He believed that the rear admiral wanted the same thing that he wanted—justice and the truth, wherever that led.

Joe was shown to the rear admiral's office by his assistant. As Joe walked through the door, the rear admiral stretched out his hand. "Hi, Joe. How are you? I wish this meeting could be under different circumstances."

"Yes, sir, I wish it could be as well."

Already in the room, sitting at the conference table, were several officers with higher pay grades than Joe. Somehow, that seemed to calm him. He believed they were gathered to plan what they should, or even could, do regarding the situation. Joe outlined what Tom's daughter had told him over the phone. At this point, he didn't have much information but he wanted to at least tell the assembled officers what Tom represented and what he meant to Joe personally and to all those others that he'd faithfully trained over the years.

"I don't believe that Tom was a drug dealer," he declared emphatically. "And if I don't get there fast, the Orlando detective in charge of the investigation will close it down because, as he told Claire, 'they don't waste resources on drug dealers.'"

Throughout Joe's impassioned presentation, Rear Admiral Barnes never said a word. There were several questions from the other officers and Joe handled those without hesitation. He was trained for these occasions. He finished by saying, "If the evidence points to Tom's involvement with drugs, I'll bring it to a swift conclusion and let the chips fall where they may, if I'm given the assignment."

Joe had never met the rear admiral as he'd only been back in the Coast Guard for the second time for only a few months. Joe *had* spoken to him on the phone when he was offered his current assignment in Islamorada. Joe had left the service several years ago to get his MBA from Rensselaer and to go to work back in Albany. He knew that the rear admiral was well aware of his background and that Joe had been presented with the second highest award offered by the Coast Guard for valor in a noncombat situation for his part in breaking up the

Mexican Mafia drug and money-laundering ring back in Albany.

The rear admiral told the gathered staff that Joe had received the US Coast Guard Commendation Medal with a Ribbon. "It's the highest award issued for heroism, not involving combat with an enemy outside the country, by the United States Coast Guard."

The assembled group clapped and Joe felt embarrassed.

"Joe, if that was what it took to get you back, we should have done it earlier." The rear admiral smiled. "You've got our full cooperation in this matter. I'll call the captain of the port up in Jacksonville and the chief warrant officer at the Coast Guard Station in Port Canaveral. It's the closest field office we have. Frank Cortez is in charge and he's a good man. He'll be of great assistance. I also believe we need to free up Mark Silva as well. Is that correct?"

"Yes, sir. Mark and I've been a team forever and we need each other to get to the bottom of this. Will you also call the Orlando Chief of Police to let him know that we will be looking into this, not to whitewash it, but to seek the truth? That would be appreciated. I believe that the detective in charge, Jim Butler, won't be happy. He even told Claire, Tom's daughter, that there would be no in-depth autopsy because Tom was a dead drug dealer, but she'd still have to identify his body."

The rear admiral nodded. "If this investigation goes federal let me know," he said. "If you find drugs or any other circumstances that would involve crossing state lines, it's Homeland Security and the FBI's case. We're part of that so you would wear your federal hat as well. Good luck, Joe. Let us know what you need once you get there."

"Thank you, sir. This means a lot to both Mark and me. We won't let you down, sir."

CHAPTER 3

Joe thanked everyone at the meeting, especially the rear admiral, for allowing him the opportunity to hopefully clear Tom's name, if that was the case.

When he hopped into his car after the meeting, it was already 10:00 a.m. He didn't realize how long the meeting had lasted, but it had gone well, and that was all that mattered. Before heading out, he called Mark and told him that he'd pick him up just before 11:00 a.m. at his office in Dania Beach. Joe got back on I-95N and headed to Fort Lauderdale and to the Dania Beach station. He pulled up just about ten minutes to 11:00 a.m.

Mark was sitting on the front steps of the facility. His bags were packed and he was ready to go. He and Joe had been doing this together for a long time and he knew exactly what to bring, the weapons required, and his credentials, including his US Coast Guard, Homeland Security, and FBI liaison credentials—just in case there were any federal-versus-state issues.

When Joe'd rejoined the Coast Guard only a

few short months ago, he was assigned to work with Mark, since they'd previously been the premier drug-enforcement-investigation-and-take-down team in Florida and the Keys. Mark had taught Joe not only to speak fluent Spanish, but he also gave him all the Mexican infused dialect and street smarts needed to do the job. In turn, Joe gave Mark credibility and helped him with the higher-education components that Mark so desperately needed.

Mark had joined the Coast Guard at age twenty-seven, the oldest age you could be for entering any military service. He was a gangbanger from San Diego and had had his last run in with the law. It was join the service—any service—or a minimum of two years in jail for assault. Mark turned his life around, married, and had two remarkable children, one of which was Joe's goddaughter, Jennifer.

The combined talents of Joe and Mark became even more valuable as Joe became fluent in Russian as well as Spanish and, together, they were able to stop a Cuban-Russian Mafia connection before it took off. All of Florida, including the Keys, was now a Russian drug-and-money-laundering empire in partnership with the Cubans, both in Florida and on the island of Cuba, itself.

Mark was antsy. "Hey, Joe, right on time."

"Traffic up 95N was okay. There were no major holdups," Joe said. Major highways in south Florida were either smooth sailing or the world's largest parking lot, depending on the weather, day of the week, and time of day. "I still have a few buns I picked up on the way. Are you hungry?"

Mark knew, just as Joe did, that you ate when you could, slept when you could, and took advantage of every opportunity for rest because you never knew what the day would bring. He grabbed the bag, and opened a bottle of water he had on him. "Let's go. What're you waiting for?"

Joe just stared at him and grinned. Nothing ever changed, not in almost fifteen years. Joe drove the 185 miles in just under three hours, pulling into the station at Port Canaveral to meet the Chief Warrant Officer, Frank Cortez. It was almost 2:00 p.m. and Joe only wanted to make a quick stop and then head to Orlando to meet Tom's daughter, look around the apartment, and then go to police headquarters to meet the detective in charge of the investigation, Jim Butler.

Joe and Mark ran up the stairs and headed toward Frank's office. Frank was waiting for them and he couldn't have been a nicer guy. Joe hoped Frank had more than niceness going for him and, after a short conversation, was well aware of what Frank thought about what happened to Tom.

Joe hadn't realized that Frank had also trained under Tom many years earlier. Frank was a few years older than Joe, but younger than Mark, and he was every bit as well-trained as both of them. He'd faced danger many times but he was also well aware that Joe and Mark faced it every day, under more trying circumstances.

"Since we're only about fifty miles away, you should get going. I'll follow and assist you for the day," Frank suggested. "We will have an office set up with the technology required to do any investigations from the Port Canaveral site. I'd like to take credit for the fast service but I got a personal call from the rear admiral and my own boss in Jacksonville, telling me to fully cooperate."

It was clear to Joe and Mark that Frank's cooperation was already there. Joe set the GPS for Tom's address. They took Fl-528W to Fl-417N for fifty-two miles, headed to South Primrose Drive in Orlando to meet Claire and go through the condo that Tom had called home for the last several years.

Joe knew that it would be tough for Claire to go through Tom's things but Frank volunteered to stay with her outside and get as much information as he could while Mark and Joe went quickly through the condo.

The drive took almost an hour and they arrived at Tom's front door a little after 3:00 p.m. Claire was already parked on the street. She had her two children with her.

He pulled up right behind her and then Frank drove around them and parked a few spots down the street. Claire opened her door, just as Joe got to her car, and gave him a big hug.

"Thanks for coming, Joe. I really appreciate it,

especially on such short notice."

"No problem, Claire. You know Mark, and this is Frank Cortez who'll be helping us out."

"Nice to see you again, Mark. It's a pleasure to meet you, Frank," Claire said. "Thank you both for coming with Joe. I can't thank you enough. This is all too much for me, especially with the kids and my job."

Mark stood by the side of the car and waved, letting Joe handle the emotional scene. After a few minutes, Claire composed herself and Joe said hello to the kids.

She handed Joe the key. "I'll wait for you to finish."

"That's not necessary at this point but give Frank as much information about Tom's case as you can," Joe told her. "Get the kids home and then meet us at the police station to see if we can identify the body. If it's too late in the day, then we can do it in the morning."

"I still have to go to work tomorrow to let my boss know what happened to Dad and ask for bereavement time off. I don't see any problem but I want to get it done the first thing in the morning, so identifying him this afternoon would be better."

"Okay," Joe said. "We will meet Jim Butler as soon as we finish at the condo. We will meet you at the station. After the identification, I'll bring you back to the station and then go look for a hotel close by. As soon as we find a place to stay, I'll call you and let you know what's really going on and what I can tell you officially." He grimaced. "It's not my investigation yet and I can't make any promises."

"I understand, Joe," she said. "I'm just glad you're here."

"I'll get the key back to you tomorrow, after I make a copy of it."

She left in the car with the kids, saying she would meet him at the station.

✂✂✂

Joe opened Tom's front door. The living room smelled of death. It was the smell of iron in the blood that never seemed to go way. There was a big spot on the living room floor where the impression of Tom's body was, or so Joe believed. He was surprised that there was no taped off areas outside or even inside the condo. He turned to Mark and Frank and they all seemed to have thought the same thing at the same time.

They were trained to go through rooms quickly and efficiently. They had their investigation kits with them. They'd put on gloves even before entering the home but they also didn't want to raise any eyebrows from the neighbors or those walking up and down the street. This was to remain quiet for as long as possible. If the media got a hold of what they were really looking for, it could blow up in their faces. Joe could read the headlines now. *COAST GUARD COVER UP OF DRUG DEAL GONE BAD.*

There were only five rooms to look through, including the living room, kitchen with eating area, two bedrooms, and one bathroom. Joe immediately went to Tom's bedroom, since he'd been there before and knew which was Tom's and Mark and Frank didn't. Joe went over the entire bedroom with a fine-tooth comb. They weren't checking for hairs at this point because if the investigation was done properly, the police would have already gathered evidence. Joe flipped the mattress and box spring against the wall and looked under the bed. Against the wall at the foot of the headboard was a pill jammed between the wall, the headboard, and the carpet.

Joe left the pill right where it was and took a photo of it from several positions. "Frank, Mark, come here, now."

"What's up?" both of them said in unison.

Joe showed them the pill. "What's that look like?"

Frank had no clue.

"Is it meth?" Mark asked immediately.

"Yes, it's meth but look at it closely." Joe showed him the pictures taken by his phone as well as having him get down on his knees, like Joe had, to inspect it personally.

Mark looked and then Frank looked, but Frank

admitted he didn't have a clue.

"I've seen this type of pill before, but I don't remember where or when," Mark said.

Joe was known for his photographic memory. "We had a takedown seven years ago, in the fall of 2007, I believe, outside Miami," he told Mark. "This pill and those we took in the seizure that day had 'TN' printed on one side. Those, gentlemen, looked exactly like this one on the floor, and it stands for 'The Nations' which is the poorest section of Nashville, Tennessee. It's a marketing ploy. If anyone wanted a 'TN' meth pill, it had to have the 'TN' on it or it was not the real meth deal. Most people believed it stood for Tennessee but it really stood for 'The Nations.'"

Joe frowned. "What we have here, regardless if Tom was a drug dealer or not, is a federal crime not a state crime because this drug was taken and sold across state lines. When we go to police headquarters, let's see if we can get a comparison to what the cops found under the mattress that they told Claire about, accusing Tom of dealing drugs. In any case, it's now federal."

Joe took out a pair of tweezers and placed the pill in an evidence bag. "Let's head out right now and see if we can catch Detective Butler before he goes home. Claire is meeting us at the station and we can go identify Tom's body, hopefully."

They all hopped in Joe's car. Frank left his where it was. It was only a few miles to police headquarters and they got there in ten minutes, despite the late afternoon traffic. They parked around the corner from the station and Joe fed the meter. He always carried a roll of quarters with him to avoid situations that needed further explanation like, "Who do you think you are, parking in an official spot?" They headed up the stairs, went to the front desk and asked to speak with Detective Jim Butler.

Claire was already sitting on the front bench, waiting for him. She never said a word to anyone about why she was there. The desk sergeant asked Joe what it was about and Joe gave him the briefest explanation possible. The sergeant told them to wait on the bench at the front of the facility and someone would meet them there.

Joe sat next to Claire and smiled at her. He took her hand and said he was there for her. They all were.

They waited almost twenty minutes, and finally, the desk sergeant pointed them to the detective section down the hall.

On the frosted window next to the door, the sign read *Orlando Police Department, Violent Crime Section*. Joe guessed that at least they were headed in the right direction.

ဢၘဢ

Butler greeted Joe, Mark, and Frank as soon as

they walked through the door. "Why are you here?" he asked immediately. "Who's this woman?"

Butler appeared to be in his late forties, wearing a rumpled suit with a loosened tie hanging from his unbuttoned short-sleeved shirt. He was tall, about six-feet-three, and well over 250 pounds. His nose was a little red, as were his eyes. Joe thought he might be hanging on by a thread, so he'd better not antagonize him—yet.

"Is there some place we can talk?" Joe asked.

"I don't have a lot of time. What's this about?"

"It's about the Tom Jones's murder."

Both Frank and Mark stared at the detective, looking for any reaction whatsoever. The reaction was not pleasant. Joe introduced Claire as Tom's daughter to whom Butler had spoken on the phone. At least the detective told her that he was sorry for her loss, but that was it.

"Why are you interested in a dead drug dealer?" Butler demanded. "Just because he was in the Coast Guard? Isn't that great? Don't you guys have anything better to do?"

"We didn't come here to argue with you," Joe said. "But we'd like to understand where you're going with this and see if we can be of any assistance."

"I don't need any help with a dead drug dealer. We're closing the case. We don't have time to waste. I got enough shit to do without worrying about a bunch of fucking sailors in my face."

Joe looked at Claire's face and got really pissed off at the pain he saw there. "When will the official autopsy be held? And when can we go to the Medical Examiner's Office to identify the body?"

"You can go anytime you want," the detective said. "I'm not going with you as there's no in-depth autopsy scheduled."

Joe was now infuriated, especially after looking at the tears pouring down Claire's face. *How can anyone be such an asshole*? "Do you have to practice or does being a moron come naturally to you?" he snarled.

With that, the detective grabbed Joe by the arm and jerked him closer to him.

Joe stared at him and then looked down at his arm. "Do you really want assaulting a federal officer in your jacket?" he growled. "You look like you've got more than enough going on to worry about." He then removed Butler's fingers from his arm.

"What do you mean? What federal officers? All I see is a bunch of over-dressed pussies," Butler scoffed.

Joe could barely contain himself. *Thank God I left my gun in the car*. He flashed his FBI and Homeland Security credentials. "Guys, I tried, but this officer won't cooperate. So we're heading to his chief's office, and we will see what cooperation we get there."

Mark and Frank shook their heads and smiled.

"Pissing off Joe was really not your best move," Mark told the detective.

They turned around and went directly to the chief's office, leaving a stunned Butler staring after them. The chief was holding a meeting. Joe opened the door and asked if he could speak to him for a minute.

The chief was flustered but composed himself quickly. "What's going on?"

Joe gave him the short version. "Did the rear admiral call you?"

"Yes."

"You'd better talk to your detective before he gets arrested," Joe told him.

The chief called Butler, told him to get to his office immediately, and then dismissed those attending the meeting that Joe had interrupted.

Detective Butler sauntered into the chief's office and sat down.

The chief shook his head. "What's going on, Detective?"

"I'm wrapping up the case," Butler said.

As soon as he said that, Joe threw his evidence bag down on the table in front of the detective.

"What the hell is this?" Butler demanded.

"Evidence, physical evidence, taken from the condo just an hour ago. Both you and your team overlooked it. That is, if you even looked for any other evidence after finding the money and drugs. Chief, this is now a federal investigation because as you can see this pill is labeled 'TN' and stands for 'The Nations,' that part of Nashville where these drugs are made. That's a federal crime, as the pill's crossed state lines. We could sure use your help. But closing a case because you don't give a shit doesn't prove anything. Your detective here didn't even schedule an in-depth autopsy for a murder victim. We aren't here to clear Tom Jones if he dealt drugs, but he *was* murdered and that was, apparently, in connection with a federal crime. And when the culprit is found, it can mean the death penalty."

Joe then turned to Detective Butler. "We need your help. You've the experience and knowledge of the Orlando area, but I'd expect much more than you've shown. Calling it in, the way you did, doesn't really help. Not being polite to Claire Murphy only made the situation worse. Being totally unprofessional didn't help either."

The chief glared at the detective. "Well, you were supposedly in charge of this case, but I'm not happy with your work. You can help these men solve this crime, or you can find your ass out the door. Am I making myself perfectly clear, Detective?"

"Yes, sir. You're very clear. I'm sorry about this and I'd very much like to get another chance to see it through."

Butler seemed taken aback by the direct statement from his superior officer. He turned to Joe.

"As soon as we're finished here, I'll drive you to the ME's office and then schedule an immediate in-depth autopsy if possible, maybe tomorrow morning. We can meet briefly now and they'll wait for us at the ME's office. It's only five minutes from here."

"We've no problem with your detective, Chief," Joe stated. "That is, if he meant what he just said. We aren't familiar with the territory here but we've all the technology, equipment, and access to find those responsible for this crime." He turned back to the detective. "We'd welcome you aboard if you would do the same."

"I will," Butler agreed.

With that, the chief shook their hands. Joe turned to Butler and shook his hand as well.

Butler nodded. "Let's get to work." He took the three men and Claire to a small conference room down the hall from the chief's office. "Can I get you guys and ma'am anything, before we start?"

"No. We're fine," Joe said.

Mark, Claire, and Frank said "No" as well.

Joe turned to Claire. "Are you ready to identify your father's body?"

"Yes."

"You don't have to attend the autopsy. Detective Butler and I will be there for the entire procedure."

Claire decided to sit in the waiting room and collect her composure while Joe and the others met with Butler. Identifying the body would be the hardest thing she ever had to go through, other than the birth of her children. She was grateful that Joe was there. She didn't know what she'd have done without him.

"I'll be right back with the evidence that we've already collected at the scene," Butler said and headed out the door to the evidence room, which was under lock and key.

Claire left the room and Joe turned to Mark and Frank. "The pills better match or we're in deep crap," he whispered.

Both men nodded.

"We'd better get a game plan started," Joe added. "But I'm totally unsure of where we are at this point,"

Frank and Mark said they didn't know either.

Joe decided that as soon as the meeting broke up, and after he and Claire had identified Tom's body, he would call the rear admiral and explain the circumstances and where they stood. He'd then call Joan at the Islamorada office and let her know that he'd be in Orlando for a while and, once again, ask her to keep an eye on Tillie while Julie was away.

Julie wouldn't be back from her New York City book-signing tour for another few weeks. Joe had been going to meet her for the weekend coming up but that was out of the question now.

He had just turned nineteen when he'd met Julie

and Tillie. They'd bonded for life. Both of Julie's parents had died suddenly, and under very trying circumstances. Julie had lived with her grandmother since she was a child, until last summer when Tillie sold her home of over forty years and moved into a brand new senior apartment complex. It was only a short distance from her old house in Key Largo.

Julie had just sold her first novel, after graduating from Brown University, and had just survived her first year in the Monroe County School District as a teacher's aide, while completing her book. She was now traveling on the road for book signing events before school reopened.

When she went back to her school district position in the fall, she'd have to decide if she wanted to live with Tillie once again, get her own place, or move in with Joe her now-official significant other. It took a lot of convincing for Joe to move from being her best friend and surrogate brother, to this new romantic relationship. The nine years' age difference—at ages nineteen and ten—had been huge, but now with Joe at age thirty-three and Julie at age twenty-four, it was insignificant. Julie had loved Joe since the day they'd met. He finally admitted that he felt the same way but was reluctant to discuss it with Julie because of the age difference. Now, he realized how much she'd always meant to him. Tillie was also like his second mother, especially after Joe's own mother died of breast cancer only a few short years ago.

If everything continued the way it was going, Tillie would be Joe's grandmother-in-law—he smiled—if there was such a thing.

Butler came back with a sealed bag and the murder book, where all the investigative data was kept. The book was in good shape, in spite of the deep-six Tom's murder had received by the lead detective and his fellow officers. Joe, Mark, and Frank signed off with the date and time for the review. Everyone put on gloves, and Joe immediately went to the evidence bag. He emptied the contents onto the table. There were a few odd hairs and a brush from the bathroom in order to eliminate Tom's hair from any others they found. Joe assumed that Tom's daughter, her husband, and the kids would have to be eliminated as well.

The bag contained the cocaine-laden money and the white pills. There was $1,500.00 in hundred dollar bills and a large handful of white, round pills. Joe counted the pills and they added up to enough for a felony conviction. Joe inspected the pills, individually, and then handed each one to Frank and Mark for further inspection.

"They all have the 'TN' trademark embedded into each pill," Butler said.

Thank God. Both Frank and Mark nodded in agreement and the detective was handed back the bag for his inspection.

"It looks like all the pills here match the pill you

found in the bedroom and each one has the 'TN' label," Butler agreed. "Either Tom was a drug dealer or he was completely set up by someone. But why?"

Joe studied Butler. "Tom was a drill sergeant first and foremost. He was our friend but he could be a royal pain in the ass. He had to have done something to piss someone off enough to kill him. This didn't just happen by random. Tom was big time into electronics and technology since he retired from the Coast Guard. The last time I was here, he showed me his state-of-the-art computer, iPhone, and iPad. All were hooked up to a wireless connection and all his data was stored in a 'cloud.' When we quickly went through his condo, I didn't see any of those items. Did you see them and put the items into evidence bags?"

"All we seized is right in front of you. As a matter of fact, we didn't see any of those items, either. In any case, finding the equipment could go a long way in finding out what happened. I want to go back with my evidence team tomorrow morning and start the search over for the entire condo, looking for those items as well. In the meantime, if he had what you said he had, I'll get a subpoena for his providers for phone and Internet service for the records. I'll have the subpoena by tomorrow morning. I'll call the judge right now and stop by his office before we go to the condo tomorrow. Is that good with you guys?"

31

"Thanks for your cooperation, Jim," Joe said. "It's appreciated."

ɔɔɔ

It was not inconceivable that Tom had been a drug dealer. Joe and Mark both knew him extremely well—Frank to a lesser degree—but they all knew that everyone had a dark side now and then. It was very easy to get hooked on meth and then pay for the habit by selling the drug as well. Regardless of one's status in life, everyday someone got hooked on meth, including people like Furgy, of the Black Eyed Peas; Elvis Presley; Charlie Parker; Judy Garland; Charles Manson; Eddie Van Halen; Robert Downey, Jr.; and the biggest of all, Rush Limbaugh. Some came back from a great fall in status. Others simply died a tragic death. Butler wasn't completely wrong about that, but he'd let his personal bias get in the way of this investigation and it got away from him. At the end of the day, there was still someone who'd been murdered, regardless of the circumstances.

The meeting only lasted a half hour. Joe, Claire, Mark, and Frank all hopped into Butler's police car and drove to the ME's office to identify Tom. The detective was right. It was less than three miles, door to door. They got out, went up the stairs and met with the chief ME. At least he was not condescending to Claire.

32

The doctor reached out for her hand. "I'm so sorry for your loss."

He then walked Joe and Claire down the hall for the identification. Mark, Frank, and Butler stayed behind. Butler looked like a deer caught in the headlights, after his dressing down by his chief. So neither Mark or Frank told him what a jerk he was. They suspected he already knew and was trying to make up for it. "The proof was in the pudding," as the old saying went.

Joe took Claire's hand. He wished that her husband Brian was here but he's stayed home to watch the kids, feed them, and get them to bed on time. That was a hell of a lot harder for Joe than doing this. Of course, this was Claire's first time so she didn't know what was coming. Joe had done this a lot in the last fifteen years, more than he cared to remember.

⋐⋑⋐⋑

While they were gone, Mark told Butler that there was much more to Joe than appeared on the surface. He explained to Butler quietly, with Frank listening in, exactly what came down in Albany and just recently in Key Largo, not including all the drug runners they'd brought to justice.

Butler's eyes went wide. "I'd have never guessed that in a million years."

Perhaps, this was the turning point Butler needed.

The doctor opened the door to the morgue, went to the drawer, and pulled Tom's body out. It was covered with a sheet from head to toe. The doctor looked at Claire. "Are you ready?"

"Not really. How could I be?" she said then nodded. "Let's do it, though."

Joe nodded as well. The doctor pulled down the sheet. Claire began to cry and nodded to confirm that it was her father.

"You have to give me a verbal response and then sign the identification paperwork," the doctor said.

Claire gathered herself. "That's my father, Thomas Jones."

She fell into Joe's arms. He held her up, brought her over to the closest desk, and had her sit down to sign the papers. She signed, and Joe did as well. Then he took her to the door and asked Mark and Frank to help her to the car.

Joe turned to the doctor. "Can I get a closer look at Tom's body?"

"Are you all right," the doctor asked him, but his eyes said everything.

Joe wasn't crying. He was mad. He looked closely at Tom and saw the welts on his face and the marks where the knife had penetrated his heart. He counted three jagged cuts. It looked as if the wounds were made by a serrated blade. Tom had defensive wounds on his arms, hands, and on two of the fingers on his right hand. Tom was right-handed. Joe knew this since he watched people closely. "Can you do the autopsy as early as possible tomorrow?"

The doctor scheduled it for 7:00 a.m. Joe left the morgue, hopped into the car, and they headed back to the station. Joe would bring Frank back to his car parked at Tom's place. First, Joe walked Claire to her car. "Are you okay?"

"As good as can be expected I guess."

Joe said he'd call her later and let her know if he had any news. He'd tell her what he was allowed to. "There's no question that your father was not a drug dealer and was a victim of a crime," he said, trying to comfort her. "I can't sugarcoat why Tom was a victim but I'll try get to the bottom of this. He might have been in the wrong place at the wrong time or even brought it upon himself."

Again, she hugged him, said thanks, and headed home.

CHAPTER 4

Frank had to leave and get back to Port Canaveral. Joe and Mark had to find a hotel near the police headquarters and then he had to call Claire to let her know what had happened with Butler after she went outside. As soon as they headed for the car, Joe called the rear admiral's office and set up a conference call for 6:00 p.m. to let him and his staff know what was going on. Mark drove Frank back to his car, which was parked outside of Tom's condo.

"I'll make as much time as you need," Frank said. "I can be helpful from my own office, especially with the connection to the Coast Guard investigative unit up in Virginia. Whatever you need, I'll make it a priority."

It was especially helpful having Jack Forest, one of Joe and Mark's closest friends, in charge of the Virginia intelligence facility. Jack could also be counted on for anything they needed. He'd been extremely helpful in two other situations, the first when Joe was back in Albany and needed to identify members of the Mexican Mafia, and second, back in Key Largo, when his analysis helped identify Julie's father as being still alive after it was thought he'd drowned seventeen years earlier.

Joe used his iPad to look up hotels close to police headquarters. There were three possibilities in the downtown area, only a few blocks away. Joe called the Embassy Suites, located less than a mile away, on East Pine Street, in downtown. He got a room for Mark and himself at a government rate, which included breakfast and two queen size beds. They had a living-room area where they could spread out their equipment to continue the investigation. The room was $148.00 a night for both and had WiFi included. They could leave their car in the garage, when not in use, and walk the mile to the police department in less than fifteen minutes. After dropping Frank off, they parked near Tom's condo. Joe wanted to go back in for one last look before checking into the hotel and having the telephone conference call with the rear admiral.

Joe opened the door one more time and he and Mark looked around. Mark went to Tom's bedroom and Joe checked the rest. It was the reverse of the afternoon's investigation when Joe found the one pill that made all the difference. Once again, they didn't find Tom's computer, phone, or iPad. However, a cable wire was still connected under Tom's desk, which had probably held his computer connection. The WiFi box, connected to the cable, was left dangling off the end, proving that there had been a hookup. Mark found the chargers for the iPhone and iPad in Tom's bedside table drawer.

Well, I guess we weren't crazy and those items are really missing, but why?

It just reconfirmed in Joe's mind that Tom had put his nose in where it didn't belonged and something had happened to him. Hell, it was Tom who'd pounded into Joe's head many years ago that everything happened for a reason. There had to be a reason for his death. This was no home invasion.

Mark came out of the bedroom and handed Joe some monthly bills that were just recently paid by Tom. The monthly condo payment included the Time Warner payment for cable television, phone, and Internet service as part of the rental agreement. Mark also found Tom's checkbook in his top drawer where he kept his checks and folders with his other paid bills. They were separated in folders by months and there was a cover sheet that listed all the bills he had monthly, and when they were paid. Tom was remarkable when it came to keeping his life in order. That was why this was so puzzling.

Tom, a drug dealer? No way. If Tom was a drug dealer, he'd probably have all his damn customers in alphabetical order with the size of the purchase and dollars received year to date. He was that anal. More anal than me.

"Enough for today, Mark. My tiny little mind can't take any more. Let's head to the hotel, make the call, and then go to dinner. Later, we can make a list of what we need to do and check to move forward."

"Sounds like a plan," Mark agreed.

They checked in and called the rear admiral right on the dot at 6:00 p.m. He was pleased that Joe and Mark had found the one piece of evidence needed to move this forward as a federal case. Joe promised him daily updates as best as he could and hung up.

They went to dinner around the corner and then headed back to the hotel to call Mark's wife and kids. Joe called Julie but she was out. Her trips were getting frustrating because he could never seem to get hold of her. He wasn't complaining. He was just a little frustrated. He wound up calling Joan, who'd in turn call Tillie, and she'd tell Julie as Julie called Tillie every night.

Perhaps that was best. They were moving pretty fast for only being together for a short time. The distance apart was a blessing, but not always. They were just learning to be with each other as a couple and not as friends. Joe liked both, but he was in love with her and not just a friend, and he hoped she felt the same way. It had taken him long enough to realize that he loved her in a romantic way.

After getting back to their room at the Embassy Suites Hotel, Joe and Mark started a list of things to do for the next day. It finally hit Joe that they went through Tom's condo but they never thought to look for his Ford Explorer. Where was it?

Joe immediately called Claire. "Do you know where Tom's SUV is located?"

"It's probably still in the parking lot right behind my father's condo," she said.

Talk about messing up.

"We exchanged cars every few days and his Explorer has two car seats in the back for the kids, identical to what I have in my car," Claire continued. "He never kept his house key on his car key ring and I never thought about the vehicle when I met you at the condo. On the days that he babysat, so that I could work full time, we simply switched vehicles, if the kids were asleep in the back."

"I didn't see any keys when I was searching the condo, so maybe whoever killed him, took the keys with them."

"I've my own set with the fob automatic car opener and I'll drop it off at the hotel early in the morning on my way to work, tomorrow," Claire said.

Joe thanked her and was actually quite embarrassed. *How could we've overlooked something as obvious as a big Ford Explorer? Well, at least the cops didn't think about it either.* Though that didn't make him any happier.

Joe was even less happy when Claire told him that Tom had a girlfriend living in the same complex as well. "I should have said something but I was still in shock over Dad's death. I don't even know if Gladys even knows about his death. I think she's been out of town, visiting relatives, and won't be home until the end of the week. At least that's what Dad told me the last time we spoke before he died."

"Gladys who?"

"Gladys Fenton. She's the same age as Dad and just retired as a third grade elementary school teacher at a school right around the corner. She continues to volunteer after she retired and she and Dad have only been seeing each other for about six months."

Again, Joe was embarrassed. This was not his finest hour. *What else didn't I know about the man? It could probably fill a book. A call once a month over the last few years, with a visit now and then, was really inadequate if we were good friends.*

Joe would have to put that into the back of his mind in dealing with the case.

"I'll call Gladys' cell phone, let her know about Dad, and tell her to expect you to stop by to talk to her tomorrow," Claire said. She gave Joe the phone number and address and emailed a picture of Gladys and Tom together so he'd know what she looked like. She was fifty-five years old, very nice looking, and they seemed happy in the picture. Joe shook his head one more time.

Don't screw up anymore, he thought.

She'd be back in Orlando tomorrow so he'd better drop by to see her.

CHAPTER 5

Mark and Joe got an early start the next day. First, they'd be at the ME's autopsy at 7:00 a.m. and they expected that an hour and a half would be sufficient to see if any new evidence turned up. There could be DNA under Tom's fingernails, if his defensive efforts included grabbing at the murderer. Joe wanted to be sure that, if there was DNA evidence, the perpetrator wasn't someone that Tom knew. But he just wouldn't let someone into his home without knowing the person. At least, Joe hoped so.

They were meeting Butler and his evidence team at Tom's condo at 8:30 a.m. Joe had given Butler the house key the previous day because the detective would be there earlier than Joe, while he and Mark were at the morgue.

Joe spoke to Butler before they left. "I'll pick up coffee and donuts on the way for the team and be there after the autopsy around 8:30 a.m.," he said.

Butler thanked them. "We're on our way."

Joe stopped at the desk and got Tom's Explorer keys left by Claire on her way to work. They headed to the morgue and arrived just in time for Joe to dress in his medical gear, just like the doctor. Mark went out to make some calls to update everyone while Joe watched everything going on in the autopsy very closely, in case there were any new revelations. Just as he'd thought, the cuts were from a serrated knife. There were three deep wounds to the chest that appeared to be placed at an angle, suggesting that Tom was lying down after first being struck in the face with a blunt instrument or even a hard fist. At least that's what both the doctor and Joe concluded. There were defensive cuts on Tom's arms and right hand, but there didn't appear to be any DNA evidence under his fingernails.

They also dusted the body for prints and Joe took the clothes Tom was wearing to send to Jack Forest up in Virginia to do further DNA research. The Coast Guard had one of the best, if not *the* best, investigative units for DNA in the world. The clothes were wrapped up, sealed, and signed off by both Joe and the doctor as a chain of evidence before going to Jack. The autopsy was over and Joe thanked the doctor for allowing him the opportunity to stay and watch. He left with Mark and headed to meet Butler and his crew at the condo.

Dunkin' Donuts was two blocks down the street from the condo so they loaded up two cardboard carry trays with breakfast items. Joe couldn't break the habit from his stint in Albany. He stopped every day at the Dunkin's near the Albany Coalition for Families headquarters. Joe never had time to make breakfast at home. He was always the first one in and had downed two cups of coffee and two donuts before anyone had even arrived. It was expensive, but after his Coast Guard pay, the $50,000.00 a year he made at the Coalition had felt like a fortune, especially with his reduced rent he paid for his apartment by working at the Troy Education Consulting Group. Having a few bucks in his pocket felt good.

Although the Coast Guard gave Joe a government VISA card to cover all his expenses while he was on the road, he still needed cash for incidentals. He was not handing over his card for a donut. The paperwork and receipts required monthly were a pain in the ass but at least he didn't have to shell out any large amounts of his own money while on the road.

When Joe pulled up in front of the condo, the team had already been there for a while. Before going in, Joe passed out the food and drinks to a grateful crew.

Frank pulled up as well and parked across the street. Joe had called him late last night, told him what was going on, and how he forgot about Tom's Explorer. Frank laughed and said that was no big deal. He also got a message from the rear admiral's office and his own boss in Jacksonville that it was now officially a federal case and Frank was to assist. The rear admiral also called Homeland Security and the FBI to tell them that Joe was officially in charge of this investigation to make sure there would be cooperation up and down the line of command.

Even though all three organizations were connected, it didn't always go that way. The FBI always thought they were in charge and Homeland Security thought they were in charge of everything. The rear admiral cleared that up quick. Tom Jones was one of their own—a lifer—and they'd solve the murder themselves.

After seeing what work had been done—and it was extensive—Joe was embarrassed to admit that he'd forgotten about Tom's Explorer. He, Mark, and Frank went to the parking lot in the rear of the condo building where Tom's 2008 Ford Explorer was parked. They knew it was his before hitting the key fob to open the door. It had a boat hitch on the back, two children's car seats all hooked up in the back seat, and an iPad plugged into the power outlet on the dashboard.

Joe immediately went back to Butler in the condo and asked if he could borrow one of his team members to help them dust for prints on the vehicle. Butler looked sheepish, as if he'd never even thought about it.

Before he said a word, Joe told him that he, himself, had screwed up and didn't even think about it until last night. If the vehicle was missing, and it was not, they'd have been in deep crap, giving the murderer a few days head start in Tom's own vehicle. Thank God, that was not the case.

Butler thanked Joe for his honesty and admitted that he wanted to make an apology and a confession as well. "There's no excuse, Joe. I feel bad after our first meeting, and especially the way I treated Mr. Jones's daughter. I want to explain myself to you before there are any more incidents. My wife just left me after twenty-five years and my own kids won't even talk to me. I drink too much. I don't enjoy being a prick all the time, but it comes with the bottle," Butler said. "After this investigation, I'm going to pull the plug on my career because I just can't do the job anymore. It's made me into something evil and I can't get out of this funk." He sighed. "I'll take some time and clean up my act. I'm going to apply for a job at Disney to supplement my retirement income. I won't get much, since half my retirement pay will go to my wife. I'm not bemoaning that fact, but I can't live on so little and I'd still want to kick in some more to help out my wife during the separation, and after, if our marriage ends."

Joe really felt bad for him. This was a different side of Butler—much different from the son of a bitch he'd met only a few days ago. He shook Butler's hand. "After you retire, clean up your act, and remain clean and sober, I'll ask Claire and Brian Murphy to help you get a Disney security position. You probably weren't aware, but Claire is the administrative assistant for the head of the Hollywood Studios, and her husband's the chief accountant for the Walt Disney World Airport Division."

Butler smiled. "What goes around comes around, and I'd be grateful for any assistance I can get. I know I don't deserve any, but I sure need a second chance."

Joe nodded his approval. They shook hands and one of Butler's assistants was freed up to help with the Explorer.

Back at the lot, with gloves on, the police investigator dusted everything for fingerprints. And there were a lot. The SUV hadn't been washed in sometime, adding to the difficulty. After the iPad was dusted. Joe powered it up and tried to open the Internet connection. There were ten different network names on his iPad and each needed a separate password. He called Claire to see if, in addition to the WiFi networks, she knew Tom's email password and she did. Joe wrote it down. Tom used the same password for everything "CGCM1979." It stood for Coast Guard Cape May—where he was stationed for twenty years—and 1979 for when he joined up. It was easy for him to remember and didn't mean much to anyone else. She also said that the WiFi connection's network was "JONES" and the password was Tom's ten-digit telephone number that included the area code.

She further explained that, since the cable, internet, and telephone service came as part of the lease, each tenant had to follow the apartment complex management rules that required last name and phone number for the network, so that in case there were any issues, they could address those issues immediately.

Joe clicked on the network named "JONES" and put in his ten-digit phone number. The WiFi opened and the Internet came on. Joe found Tom's emails and there were only a handful including Joe, Claire, Brian, Gladys, and the manager of the complex reminding Tom of various meetings and functions for the month. Joe was still very curious as to the reason why ten network names popped up on Tom's iPad and he decided to meet the complex manager for an explanation.

ↄ৵ↄ৵

Joe opened the apartment office's door and walked in. Sitting at the front desk was Sandy Kopinski, the apartment manager. She looked quite busy and had several lines ringing at the same time. After a few minutes, the phones stopped. She looked up at Joe. "It's a very busy day, today. My assistant, who normally answers the phones, is out and we're getting tons of calls. The calls from reporters are coming out of the woodwork and it's bad for business."

Joe smiled at her and flashed his Homeland Security badge. He'd have too much explaining to do with the other IDs.

"How may I help you?"

"I'm leading the investigation into Tom Jones's death." He left it at that. He didn't call it a murder or a drug bust or even a home invasion.

She was pleasant but guarded. "So, how can I help you?"

"I'd like to know how your Internet service worked for the entire complex and I'd like to find the addresses associated with these networks, which I assume belong to residents of this complex."

"Do you have a warrant?"

That actually surprised him. "No, not at this point. But if I need one, I can get one in fifteen minutes, and you'll have fifty FBI agents going door to door to ask about a drug bust gone bad and a murder that took place right here only a few days ago. It will then be blown up, all out of proportion, and in the newspapers by tomorrow, if that what you want. You think you got reporters calling now?"

"No, I don't think it would go over very well," she said. "Can you give me a minute? I'll put on the answering machine and lock the office door so I can get you what you need. Would that be all right?"

"Perfect. Thank you." *Cooperation is a lovely thing*.

She pulled the ten files, which were easy, since the network names were the last names of the residents. She handed the files to Joe who reviewed each one. In the files were the tenant's previous addresses, current phone numbers, cell numbers, work addresses, work phone numbers, and whether their rent was up to date. It also included their vehicle information registration, plate number, and a picture of the vehicle parked in the lot with the complex parking sticker number that was placed in the rear driver's side window. The file also had references, if any were available. Not all files had references. In addition, some condos were fully furnished while others weren't. The monthly rent charged reflected the difference.

As Joe was reading, he looked up. "Who is Lacey Bradford?" he asked, noting that she came from Nashville—the source of the pills, labeled "TN"—and wondering if there might be a connection. "She resides in a furnished condo two buildings over from Tom's."

"She's been here only about six months. She said she'd inherited some money from her grandmother upon her death and wanted to start over in Orlando. She said she was enrolling in the local community college and was looking for a part time job."

All files had local police reports, if any, but since Lacey was new, there weren't any incidents. There was no report from her previous address in Nashville.

"I'm going to knock on her door and see if she's home," Joe told Sandy. "If she's not, I want to look around for a minute and then check out her car if it's in the lot."

Joe went to Lacey Bradford's condo and knocked on the door. He rang the bell and knocked again. There was no answer. He went back to the office and had Sandy accompany him back to the condo. She opened the door and they went in. This was a fully furnished rental so nothing looked out of place. The furniture was second tier but fine for an apartment or condo. Joe looked around and went to her closets. There was nothing there. He went to the bathroom. There was nothing laid out, no cosmetics or shampoo, nothing. There was no computer and no television. The apartment came with everything but a television, which could be easily broken—and left broken and unnoticed when tenants left. He turned to Sandy, who by this point was wide-eyed.

"She's not here," Sandy said. "She moved and never said a word. There's nothing of hers here. I still have her breakage and the last month's rental deposits. Where did she go?"

"Let's go to the lot and see if her car is still here," Joe said.

It was not. From the picture in the file, she owned a 2009 Nissan Sentra, which still had Tennessee plates. After six months, the state of Florida required a new Florida registration for those moving in permanently. She was at that point but evidently left abruptly.

"Does this have anything to do with Mr. Jones?" Sandy asked.

"I really don't know at this point but we will follow it up," he said.

Joe ran over to Tom's condo where the team was winding up their duties. "Can you put out an all-points bulletin on a Lacey Bradford and her automobile with Tennessee plates," Joe asked Butler. "It's been a few days so she could be almost anywhere."

Butler called it in and Joe went back to the office. "Do you have any cameras working in the complex?" he asked Sandy.

"We do," she said and it was probably the first thing she was sure of all day. "We keep the videos for one month and then start over again."

"Where are the cameras placed?" he asked.

"At each door of every building and in the parking lots in each corner and on the middle light pole. We've had problems in the past and this has helped with break-ins."

They found the video for the day Tom was murdered and ran it. After a half hour of looking at the front door Lacey's building and the parking lot, they saw Lacey walking out the door and to her car. Standing next to her car was a man. Tall and white, he looked to be in his late twenties or early thirties. He had several tattoos, but the markings were unidentifiable at this point. Jack Forest would have to do some heavy lifting to bring the tattoos into focus. The video showed that Lacey and this man had hopped into the car and left. It appeared that she had luggage in the back seat and some clothes hanging from the back straps. You could barely see the top of a television set sticking out near the back window.

They looked at video from several different angles and copied the pictures into a file so Joe could send the files to Jack to do facial recognitions, if possible. This might just be the break they needed.

Joe called Jack. "I'm sending you an email immediately with the attached photos."

Jack had already gotten the heads up from Joe earlier, in case they found something that needed his expertise.

Jack got the files and placed the pictures into his facial recognition software that was tied to the FBI files. Within twenty minutes, he'd matched Lacey Bradford to a police report in Nashville for a minor drug violation when she was in her late teens. It had her picture, fingerprints, and other personal information. Next, a few minutes later, came a picture of Jefferson Banks, a real bad guy. He'd been in and out of prison several times for assault, drugs, and for a manslaughter charge that didn't stick, all back in Nashville. The address they had at the time was for a house sitting right in the middle of "The Nations" section of Nashville. This was the heart of meth manufacturing, from where a large portion of the southeastern region of the United States was supplied. Jack sent along Jefferson's fingerprints as well.

Joe called Butler immediately and caught him and his crew before they left. He asked them to meticulously go through Lacey Bradford's apartment for any DNA to associate Jefferson Banks to Lacey Bradford and then to Tom's condo if they found anything the second time. He also asked them to put an APB out on Jefferson Banks and gave Butler the report sent by Jack.

Butler looked at Joe as if he had two heads. "You weren't kidding when you said you had better resources, were you?"

Joe laughed. "Told you so. Now get moving. By the way, do you know if either of them had cell phones? I didn't find anything listed for Lacey at the manager's office and I wouldn't have a clue if Banks had one either."

Butler told him he'd check out local cell phone companies and have someone look into cells with Nashville area codes to see if either suspect had one. At this point, Joe could be pretty sure that Tom had no part in any drug deals, but he wasn't one hundred percent certain. He still had to talk to Tom's girlfriend and see what evidence popped up this time so they could move forward. Joe was pretty sure that Butler no longer believed that Tom had anything to do with drugs and was, in fact, a victim. *What the hell did Tom do to get himself killed?*

Joe thought back and it finally came to him that

the last time they'd spoken, about three weeks ago, Tom said something but Joe was only half-listening. Joe now remembered that he'd said he was working on something and wanted to discuss it with Joe and get his opinion, but he wasn't quite ready yet. He said he would be soon, and would call Joe when he got enough evidence. Joe remembered clearly that Tom said "evidence."

Was this what he'd been talking about? Had he wandered into a drug ring selling meth out of his own condo complex and then tried to solve the case himself?

Joe thought it would be just like him to do something like that. Joe would probably do the same stupid thing, but his training would've kicked in and protected him. He wasn't sure that being a drill sergeant would qualify. Did Tom's own pride get him killed? What the hell was he trying to prove?

Joe knew that he might never find out Tom's motivation.

CHAPTER 6

It was now late afternoon and no one had eaten. There was a McDonald's a few blocks away so Joe picked up some burgers and drinks to re-supply the guys still there, now going over Lacey's apartment. He went through the drive-through and the bill was $58.95. *What the hell did I buy*?

He got back and parked in the lot next to Tom's Explorer. Everyone came over, got their lunch, and sat on the ground to eat. Joe still wanted to see Tom's girlfriend Gladys Fenton, who was supposed to return by that evening.

Claire had called earlier and Joe told her, once again that, if it was any consolation, Tom was not a drug dealer and, in fact, it looked like he was trying to solve a crime on his own and it backfired.

"Gladys will be coming home around 5:00 p.m.," Claire reminded him. "I spoke to her this morning and told her about Dad. Gladys was quite broken up and thanked me for telling her. She said she had no idea, that she was visiting her family in Ohio, never thought to look at the news, and never heard a word about Tom. She never even checked her emails. She said she got one the day Dad died, but she never thought anything about it. She opened the email while I was on the phone to see if it had anything to do with his death and it was simply to say that he missed her and that he'd see her when she got back. I guess it was the last thought he ever had about Gladys."

Claire was making plans for the memorial service at the Benton Funeral Home and Crematorium, on Michigan Street, which was located about five miles southwest of Tom's condo. There wouldn't be a church service but there would be a memorial service at the funeral home.

"Would you and Mark participate in a ceremony near Titusville, where Dad kept a small boat? My husband and the kids would attend. I invited my mother but she failed to reply."

So it looked like Joe, Mark, and Frank from the Coast Guard would dress in full uniform with only the family participating.

Butler overheard the conversation. "Would it would be all right if I attended as well?"

"I don't see any reason why not, but I'll ask Claire and get back to you. We'll meet Saturday morning at the dock, say a prayer of remembrance, and place some of his ashes in the ocean near his boat, allowing them to float away. Claire will keep a vial filled with his ashes, sealed, and worn close to her heart on a chain around her neck. She also said most of his ashes would be placed in a burial vial and would then be placed in the Florida National Cemetery for war veterans. The ceremony will take place after all this mess has been resolved, just in case Tom was involved with drugs."

It was a very nice gesture and reminded Joe how close Tom was to his daughter and her family after almost losing her after his divorce. Tom had been divorced from Claire's mother for many years. She'd remarried and moved to the west coast. There was very limited contact between Claire and her mother, but she'd felt fortunate that at least her father was around to see her own kids grow up. Whatever Tom was as a father, he more than made up for it as a grandfather to her two kids—Ryan, age five and in kindergarten, and Shannon, age three. Tom's whole life had been the Coast Guard and now his whole life was his daughter and her family.

Tom was thrilled to babysit at the drop of a hat. He filled in two days a week for Claire so she could work full time at Hollywood Studios in Disney World as an administrative assistant to the head of the theme park. Her husband Brian was an accountant working for Walt Disney World off-site in downtown Orlando. The Walt Disney World Corporation actually owned a third of the Orlando International Airport and Brian was the chief accountant for that division.

It had come full circle and Joe would always remember that. Just then, Claire pulled up with the kids and gave Joe all the details for the memorial and with the ocean-side ceremony scheduled for Saturday morning. She was very gracious in allowing Butler to attend, especially after the way he treated her when they first met. Jim thanked her and, once again, apologized.

CHAPTER 7

It was after 5:00 p.m. when Claire drove away. Joe went to Gladys Fenton's condo to finally meet the woman, whom he knew nothing about. It was odd that Tom had never mentioned her and she only came to light through Claire's off-handed comment about Tom's girlfriend. Joe hoped that she might have some idea about Tom's last days and what he was doing at the time. If she knew him well, she knew his personality and may-be she could shed some light on the situation.

Her place was actually in the back of the com-plex, not far away from Tom's condo.

Claire had filled Joe in on Gladys' personal background. She was fifty-five years old, the same age as Tom. She'd been a widow for almost eight years, since she was forty-seven. Her husband of twenty-five years, who was fifty at the time, dropped dead of a heart attack, with no warning. She'd been devastated. She had two children, a daughter, now age twenty-five, and a son age twen-ty-seven. They both lived in the Orlando area and saw their mother on a regular basis. Gladys had loved her husband very much and the kids treated her well.

She was pretty, well rounded, and now just retired as a third-grade teacher at an elementary school just down the street from the apartment complex. She volunteered as a reading teacher a few days a week, and substituted when needed. She had a full life but was lonely and Tom filled that role. He'd met her at a tenant meeting. He was surprised that they hadn't run into each other before that. Tom had been there since he retired from the Coast Guard, for almost five years. After a meeting, they started talking about life in general. After he told her that he'd retired a few years ago from the Coast Guard, she told him that she had retired as well and invited him over to the school to talk about the Coast Guard experiences with the third grade kids.

Joe found the story very interesting since that's what happened to him when he first started in the Coast Guard and met Julie during a fifth-grade career day presentation in Key Largo, when he was a first-year apprentice seaman.

Joe walked up to Gladys's door and rang the bell. She opened the door on the second ring. She was expecting him.

"Hi, I'm Joe Traynor, a friend of Tom Jones. Did his daughter, Claire, tell you that I'd drop by?"

"Yes, she did. Please come in. Can I get you something to drink or eat, Joe?"

"I'd love a glass of water if you don't mind, lots of ice if you would. The humidity is starting to get to me."

It was over ninety degrees and the humidity was about ninety percent. You had to really love Florida and warm weather to live there all year around. He was finally getting used to the weather after just coming back from Upstate New York. Joe followed her out to her eat-in kitchen. She handed him his drink and offered him a blueberry muffin that she'd just bought.

"Thank you," he said.

He then went on to tell her how sorry he was about Tom's death. She knew about Joe's long-time relationship with Tom. "I was in Ohio, visiting my mother who's eighty-five years old and living in a rest home. I offered to move her to Orlando but my mother doesn't want to leave. My brother is still there and looks in on her from time to time. I stayed with my brother for about ten days and just got back a little while ago. The Orlando airport is close to my condo and I took a cab home," she said. "I was shocked when Claire called me about Tom. I'm very upset about his death and I'm not really sure what happened. Claire said that you would fill me in when I got home. Claire invited me to the memorial at the funeral home and to the ocean-side ceremony on Saturday to spread some of Tom's ashes at sea."

Gladys told Joe that her last conversation with

Tom was pleasant and that he looked forward to her coming home. "He mentioned that he wanted to take me to dinner the night I returned. That was our last conversation."

Before Joe told her his observations, he asked her to fill him in on Tom's habits, that she knew about, what he was working on, if anything, and if she knew anything that could have led to his death. He asked her these open-ended question because he didn't want to sway her memory or move it in any direction that could lead to false conclusions.

"I liked Tom very much," Gladys said. "I'm not sure if it was love, at my age, but the companionship was special to me and I liked being with him. We got along great. I still haven't gotten over my husband's untimely death, but I was open to a more intimate relationship with Tom. I knew about his divorce and that his wife took off for California and never looked back. I've met Claire and can't understand how a mother could abandon her own child. It was the wife's fault and not Claire's, obviously. Claire and Tom had rebuilt their relationship. Tom adored his grandchildren and watched them every time he could. They were his life."

She went on to tell Joe about Tom's passion for technology. "I can barely use my cell phone and don't know one app from another."

"Do you know what Tom was doing on his computer, iPad, or iPhone?" Joe asked.

"I was starting to get the gist of what he was doing before his death," she said. "I was a little upset with him because he told me he'd learned how to hack into other tenant networks and emails and might have stumbled on to something. I wasn't sure, but I told him flat out that if he was watching Claire's kids a few days a week, he should stop doing what he was doing, for their sake. Tom dismissed it as small potatoes but I was going to tell Claire the next time I saw her that I didn't like what was going on."

This raised Joe's eyebrows a few notches. "Do you know the specifics?"

"I think he found someone in the complex dealing drugs. He'd hacked into their WiFi network and looked at a few emails that gave him the idea of what was going on."

Joe just shook his head. *Boy, was Tom ever in over his head.* He was a drill sergeant not an investigator. He knew nothing about investigations or how to build a case. This must have been what he was going to tell Joe, the last time they'd spoken. Joe was only half-listening at the time and now he could have kicked himself.

"Tom had a file in the bottom drawer of his desk with the printouts from websites he'd researched," Gladys said. "I glanced at it once and saw pages on meth, on drugs, on gangs in the Orlando area, and a folder on someone named 'Lacey' but I didn't know what it contained."

Bingo thought Joe. The only problem he now

had was that there wasn't a folder or any folders in Tom's desk drawers. Those folders were gone. The drawers were empty when they went over his condo. He'd go back and look again, and tell Butler about this conversation.

Joe thanked Gladys and gave her a hug. He gave her his cell number, email address, and told her to call him at any time if she remembered anything. Then at the last minute, he asked her, "Did Tom ever use your computer?"

"He checked emails, while I was cooking dinner," she said. "But I didn't think it was a big deal at the time."

"Do you mind if I look at your computer to see if there's anything on it that might put you in danger?" he asked her before leaving.

"I never thought about it like that, but it's better to be safe." She went to her computer in her bedroom, which had the same hookup as all the other complex tenants. She turned it on, put in her yahoo address, her password, and network, and turned it over to Joe. He carefully went over her safari history and there were several files that stood out. There was a file on Nashville, Tennessee, the Tennessee Bureau of Investigation, "The Nations" section of Nashville, and a meth hotline in Nashville. There was also a violent-crimes list of those convicted of meth use and the sale of meth. Evidently the meth list was similar to a sex-crimes list published for local citizens to see if any of those convicted lived near them. The meth problem in Tennessee was so prevalent that they started a meth convictions hot line and convictions list. Joe went down the list of names and there was a check mark, most likely placed by Tom, next to the name Lacey Bradford. She had several minor drug possession convictions for meth.

"Shit," Joe said out loud.

"What is it, Joe?" Gladys said.

Joe turned the screen around. "The name with the check mark is 'Lacey Bradford,' someone who lived in this complex and just moved out on the same day as Tom's death. This woman gave no notice and the apartment manager and I went to her place. It was cleaned out of all her personal possessions and her car was gone from the lot," he said. "We put a BOLO out on her and the car."

"Why would he put me in this danger?" she said. "I really liked Tom and I don't want to have his memory tainted but how can I not, now?" she asked Joe.

"I loved Tom like a father, and he was a very close friend, but this is just wrong," Joe said. "What the hell was he thinking, if anything?"

Joe was officially pissed at Tom for putting Gladys, Claire, and the kids in jeopardy. He was now mad at himself for not knowing anything about this situation. Once again, Joe said he was sorry. It was like he was apologizing for even knowing Tom. Nonetheless, Tom was a murder victim, even if he caused his own demise. Joe would do everything he could to find the perpetrator and then worry about his feelings later.

He told Gladys what he was thinking and she nodded. He kissed her on the cheek and left her apartment.

She was standing by the door with tears rolling down her cheek. Was it anger or grief from losing a loved one? *Will she show up for the memorial service and Saturday ceremony? Who could blame her if she doesn't?*

᥊᥊᥊

Joe had to get back on track after leaving Gladys. He went to the parking lot and spoke to Mark and Frank about what he'd found. They both shook their heads and looked pissed. It was hard to be pissed at a dead person but that's the way it went.

"I'll probably wind up in Nashville by the end of the week if they get a hit on any of the evidence," Joe told Mark. "After reviewing the checklist, that you and I created the other night, we haven't done anything about finding the computer and iPhone. The iPad was in the Explorer and led to where we are now. We have two suspects, probably headed for Tennessee."

Joe turned to Frank. "What do you know about the meth trade in Orlando and about gang activity and drug dealers?"

Frank was in charge of the facility and had a little knowledge of the area. "I'll get in touch with the north Florida Coast Guard investigation team and get all the information I can."

"I want to specifically know about the 'TN' trade-marked meth pills and where they landed in Orlando. It might not solve the murder but it could lead back to the manufacturer in Nashville. If we catch someone who'd make a deal, in lieu of a long prison term, it could lead to finding the distribution link or links."

"I'll get right on it," Frank said and headed back to Port Canaveral to start the ball rolling.

Joe called Butler and gave him a lengthy explanation of his day's findings. The detective did as well."

"In light of what you found, your original feelings about Tom being a drug dealer were warranted," Joe told him. "Tom was definitely not a drug dealer but simply a jerk who put his friends and family in jeopardy for no reason. Whatever he was trying to prove only got him killed."

"No, I was wrong and should never have said what I did when you first showed up at the station." Butler sounded like he felt bad for Joe. "Tom wasn't any bigger a jerk than I was."

Joe started to laugh and felt better. Butler laughed too. "Why don't you and Mark come to dinner, on me?"

"Great and, if you would, pick us up at the hotel at 6:00 p.m. That would work out fine."

At dinner, Joe went over everything with Mark and Butler. Joe felt that he was not getting to everything as quickly as he could and, for every day that passed, they'd lose ground and never find Lacey or Jefferson Banks, if, in fact, they were the killers. Joe told both of them that he thought they knew exactly what Tom had done and confronted him that night he died. He believed that Tom would never have opened the door if he saw Banks pressing the bell. However, Joe believed that if Lacey rang the bell, Tom would immediately open it. Joe didn't believe Tom knew what either one looked like. Joe believed, after the visit to Gladys, that Tom only had the name Lacey and hadn't gotten far enough to know what she looked like.

"I think that Tom opened the door for Lacey and that Banks came around behind her and hit him in the head with a heavy object. He then dragged him into the living room, stunned but awake, had Lacey close the front door, and then Banks tried to knife him to death. The defensive marks on Tom's two arms and his right hand and fingers proved that he fought back but succumbed to the stab wounds right into his heart. I also don't believe that Lacey knew what was coming because she probably never saw how violent Banks was. She knew he was a drug dealer and only had a tenth-grade education, but she was probably in love with him and wouldn't believe that he was violent. Then Banks probably went through Tom's house, taking his computer and phone and the files from his desk. I think that he put the $1,500.00 in cash sprinkled with cocaine and the meth pills, enough for a felony, and placed both between Tom's mattress and box spring, in the bedroom."

Joe turned to Butler. "Was the dead bolt engaged or the door was simply locked when you first showed up?

"Just locked."

"I remember that Tom always turned both the lock and the dead bold when he was home." It was part of Joe's photographic memory. "They probably left and simply closed the door, with it locked. When I saw them leaving the parking lot together, on the video in the manager's office, it was probably a few hours after the murder and it gave them enough time to pack and leave after the manager left the office for the night. No one else would probably notice a thing. Apartment complexes are notoriously transient by nature and filled with young adults who lead their own lives. They're only there to sleep normally."

Both Mark and Butler stared at Joe, astonished after he finished his story. They couldn't believe how he took all these separate events and pulled the pieces into one plausible story. They looked at each other and shook their heads.

"What?" Joe said. He then went on. "So our

next step is to find the phone and computer, check both out for fingerprints because at this point those would be the only two items tying Banks and Lacey to Tom's condo. Finding the files with a big thumbprint on the cover would certainly help but I don't think that's going to happen. We've built one hell of a circumstantial case for now. One more direct piece linking them together would be icing on the cake."

"So far, the second trip through the house didn't reveal any new evidence tying anyone to the crime," Butler said. However, he was clearly happy to have both Joe and Mark, as well as Frank, helping him. Or was it he helping them? He couldn't be sure.

ભભભ

After dinner, and back at the room in the Embassy Suites, Joe called the rear admiral's office and left a lengthy message on his answering machine, telling him he'd call the first thing in the morning.

Mark called Louise, his wife, and the kids and let them know that he and Joe were making progress, if slowly, and he was unsure when he'd be home. He knew Louise would call if she needed anything. Joe called Joan and gave her the same message. She'd spoken to Tillie and Julie earlier in the day and would keep them informed.

The next morning Joe and Mark met Butler at the police station to set up a system to find both the computer and iPhone. Joe knew that Tom had the state-of-the-art equipment at his condo. The last time Joe was there Tom had been bragging about it and Joe knew he should have been more attentive.

Other than his grandkids, technology was Tom's life and it looked like he paid for it with his death. Joe was very computer savvy and Mark was as well. When they were doing drug investigations, both could manipulate data better than most and were also very effective because of their bilingual skills. Simple chatter to most would be a symphony to them in English, Spanish, and Russian.

They could pinpoint exactly where pickups at sea would take place. They knew how to find foreign ships through GPS and through electronic listening devices. They even took part in the takedowns because ninety percent were either Hispanic or Russian drug runners or even both together, out of Cuba. Joe and Mark knew what they were looking for and had very few failures once the investigation was underway. This was different because it had to do with one of their own, but it had the same methodologies employed.

CHAPTER 8

T om had an iPhone 4 with GPS capabilities. It had both GPS tracking and GPS navigation systems. Both would be helpful in finding the phone. It didn't matter if the phone was turned on or not.

The computer was a different story. Tom's laptop had its own WiFi capabilities, but Joe didn't believe that Tom had it hooked up since he left the laptop on his desk most of the time and used the iPad on trips in his car. Why pay extra for an additional WiFi when it came as part of the lease?

However, the Apple iPhone 4 was Tom's pride and joy and it was state-of-the-art. It featured a thinner case—by 24%—than the iPhone 3GS, had more squared-off edges, a metal frame, and separate buttons for volume control. It featured a front and back camera. The back camera took nicer pictures, with 5 megapixels, and included an LED flash. This version had a higher-resolution display—960x640 pixels, 4 times more—in the same-sized 3.5-inch screen. It was powered by a super-fast proprietary Apple A4 chip and had a larger battery, lasting as much as 40% longer. Tom, of course, had the 32 GB model, the most expensive.

Of interest to Joe were the navigation and GPS features. The stainless steel frame doubled as an antenna for the iPhone's various receivers, including GPS. This boosted the iPhone's GPS reception. The upgrade to a much higher resolution display helped sharpen up the complicated map and navigation displays. The iPhone 4 ran on the iOS4 operating system, which permitted multitasking.

The HD video capability of the iPhone 4 included *geotag* videos. This was what Joe wanted to know. This *geotag* video feature would turn on the phone, give the coordinates of where it was currently positioned, and could potentially snap pictures of the immediate surrounding area, if that helped. Joe wasn't sure if it was in a pond, on the ground, or broken into a million pieces. He thought that if he were on the run, he'd stop in some rural area and heave it as far as he could. If there was an isolated stream, that would have been even better. If it was simply broken, Joe knew that someone, somewhere, had the ability to put it back together in working order.

He knew that he needed the box that the phone came in that held all the specifics, including the model number, the serial number, the software, memory, graphics, and other features to call into the Apple 800 helpdesk hotline to have them set the GPS so they could track it on Tom's iPad. Joe had stopped late last night at Tom's. He went through his closets and found the boxes that held all his electronic equipment from when he purchased the items. Evidently, no one even gave the boxes a second glance when they were going through the condo. Tom knew the value and kept everything.

When Joe got back, Mark asked him if he ever slept. Joe smiled. "I'm going to bed right now."

Mark turned over in his own bed and started to snore.

☙❧☙

Joe, Mark, Butler, and the police chief sat in the chief's conference room as Joe dialed the Apple hotline. He knew that if he had the information required by the technician, he didn't have to identify himself as the investigator. Apple asked him his name and the pertinent information, including passwords, networks, and a list of questions supposedly only known by the owner.

"What's your mother's maiden name?"

Joe remembered that it was Wamsley. How he remember that he had no idea. Everyone looked at Joe, who turned and said, "What?"

Daughter's name and grandchildren, no problem. Date of birth, no problem.

"Favorite town?"

Cape May, what else?

The chief just shook his head. Joe had Tom's

iPad turned on, which was already interfaced with his phone and computer. The iPad started to work and the GPS system came on. A beep, beep, beep, came across the screen and a picture of a tree came into view.

"Great," Joe said.

"Where's the phone, Joe?" asked the chief.

"We found it, Chief. It's right next to this tree," Joe said and smiled. *Told you so.*

"No, Joe, where is it?"

"Don't know. It's obviously in a ditch looking at a tree. Here are the exact coordinates."

Joe immediately fed the coordinates into his own GPS system on his own iPad, so as not to lose the phone connection and found out that it was one hundred feet from a main highway, five miles outside of Chattanooga, Tennessee. Joe went to the law enforcement web site and found out who was responsible for that section of road—and since it was the state highway, it was under the authority of the Tennessee Highway Patrol. He got the number for their main headquarters and handed it to the police chief who left to make the call.

Then they all sat back, sighed, and hoped for the best. The chief went to his office, was on the phone for a long time, and came back to the conference room.

"I spoke directly to the head of the division that patrols the highway and they'll send a team right out to the site," the chief told them. "They were only ten miles from the GPS coordinates. The team is well aware of the BOLO that was out for Lacey and Banks and wanted to know if this was directly related to the murder. I told him everything I knew and that it's now a federal investigation. I gave him your cell number, Joe. They'll call you when they have the phone."

The meeting broke up and the chief asked Joe to come down to his office. He wanted to know about Butler's performance, in light of the initial problem.

Joe told him everything that had happened. "I believe that working on this investigation is changing his life for the better. I admit that I, too, could have handled things better, but being Irish stood in my way."

"I'm half-ass, too," the chief said, meaning half-Irish. "And so is Butler."

Which explained a lot. All three were half-assed, apparently. Joe thanked him for everything and left the office. Tonight would be the memorial service at the funeral home on Michigan Avenue. He knew that a bunch of Coasties were coming, including the rear admiral's staff assistant.

Joe was grateful, in light of his findings, that they'd still attend the service for Claire and her family's sake at least. Gladys had called Claire and taken the higher road. She'd be at all the functions that Claire had put together.

What a nice lady.

Joe got his clothes from the laundry service at the hotel and had his full dress uniform dry-cleaned and ironed for the event. Hopefully, it would hold him over for the ocean-side event Saturday as well.

CHAPTER 9

Joe was heading back to the hotel with Mark when his cell phone beeped. It was the Tennessee Highway Patrol captain who'd gone to the physical GPS coordinates to find Tom's iPhone.

"We found the phone exactly where the GPS coordinates said it would be," the captain said. "We placed the phone in an evidence bag for processing. Is there anything specifically that you were looking for on or near the phone?"

"It would be virtually impossible to heave the phone any distance without placing a fingerprint on it unless he or she was wearing gloves. I'm hoping for the best. When you pulled in on the side of the road, were you careful not to run over any tire prints that may have been there?"

The captain laughed. "Do you think we're a bunch of shit-kickers from Tennessee?"

Joe laughed sheepishly. "No."

"My staff and I parked almost one hundred yards away on both sides of the coordinated area. We found tire tracks and did a casting. We'll compare tires if we find the car."

Joe thanked him and asked the captain to process the phone and prints, if any.

After getting the captain's email address, Joe emailed him the information on both Lacey Bradford and Jefferson Banks. He also sent pictures of the car, the registration, Tennessee plate number, and vehicle ID number. It wasn't twenty minutes later that Butler called Joe on his cell. "Joe, it's Jim."

"Yes, Jim, what's up?"

"The Tennessee Highway Patrol just called about the BOLO on Lacey and Banks. They didn't find the car but they found a young lady by the side of the road, maybe twenty feet from the highway. She's dead, Joe. She was knifed to death."

"Wow, I didn't see that coming. Did you? Did you send them the package on Lacey to match her picture and fingerprints?"

"I didn't see it coming, either," Butler said. "But it sure helped your theory about what happened to Tom. About the package, I did it right away. See? I can be on top of things when I'm not drunk or vindictive."

"I get your drift, Jim. Sorry. I'll stop asking obvious questions. I just got called on it, a few minutes ago by the captain of the state police in Tennessee. He wanted to know if I thought they were shit-kickers. I better lighten up."

Butler laughed.

"So do you think she was a willing participant

in drug dealing but not murder?" Joe asked.

"Yes, that's exactly what I believe now," Butler said. "Do you want to head up to Tennessee right now?"

"We can't, Jim. We have to go to Tom's memorial service tonight."

"Shit, that's right. How about right after the service? We should take separate cars in case I have to come back and you have to head north to Nashville."

"Sounds good. I'll leave Mark here to investigate the gang angle. You know he's Mexican right? It could be helpful if Hispanics are involved. Mark is the best of the best in these kinds of investigations. Of course, I didn't tell you, but I'm as fluent in Spanish as he is, since I learned it all from him. We worked as a team, speaking Spanish about ninety percent of the time. Now, Russian's been added to our repertoire as well."

"I don't believe that there are many Hispanic gangs in northern Florida," Butler said. "They're mostly in south Florida in the greater Miami area. Outlaw bikers have been around Central Florida longer than Walt Disney World. For as long as I can remember, almost twenty five years on the Orlando police force, local bikers blew up rivals' headquarters, sold guns and dope, and shot at one another. Bikers are the most likely to sell meth in the area. In its heyday during the early 1990s, Orlando had its share of Warlocks, Outlaws, and Hells

Angels and it took a ton of federal investigations and prosecutions, resulting in numerous convictions, to get gang activity under control. However, all of them are still in the area, selling dope."

"Good to know. I'll see you tonight. I asked the highway patrol officers to be especially careful while looking at the knife entry and type of wounds on Lacey. If it's a serrated knife wound, we can probably match both wounds, Tom and Lacey's, exactly and then we've the proof we need to convict for both of them."

"You don't need the actual knife if both wounds are identical and Banks would have been the last one to use the knife," Butler said.

"Good thought, Jim. You're right, this ties up everything, but I still want to get that son of a bitch," Joe said.

"Me, too. I'll see you tonight."

☙❧

After Joe packed up at the hotel for his trip with Butler, he and Mark headed to the memorial service at the funeral home. Mark would be staying in the area and would get a government car from Frank the next day. He was to start investigating the meth trade in Orlando. The little information Butler had given them about biker gangs would be very helpful in determining who was distributing meth in the greater Orlando area. If Joe was successful in finding the distribution point up in Nashville, they might be able to trace the flow right back to here. At least that was what he was hoping.

As they walked into the front door of the funeral home, Joe and Mark ran into Butler.

"I'm ready to leave for Chattanooga as soon as you are," Butler said.

There were two memorial services that night—Tom's, in the parlor on the left, and one for an eighty-year-old widow, in the parlor on the right. There were only a handful of people in that parlor. To the left, Joe and the others signed in before entering Tom's viewing room. As Joe looked around, he noticed that Frank and his entire administrative staff from Port Canaveral had already arrived in full military dress. The rear admiral's assistant was also seated in the back of the room.

Tom's ashes were placed in an urn that was raised on a three-foot platform, draped with a black cloth. There was a kneeler in front of the urn. A picture of Tom, in full military dress, was placed next to the urn on the platform. A picture of Tom and Joe stood on a table to the side. Pictures of various graduating classes from Cape May were placed next to Joe and Tom's picture. Standing to the side was Claire, her husband Brian, and Brian's family. Claire and Brian had left their kids at home with a close family friend watching them. Gladys Fenton sat by herself near the middle of the row of chairs placed for mourners. She looked like someone who had mixed emotions about being there. How could she not after learning what Tom did to her and his own family?

Joe went up to Claire, gave her a big hug and a kiss, and shook Brian's hand. There was no need to tell them how he felt. They already knew.

"I'll be forever grateful for what you're doing to clear Dad's name, Joe," Claire said quietly.

It didn't change the fact that she loved her father but she was mad at him for what he did. Still, she wanted to find his murderer as much as Joe did. Mark and Butler gave her their condolences. Joe told her he was going to Chattanooga and, hopefully, would be back for the ocean-side memorial on Saturday. He went over to Gladys and sat next to her. He told her what was going on and that she was in no danger, or so he thought. It actually relieved her. It had weighed on her mind and she told Joe that.

Joe then went to the rear admiral's assistant and the other staff who came from Jacksonville and asked them to step outside for a minute. He briefed all of them on exactly what was happening and where he was headed with Butler. He told them about the ocean-side service, and if any of them could make it, he'd appreciate it.

The actual service at the Florida National Cemetery wouldn't be for several months. Joe mentioned the Saturday service to Frank and his team as well.

A local priest from Claire's church came by, said some prayers, and gave a brief homily. Joe nodded to Claire and excused himself. Mark and Butler followed him out of the funeral home.

"We need to get gas," Joe told Butler. "And stop at Burger King before leaving Orlando. It's a long drive up to the Tennessee border."

Butler would follow Joe all the way up. They'd keep their cell phones on and talk to each other as they drove, helping them to stay awake. Orlando to Chattanooga was a five-hundred-and-fifty-mile trip, taking over eight hours to get there. From Chattanooga to Nashville, it was only around 130 miles and two hours.

After a trip to Burger King and a stop at the gas station, they headed north up the Florida Turnpike, hitting Georgia's I-75 N for almost three hundred miles. From there it was 175 miles more. They'd be meeting with the Tennessee Highway Patrol Captain who found the body by the side of the road.

After a few hours into the trip, Joe got a call from the Tennessee Highway Patrol forensics team who had found the phone. It was their lucky day. The iPhone had a big fat thumbprint on it just like Joe thought it would. The good news was that it matched Mr. Banks. They now had a series of events that circumstantially proved a sequential timeline, enough for a conviction. Now, there would be a direct tie to Jefferson Banks, placing him with Tom's phone, taken from the condo where Tom Jones was murdered.

Finding Mr. Banks was another matter. Finding the knife would be helpful but not really needed at this point. Banks was with Lacey when she was murdered and they could prove a direct link to Tom.

CHAPTER 10

J oe and Butler, in separate cars, arrived at the scene of the crime, outside Chattanooga, around 4:30 in the morning. They'd left at 7:30 p.m. the previous night and made two pit stops for gas, to go to the bathroom, eat, and drink as much coffee as they could. They both got large to-go cups and saved a lot of time peeing into the cups while driving at 75 miles an hour on the way up. Heaving the full cup's contents out the window was another matter. They got near Chattanooga and pulled over into the last rest stop on the highway. They went to the bathroom then set their alarms for one hour and went to sleep in their cars. They'd been up now for almost twenty-four hours straight. An hour of sleep might not help, but it certainly couldn't hurt.

The GPS systems were a godsend and they both pulled up simultaneously next to four highway patrol cars parked on the side of I-24 West, right off I-75 N going into Chattanooga.

Joe and Butler got out of their cars and flashed their credentials over their heads so there was no confusion as to their identification and why they were there. They both asked for Captain Tymeson simultaneously. The captain popped his head over his highway patrol car and waved them both over. Joe shook the man's hand and so did Butler. The captain took them both over to the body. It had been there all night but no one wanted the body moved until they'd arrived. Joe uncovered her face and identified the body. "It's Lacey Bradford, age 23, of Orlando Florida."

He had already sent the fingerprints to the captain before they left Florida. They were now in the process of matching the body's fingerprints to those sent in by Joe. Wearing gloves that he pulled out of his pocket, Joe bent down and looked at the knife marks near her heart. There were no defensive wounds so she must have been surprised—if, in fact, it was Banks, who must have pulled over and stabbed her to death with no warning. It was hard to tell, at 5:00 a.m. in the morning, exactly what the knife marks looked like but they did appear to be a little jagged, not unlike those found on Tom.

Joe pulled out Tom's crime scene photos and handed them to Captain Tymeson. He looked at the body and the picture and nodded. It would be much longer at the morgue to make sure that they could positively state that the knife marks were identical in both cases. However, there was sufficient evidence to suggest that the knife was the same. They didn't *have* to find the knife, but it would go a long way proving their cases.

Just then, another officer pulled up with coffee and buttered rolls for everyone. Joe and Butler ate. Butler would find a motel nearby, get some sleep, and then head back to Orlando. Joe couldn't thank him enough.

"You'll work closely with Frank and Mark and find out where the meth in Orlando wound up, if possible, right?" Joe asked Butler. "At this point, we know who committed the Orlando murder and now we have to find Jefferson Banks.

Butler nodded. "I'll contact Claire and let her know where the case stands. It won't be closed until we arrest Banks but there isn't anything we can do for Claire in Orlando except close down meth dealers, if we find them."

Captain Tymeson's phone rang and he waved Joe over to his car. He hung up and turned to Joe. "A car, just outside of Nashville, was found still smoldering. It was obviously set on fire using an accelerant, probably a full can of gasoline. The car didn't have any passengers. It appeared to be a Nissan Sentra but it was badly burned. Three of the four tires were melted. The serial numbers had been removed."

"Did they see anything in the car, like luggage?"

"There's a big hunk of plastic melted in the back seat with shattered glass down on the floor.

There's a bar across the back seat that looked like it held clothes, but that was melted and hanging down as well."

"When I saw the car in the parking lot picture," Joe told the captain, "it was a 2009 Nissan Sentra and had a television set that you could see the top of through the rear window."

The reply from the investigation team was a positive that it appeared to be a melted television set. Joe asked them to remove the good tire that wasn't melted. "Maybe we can compare it to the plaster cast they took of the track marks where the iPhone was found right on the Tennessee border. I'm heading toward Nashville to where the car is located and please don't remove it before I get there."

After last night's trip, it was only a hop, skip, and a jump to Nashville. Joe's GPS said it was 130 miles and about two hours away. He got gas and headed toward Nashville. On the way, he called the chief of police in Orlando and told him what he'd found. The chief would tell Mark that Butler was headed back and would meet him at the Embassy Suites Hotel later that day after he got some shut-eye.

Joe called the rear admiral and gave him a lengthy explanation of what they found, where he was, and that he'd be getting some rest after he saw the burnt-out car and met with the head of the Tennessee Highway Patrol and the TBI. He wanted to find Banks, desperately.

He called Joan Talbot for an update.

"Everything is fine on the home front," she said.

He called Julie and had to leave a message. She had a speaking engagement every day that week in New York City at several girls' charter schools. Her book was being used as a model of success for teenage girls to improve their lives. Joe couldn't argue with the results, but the timing sure stank. He also had to be back Saturday for Tom's ocean-side memorial. He'd leave his car in Nashville, fly back and forth to Orlando, and hitch a ride to the service.

రారా

The 2009 Nissan Sentra was parked about a half a mile in from the main highway going in to Nashville. Joe took I-24 W to the last exit before I-65 N. He took what looked like a deserted back road, all dirt, into a copse of trees. He could see flashing lights in the distance and headed in that direction. Once again, there were several highway patrol cars along the side of the road as Joe pulled in. He did the same routine, holding his badge over his head. He met the sergeant at the scene who was expecting him. The sergeant looked at Joe's eyes, which were beginning to close, and gave him some coffee. That seemed to help.

"I already booked you a room at a small motel right down the road and charged it to the Tennessee

Highway Patrol," the sergeant said.

"Thanks a lot."

The sergeant also handed him two subs to eat when he got there and a large bottle of cold Coke. The timing couldn't have been better. Joe and Sergeant Normile walked over to the still-smoldering car. Joe immediately knew it was the same car as that in the picture he handed to the sergeant.

"It appears to be the same," Sergeant Normile said.

Joe looked into the backseat and saw a bunch of electronics surrounded by melted plastic. "We'll know more after we match the one tire left that hadn't melted."

Joe knew he had a big day following and was unsure of how he was to proceed. He had a murder in Orlando tied to a federal drug-dealing scheme going across state lines, coupled with a murder in Tennessee and a burned-out car that would also be considered a federal crime, following the evidence from Orlando. He guessed that a good eight hours sleep wouldn't hurt a whole lot.

"How the hell did a Coast Guard chief warrant officer from Islamorada get messed up in this?" Sergeant Normile asked.

Joe smiled. "I'll call you after I sleep a while and give you the history involved because I don't quite believe it either." He didn't want to go into the fact that he was not only Coast Guard but represented the FBI and Homeland Security as well.

CHAPTER 11

Joe barely made it to the Evergreen Motel. He walked into the office and the manager handed him a key. He told Joe that he could check in later. It was clear that Joe was driving a government car. It couldn't have been more obvious if it had FBI on the side with the lights flashing.

Joe thanked him and headed for his room, number four, less than thirty feet from the manager's front door. He left the car where it was and already had his overnight bag in his hand. He went into the room, put the drinks and subs in the small refrigerator that came with it, and hit the head. He thought it was late morning or early afternoon. He never once looked at his watch. He'd eat later, he decided, and almost passed out on the queen size bed.

Normally before Joe went to sleep, he found it always easier if he took a topic to daydream about and then sleep would take over. If he was in an investigation, he'd start with what he needed the next day and soon he'd be on his way to dreamland. Today, he started thinking about where the hell he'd been over the last fifteen years and how he came to be sleeping in a small roadside motel in Nashville Tennessee. It was quite a trip.

As he lay there, Joe realized that he was now thirty-three years old, closing in on his thirty-fourth birthday. He'd spent ten years in the Coast Guard, receiving his BS in Strategic Intelligence and Research from the Coast Guard Academy in New London, Connecticut, at age twenty-eight. Many of his liberal arts classes were taken in Florida at Miami Dade Community College, during his enlisted service, and then he completed his science courses at the academy, off and on. He worked for ten years as a noncom, mostly at the Coast Guard COMMSTA facility in Miami. After he got out of the Coast Guard in 2008, he really didn't want to go another ten years and into officer training. So he spent two years at Rensselaer Polytechnic Institute in Troy, and received his MBA in management in 2010.

He'd started what he thought would be a new career at the Albany Coalition for Families that same year, and he did very well for a late bloomer. Getting there was quite a different story. How he got from Albany back into the Coast Guard was a different tale all together.

The take-down of the Mexican Mafia nationally, starting with the Albany charity, and then wanting to protect Julie Chapman and her grandmother, living in Key Largo, brought Joe full circle, back into the Coast Guard, now as a chief warrant officer. A title he vowed he'd never wanted.

He had grown up in Troy, in Lansingburgh in the north end, just outside of Albany, ten miles north. He went to St. Augustine's Catholic Elementary School and then on to Catholic Central High School, only a few blocks away. He graduated with honors, had high SAT scores, really excelled in math, and wound up with a scholarship to Massachusetts Institute of Technology, better known as MIT, in Cambridge, Massachusetts, across the Charles River from Boston. He'd lived in Troy his whole life before going away to MIT and then into the Coast Guard.

He was raised in a middle-class construction family. His mom was very religious, his dad not so much. Joe started working construction at fourteen years old, during the summers and then on weekends during the school year. He got his commercial driver's license in an 18-wheel dump truck, at sixteen years old. He never got a regular driver's license. He had a good life, good family, good brother, good support, but that all changed at MIT. He just wasn't ready. He got all Cs as a math major but he wanted more than to just sit in class. He was bored to death. At eighteen, no one could have convinced him differently. At the end of his first semester, he knew he couldn't go on. He was first generation in his family going to college and he knew he'd disappoint his parents, but growing up in a construction family, he also knew that he could take care of himself. He could always go back to school later.

The day after his last exam at MIT, in December 1998, he went to Malden outside of Boston, only a few miles from school, and signed up with the Coast Guard for an eight-year commitment, which turned into ten. He'd just started at MIT in the fall that year, two years before the bombing of the USS Cole in Yemen in 2000, and three years before 9/11, in 2001. By that time, Joe would have been in the middle of the new terror threat on America. At the time, he thought joining the Coast Guard could make a difference, but little did he know how much. He thought he could continue his education at some point, see America, especially the coast, do some good, and gain some experience. He didn't know the real terror threat that was coming and how the Coast Guard would be changed by it. Being eighteen and patriotic was kind of a given in his family. At eighteen, you never thought too much about death or anything else for that matter. Joe woke up very quickly.

It was late January 1999 when he went to Cape May, New Jersey, for basic training. He was still a teenager and wouldn't be nineteen until April. He arrived at Sexton Hall in Cape May and most of the next few days were spent getting oriented, learning his way around, getting his uniforms, a really short haircut, and filling out nothing but forms for two days. God, he thought he was back in school.

He met his Master Chief Petty Officer, Tom Jones, upon his arrival. No, he didn't break out in song. To this day Joe thought that "Can't Sing or Dance" fit Tom well. He was not the international singing star, appearing in Las Vegas, also named Tom Jones, but simply a drill instructor—one of the best the Coast Guard ever had. He was tough, forty-one years old at the time, a lifer, and he was going to be Joe's mentor, his instructor, coach, guide, and all around pain in the ass.

They learned discipline the hard way, how to take orders, and what was expected of them. Every morning the day began the same way with pushups and sit-ups. They ran for miles and had lots of swimming. Joe guessed he forgot that the Coast Guard meant not drowning. He had swum all his life but never like this. This was not a boat in the Hudson River. He was waterlogged for all eight weeks of basic training.

After the physical training, Joe was exhausted. And then the real fun had begun. A seaman apprentice was the first step and they taught you what you needed in order to be seaworthy. They taught academics related to ships, technology, and things you would never think about. He was really glad that he was good in math. The easiest way to wash out, literally, was to not be able to swim or not know math. Both were essential to everything they did.

Toward the end of training, Joe participated in small-arms training, seamanship, firefighting, damage control, and the nomenclature they'd need know to immediately respond to various situations, on board and off. After Joe's final physical exam and then his written exam, he was ready to start his first assignment. Tom Jones had prepared him, not just for the Coast Guard, but for life. Joe was very smart but he let things slide when he could because he could always make up the work, if needed. Tom didn't let anything slide and Joe hated him for it, but, later on, as Joe grew older and wiser, he appreciated the life lessons, especially as his life was in jeopardy on every drug takedown.

As part of the original recruiting process, Joe had to pass the Armed Services Vocational Aptitude Battery, ASVAB, test and had to get a minimum qualification score of 45 or higher. Joe thought that this was pretty easy, considering a majority of the test was math. He guessed they were impressed and told him that he scored the second highest that they'd ever seen since keeping score data online. This simply meant that upon graduation, he could go for any one of nineteen different enlisted ratings for which he could actually go on and receive a degree from the Coast Guard Academy in his field during his enlistment. That was what Joe had hoped for—to obtain a degree on the Coast Guard's dime.

Upon completing the eight weeks of basic training, he was promoted to seaman, E-2. He was told at the recruitment office that if he did well on his tests and basic, a guaranteed A-school program would be within his reach, and he'd go right from basic training to his A-school choice, which was as an intelligence specialist, IS. With the Coast Guard taking an increasingly larger role in Homeland Security, he'd be one of the first defenders of US ports and waterways.

After basic training, he started his career with fourteen weeks of specialized training at the A school in Yorktown, Virginia, only a few miles from Newport News and Virginia Beach. Tom Jones followed his trainees to Yorktown to continue overseeing this group. He knew they were special. He had never been asked to move with his trainees before but this was different. They never had such a diverse group of people and the top officers wanted to see where this would go.

During his basic training in Cape May and the fourteen weeks at Yorktown, Joe made friends that that would stay with him for a lifetime. In addition to Joe, there were four other trainees in his immediate group, including Mike McGreevy, who came from Seattle; Mark Silva, from San Diego; Sean O'Neil, from Boston—they came down together since they both signed up in Malden that same day; and Jack Forest from Charlestown, South Carolina. Joe went through basic training and Yorktown advanced training with them, ate, slept, and breathed the same air. They all made it and they all graduated together.

Mark had remained Joe's best friend to this day. Back then, he'd just turned twenty-seven years old right before he joined the Coast Guard. He was a Latino and a former gangbanger when he was a kid, but he loved the sea and, when picked up by the cops at twenty-seven years old for aggravated harassment, he decided that a better option was to join the service. Twenty-seven-year-old gangbangers didn't live very long. He probably wouldn't have made it to thirty. Now at forty-one, Mark was a mentor to others and he was Joe's full time working partner in the intelligence area for all of south Florida. Joe wouldn't have come back to the Coast Guard if he hadn't been able to partner back up with Mark. After all those years away from the service, Joe's separation didn't mean a thing. It was like he'd never left or missed a beat.

Joe saw Mike and Sean at least once a year but, in addition to Mark, he continued to work regularly with Jack Forest who'd saved his bacon on more than one occasion. Jack originally grew up in New Jersey, the Cape May area, but his family transferred down to South Carolina when his dad's company moved. He still had family in Cape May and while in basic, on weekend leave, saw his grandparents on both sides, as they lived their entire lives in Cape May. Jack had just turned twenty-two years old when Joe first met him, and he'd just graduated from Rutgers University—New Jersey's State University—at Camden with a BS in computer science. Jack's computer science degree allowed him to pick the intelligence field and he wound up in Joe's training group. Jack was now in Virginia in charge of advanced intelligence and technology for the entire Atlantic Region. Having Jack as one of your closest friends didn't hurt when you needed something immediately.

Joe remembered his personal turning point with the Coast Guard as if it was yesterday. Fifteen years certainly went by fast. Into his fifth week of the fourteen-week A-school training at Yorktown, Tom Jones called him into his office.

Joe thought he was doing pretty well at the time, but what the hell did Tom want to see him for? Tom never spoke to anyone alone, so Joe was nervous.

"Joe, close the door," Tom had said. "Are you okay? You look a little pale?"

Normally, Joe joked around when he was nervous, but he really didn't know what was going on or what to expect, so he said, "No, Chief, I'm fine, just fine."

"Look, you're fine, you're doing fine for a nineteen year old, but your sarcasm gets a little bit much, you know? Happy Birthday, by the way." It was April at the time and Joe had turned nineteen. "That's not why I called you in," Tom continued. "Look, Mark isn't making it in the classroom and I need you to tutor him."

"Is that all?" Joe had asked. Being nineteen

meant he knew everything and didn't want to be bothered. Joe now knew exactly how wrong he'd been.

"No, you might have to go against your normal smart-ass instincts if you're going to help him," Tom said. "We've decided to break up into two-man teams for the rest of the nine weeks."

Tom wanted Joe and Mark to be one team, and he meant one team, a tag team. Joe was not to leave Mark's side for the rest of the training. If it worked out, both he and Mark would be assigned to the COMMSTA facility in Miami, after a short stay at headquarters in Portsmouth at the Maritime Intelligence Fusion Center Atlantic. Tom told Joe that he wanted him for his brains and Mark for his Latino background and street smarts.

"However, he might not make it and, if he doesn't, you won't either," Tom said. "No one here passes or fails on their own. You have to work closely together to be successful especially to where we're sending you next."

"Chief, I'll do the best I can, but Mark's a gangbanger from San Diego. I can't understand him half the time. He goes in and out of English and Spanish so much, I don't recognize complete sentences," Joe said. "He's twenty-seven years old and I just turned nineteen."

"This isn't a request. It's an order. Do you know what an order is, Joe?"

Joe's eyes went wide. "Well, since you explained it to me in English, I'm certain that I'll be able to follow your order explicitly, Chief."

"Good idea," Tom said. "And, by the way, you better learn to speak street lingo as quickly as you can by the time you land in Miami. Do you think the intercepted message from the Columbians, are explicitly in English?"

Tom smiled. Joe smiled. He got it. Tom wasn't just thinking of Mark. He was thinking of Joe as well.

Joe had remembered that day, every day since. Tom told him that book smarts would catch the bad guys but street smarts would keep him alive. Joe didn't like to be placed in that position, but Tom was not only his guiding light, he also became a mentor and a friend for life. Even with the age difference, it didn't matter. His friend was now dead. It didn't matter if he was the chief engineer of his own death. It didn't matter if he was killed because of some grandiose plan to stop the bad guys. It just didn't matter.

When this was over, Joe would only remember the good Tom not the Tom that placed people in jeopardy, even his own grandchildren. Although, that would be hard to forget.

ഗഗഗ

Joe rolled over and started to wake up. It was late afternoon, around 4:00 p.m. He got up, took a shower, and ate his two subs, washing it down with the two-liter bottle of Coke. He thought it was the best meal he had in a long time. He was that starved. He hopped into his car and set the GPS for the Tennessee Highway Patrol headquarters in downtown Nashville. He wanted to catch Officers Normile and Tymeson if they were there. But he wasn't sure where they were stationed.

He called Mark, who told him that Butler was just nearing Orlando. Joe had forgotten how long a drive it was. He decided on the spot that he'd fly into Orlando on Friday night for the ocean-side memorial service on Saturday. He'd have to hop back onto a plane and get right back. He'd hoped that the flight would be approved. He'd call the rear admiral's office and hopefully get his permission. The upgraded pay, as a chief warrant officer, still didn't allow for luxuries like next day flights. He was hoping he might be able to squeeze in for free, since he'd be a member of Homeland Security on the job, serving once again as an air marshal.

CHAPTER 12

Joe went to the Evergreen Motel manager's office, checked in, and checked out at the same time. He thanked the manager for his kindness and gave him his card. He asked him if he had rooms available on a regular basis because he knew he'd be in Nashville for a while but he didn't know exactly where. If it got late and he didn't have a place, he wanted to be able to count on coming back to the Evergreen Motel. It wasn't a great motel, but it was everything that Joe needed and the manager had been very good to him.

The manager said he almost always had rooms but would save one for him every day until 6:00 p.m. If he called before that, the room was his, all for $49.95 a night plus taxes.

Joe wanted to see if he could meet with the Tennessee Bureau of Investigation, TBI, and its Methamphetamine Task Force, even if it was only for a minute or two. Their local office was in downtown Nashville, with its main headquarters in Chattanooga. Joe drove to the TBI in downtown and hoped to meet the head of the Nashville office.

He set his GPS to 901 R.S. Gass Boulevard in Nashville and was there in less than fifteen minutes.

Joe went to the front desk, introduced himself, and asked to speak to the officer in charge. The assistant director, who was running late, came out of his office and told Joe, "I only have a few minutes to spare."

It was almost 5:30 p.m. and the assistant director was headed to a special event at 7:00 p.m. "I'll squeeze you in if you're quick about it," he said.

He already heard that Joe would be coming in. He just didn't know when. The assistant director picked up the phone and brought in the local TBI violent crime response team members who were still in the building. He also grabbed two members of the drug investigation division as they were on their way out the door for the night.

Joe had lucked out.

They sat in the assistant director's conference room and Joe began to tell them the tale of Tom Jones, the meth trail, the murder of Lacey, the burned-out vehicle, and the iPhone, belonging to Tom Jones, which connected Jefferson Banks to all these crimes. The only problem Joe had, as he outlined the situation, was that he was unfamiliar with the Nashville area and the state of Tennessee. There was a local FBI office in downtown Nashville in its federal building.

"I'll stop and see them tomorrow," Joe said.

He'd already stopped and thanked the Tennessee Highway Patrol for their efforts. He was very clear that he was appointed as the federal officer in charge of this federal investigation and it seemed to be growing.

Just like the sergeant who found the phone and wanted to know how Joe was involved, the staff who were sitting around the table were quite surprised as well. Joe told them about his unusual reporting hierarchy. He gave them his background, about his time spent in Key Largo and Islamorada, and how he was appointed as the one in charge of all investigations for south Florida and the Keys, and how the Tom Jones murder fell into his lap.

Everyone in law enforcement knew there were changes in federal interagency reporting, but no one knew that a Coast Guard chief warrant officer could be placed in charge of a federal investigation. They'd no idea about the ties between Homeland Security, the FBI, and the Coast Guard. In fact, most of the officers at the table didn't know that the Coast Guard was even part of Homeland Security. Joe didn't mention his connection to the CIA, who'd gotten involved in the Mexican Mafia affair, and how Joe's investigation in Albany became a national event and allowed the placing of gangbangers to be renditioned out of the country by the CIA under the Patriot Act. That conversation could wait for another day, if at all.

The assistant director told Joe to be back at his

office at 8:00 a.m. and they'd all sit down to devise a plan of attack. They were obviously interested in finding a murderer and were also very interested in closing down a major meth distribution center in Tennessee, especially in Nashville, the center of the meth trade.

Several of the staff asked Joe where this was headed. He tried to be very careful and not step on toes, as he was well capable of doing when pressed. He told them that he believed, after his own investigations in Florida, that the "TN" meth trademark stood for "The Nations" and not Tennessee.

They were all aware of that fact. They weren't aware that there were only one or two major meth distribution centers in the area, whereby all the small meth manufacturers sent their finished product—using the distributor's specifications—to a major center somewhere in the greater Nashville area. From there, they stamped "TN" on the pills and distributed the meth product up and down the entire southern eastern seaboard. In this particular case, Joe felt that Orlando was probably the most southern point, since the Russians and Cubans controlled all of south Florida. He was not aware how far north the meth went.

"In the greater Orlando area, local motorcycle gangs distribute meth. If we're able to find the Nashville distributor and close it down, it would localize the meth problem in Tennessee so you could get a better handle on it. Closing down a large distributor would, more than likely, have local meth dealers competing with each other for local business and that would be more evident as time went on," he said. "I've been thinking about how to proceed in finding the main distributor or distributors without stirring up any of the meth manufacturers locally. I need to discuss the situation with the rear admiral in Miami, but I feel that a clear solution to the issue might be found. However, I'll hold it until tomorrow's meeting. In the meantime, I'm still working the murder case. I've got Lacey's previous home address in Nashville and I'll stop by see who lives at that location. Do you mind supplying me with an officer or two, in case I have a problem while banging on doors?"

"It won't be a problem," the assistant director told him. "I'll give you a few officers after our meeting tomorrow."

"Thanks. I appreciate that."

"No problem. We want this solved, just like you."

"I want to find out prior connections between Lacey and Banks when they were living in Nashville. Both names appear on your Tennessee Meth Hot Line list. Lacey only had minor issues but Banks was a card-carrying member of the meth trade, with the jail time to prove it. I believe he probably violated his probation when he went to Orlando," Joe said. "Can you check into it and see if his parole officer can make the meeting. I believe that Banks and the distributor are connected because Banks was the connection to the Nashville distributor and the Orlando biker gangs."

The meeting lasted about half an hour and Joe thought the cooperation was very good. He believed they were very interested in taking down a major player and a distributor all at the same time. He also believed that, even though he represented the feds, he didn't come across like many in the FBI—that it was his way or the highway—but thought he got more bang for the buck by being non-confrontational.

He thanked them all and shook each of their hands. He noticed that of the eight staff, three were women, and that was a good sign. When he got to them and told them what had happened to Lacey, he bet they'd be even more cooperative.

❧❧❧

Joe was now in downtown Nashville but he wasn't in the mood for sightseeing. He had a lot of calls to make, especially to the rear admiral, who he knew would be waiting for his call since Joe had been asleep and then unable to call until now.

Joe hopped into his car and dialed the rear admiral's office. The assistant picked up the phone then the rear admiral immediately came on.

"Where the hell have you been, Joe? I've been waiting here patiently for your call. You really shouldn't piss off your senior officers. Or was that intentional?"

"God no, sir." Joe quickly went through the last forty-eight hours and how he almost passed out after driving up from Orlando to Nashville. He explained all the details that involved the connections between Tom, Jefferson Banks, Lacey, and the meth trade. "I just got out of a meeting with the TBI, its methamphetamine task force, and the violent crime response team." Then never taking a breath, Joe added, "I need a favor."

"You really do have a lot of balls, don't you, Joe? I chew your ass out and now you want a favor?"

"Yes, sir. I believe we can solve this much quicker with what I've in mind."

"Go ahead and tell me what you want and how it will move this investigation along. I believe you solved Tom's murder but you really want to move forward and get those responsible even though Tom was also responsible for his own death. Right?"

"Yes, sir, that's right."

"Okay, shoot."

"Can I borrow one of the Coast Guard drones to fly over Nashville for several days to pick up the scent of meth manufacturing sites in 'The Nations,' the west section of Nashville. This is the area that's the meth capital of the world and probably has over fifty individual meth labs banging out pills that will be sent to a major distributor for the 'TN' imprint and then mass distributed down the entire eastern seaboard. At least that was what I was told in the meeting I just had. I want to isolate five to ten of the labs and, in cooperation with the local FBI agents, the meth task force, and the Tennessee Bureau of Investigation, follow those leaving the meth labs for a week or two and see where the trail leads us. I believe that there's more than one handoff of the product before it gets to a distributor. After identifying the labs, the drone could then be assigned a lab on a daily basis and track the vehicles from the sky, unknown to the delivery guys."

The rear admiral was well aware that they used drones but he was not up to speed on how they were used. Joe knew they had started in 2005 when the Coast Guard bought several from the navy as an experiment. Instead of personnel flying out to sea in a plane that could be identified, the drones would be invisible. They were needed to follow foreign ships into port and also to identify the country of origin and the name of the ship so warrants could be issued for search and seizure at sea. There was a fine line between boarding a ship and having a legal reason to do so. Even while Joe was out of the services for a few years, he was quite intrigued by the Coast Guard's use of the drones and he read as much as he could on the subject.

"I understand that a drone, flying over a target could actually pick up the smell of individual chemicals that made up an item," he told the rear admiral. "It's very much like the nose of a bloodhound. A bloodhound can't smell ketchup but it can smell the thirty or so ingredients that make up the ketchup. The dog will smell each ingredient separately and that's how the drones will be able to detect meth—by the individual ingredients."

The rear admiral seemed quite surprised about Joe's knowledge. "I'd heard that you had a photographic memory but hearing it first hand is quite remarkable."

"I'll send you the key ingredients in the manufacturing of meth," Joe told him. "The most prevalent smell comes from ether—starter fluid mostly—which is clearly distinctive as you break down the doors to a meth house. There's more than one way to cook meth, but if you see or smell the following chemicals together, they most probably will indicate a meth lab."

Joe knew he was overdoing it at this point but he wanted it to be clear that he knew what he was talking about. He then went on to tell him what the ingredients were. "Acetone; isopropyl alcohol—rubbing alcohol or Iso-Heet fuel treatment; methyl alcohol—wood spirits or Heet fuel treatment; lye, as in Red Devil lye; crystal or liquid iodine; mineral spirits; bleach; anhydrous ammonia; sulfuric acid—car battery acid; hydrochloric acid; matches and match box strikers for red phosphorus; cold tablets containing ephedrine or pseudoephedrine;

white gas; lithium—from lithium batteries; trichloroethane—solvent for cleaning a gun; sodium metal or rock or table salt; ether—starter fluid; and toluene. Since these chemicals give off unpleasant and toxic fumes, they need some sort of ventilation device to blow the vapors out of the building, like a chimney or fans. There's no smoke or any visible sign of cooking." Joe took a deep breath and waited for either an "Okay" or a "What the hell are you doing?"

Instead, the Rear Admiral sighed. "So you're telling me that you can program one of our drones to fly over Nashville and detect all those chemicals together as coming from one location or from several locations as it passes over?"

"That's what I've been told, sir. I already called the drone engineers in Dallas and told them what I wanted to do, hypothetically of course, sir."

"Hypothetically, my ass, Joe," the rear admiral said and laughed. "You really believe you can pull this off?"

"Well, it's the best chance we have or we will lose Jefferson Banks and we will probably never find the distribution center since we haven't found it yet and we never even thought about there being a master distribution center. It's the forest and the trees, sir. We've concentrated so much on closing down one meth lab at a time, catching one cooker at a time, and putting their name on the hit list, that we haven't figured out that it's run very well—

almost like Target, for God's sake."

"What do you mean, Joe?"

"Sir, Target or, for that matter, even a milk co-operative runs the same way. The farmers, in that case, bring in their raw milk every day and get it processed by a distributor who trucks it everywhere to retailers on the same day. The farmers get the lowest base wholesale price for their raw milk and the distributor gets the wholesale price from the chain grocery store who then resells it at a good markup retail price to the consumer. I believe the meth cookers make the pills and then ship them to be stamped and distributed. Everybody's happy and they have a complete closed system for production and sale of product."

"That explanation is what I needed. How the hell did you ever figure that out, Joe?"

"Well, sir, you may not know that I got my MBA at Rensselaer and these were the kinds of discussions we had in every class. Wholesalers, distributors, and retailers all need to be on the same page if everyone wants to make money."

"Have you told anyone else about this yet?"

"No, sir. I mentioned at our meeting this after-noon that we might have a solution for finding the distributor but I had to speak to you first before re-vealing any plans."

"I'll call a meeting in the morning as well and fully discuss your proposal," the rear admiral prom-ised. "I want you to proceed as if it will happen. I don't want you slowing down at all. Tell them in the meeting that you can get a drone and a team by early next week and you'll set up another meeting when the drone becomes available."

"Thank you, sir, for your faith in me. I really believe this will work."

"I knew you were a very bright guy, Joe, but no one ever expected your creativity. At the end of this case, I want you to sit down with me and have a discussion on how we can improve the efficiency in solving these kinds of crimes, problems, and issues. Again, Joe, I'm very pleased that you came back to us."

Joe was a little flustered and embarrassed at the praise, but highly flattered. "One last thing, sir. Once we find the labs, we won't only be seeing it and following its progress from the sky. We'll need to have boots on the ground. Meth labs tend to be secretive, so we may see drawn shades or paper or foil over the windows, a guard dog, and a 'Keep Out' sign at most of the places. But we will be very sure, almost 100% sure, without breaking in to the lab, if we just watch their daily garbage. We will be sure that it's a meth lab if we see excesses in their garbage cans or large, black heavy-duty plastic leaf bags filled with paint thinner cans, antifreeze bottles, plastic soda bottles with holes or tubes at the top, acetone containers, excessive cans of drain cleaner, cases of brake fluid, reddish stained coffee filters, pizza boxes, hundreds of used rags, batteries, and cold tablets packaging."

"What're the pizza boxes for, Joe? Just curious."

"It was a joke, sir. I just wanted to see if you were listening."

"So you're funny, too? Smart ass."

"Well, actually, sir, they can't leave the premises, while they're cooking, so one guy feeds the whole team with pizza. It's the meth cooker's dinner of choice."

"Bye, Joe. Call me tomorrow after your meeting. I'll let you know how our meeting went down here. I don't expect to hear any objections."

"Thank you, sir. I mean it. I won't let you down, sir."

ભભભ

Joe stopped at a downtown barbeque joint and got dinner. He had a few beers and decided to go back to the Evergreen Motel. He hadn't gotten a chance to call the manager but Joe didn't think it would be filled. "Ever," he said with a laugh.

On the way home, Mark called him. "We found Banks's fingerprints all over Lacey's apartment, including the bedroom so it's a done deal. He's the murderer."

CHAPTER 13

Joe headed for the assistant director's office at 7:00 a.m. He always rose early, even when he'd worked at the Coalition in Albany. Getting up every day at the break of dawn, since joining the Coast Guard, was a habit that was hard to break. He stopped at the nearest Dunkin' Donuts and had his daily fix of a large regular coffee and two donuts. Today, he wanted jelly donuts for some reason. He was still tired from his trip up from Orlando and he seemed to be just going through the motions. That had happened to him on the first day he wound up in Orlando and didn't think to look for Tom's Explorer or even his iPhone, iPad, and computer. Joe was very embarrassed and decided to keep a "To Do" checklist from now on, whenever he started an investigation.

Hell, I can't remember everything, but that was very embarrassing.

He got to the assistant director's office by 7:45 a.m. and took his seat at the conference room table. A few of the meth team members were already there, coffees in hand, ready to go. The assistant director walked into the room at ten minutes to eight and started the show. Others, who got there on time, walked in sheepishly. Evidently, they all knew that he'd started his meeting as soon as he could so they better be there before the scheduled time next time.

"Okay, Joe. Get us started."

And he did. Joe outlined what he wanted to do to. He not only wanted to catch a murderer, but he also wanted to shut down a major meth distributor at the same time, if those at the table agreed. They all did.

"Unmanned Arial Vehicles, UAVs, commonly known as 'drones' are aerial systems that are remotely controlled for short- and long-ranged military and civilian purposes. Drones are usually equipped with a camera and can also be armed with missiles and guns, using infrared red and laser technology. The use of drones by the United States Government is constantly evolving. Currently, the US military, the Department of Homeland Security, of which the Coast Guard is a part, and the Central Intelligence Agency own and operate drones overseas in Afghanistan, Pakistan, Yemen, and other locations, and along the US-Mexico border. In the last decade the US Government has come to rely increasingly on drones for surveillance and air strikes. Even local law enforcement agencies have begun to use drones for surveillance. It's unlikely that domestic drones would be armed, but drones used in the United States can certainly have the same capacity as those employed in war."

Joe paused for a breath. "Amazon, one of the largest online distribution companies in the world, is in the process of testing smaller drones to deliver their packages, which weigh less than five pounds. I saw it on *60 Minutes* a few months ago. Most drones are operated from a single site in the United States by what're now known as 'human operatives,' meaning people. However, in this case, we can actually bring the human operative to Nashville to work out of a carefully placed van where needed.

"The Coast Guard uses the Boeing-Insitu ScanEagle, which is a small, low-cost, long-endurance UAV built by Insitu, a subsidiary of Boeing. The ScanEagle was designed as a commercial UAV that's intended for fish-spotting. It carries a stabilized electro-optical and/or infrared camera, on a lightweight inertial stabilized turret system, and an integrated communications system, having a range of over 62 miles. It has a flight endurance of over twenty hours. The ScanEagle has a 10.2-foot wingspan, a length of 4.5 feet, and a mass of 44 pounds. It can be operated up to 92 mph," he said. "No one would ever see what we're doing.

"Furthermore, the ScanEagle needs no airfield for deployment. Instead, it's launched using a pneumatic launcher known as the SuperWedge Launcher. It's recovered using the Skyhook Retrieval System, which uses a hook on the end of the wingtip to catch a rope hanging from a thirty-to-fifty-foot pole. This is made possible by high-quality differential GPS units mounted on the top of the pole and UAV. The rope is attached to a shock cord to reduce stress on the airframe imposed by the abrupt stop."

Joe also gave an example of how he'd personally used a drone. "I was on a Coast Guard cutter in late May 2013 that used a ScanEagle to seize over 1,000 pounds of cocaine from a fast boat in the waters south of Key West. The aircraft was able to maintain visual surveillance of the unidentified boat until a cutter was able to intercept the vessel, marking the first time a UAV deployed from a Coast Guard cutter participated in a drug interdiction. The Coast Guard hopes to begin purchases of unmanned aerial systems by 2016, with small UAVs deployed from its National Security Cutter Fleet by late 2014. Long-term goals are to use unmanned systems to augment their manned fleet, while UAVs on offshore patrol cutters would replace medium-endurance cutters."

Joe read to them from his manual, telling them that the United States Coast Guard's National Security Cutter, NSC, also known as the Legend-Class Cutter and Maritime Security Cutter was the largest of several new cutter designs developed as part of the Integrated Deepwater System Program. Eight ships were in the Program of Record but only seven were funded. "I'll be on each one of these cutters as they're rolled out in the Florida Keys."

"This is really cool," the assistant director said.

Everyone at the table said the same thing as Joe smiled at them.

"Do you mean that we will be using a Coast Guard drone to find meth labs, and then we close the labs down and make the arrests?" asked one of the officers.

"Not quite," Joe said. "What we'd like to accomplish is to find five to ten meth labs in 'The Nations,' pull a 24-hour surveillance on the sites for at least a week, and watch where it leads us. The drone costs almost $250,000.00 a week to deploy and operate and I don't think you guys want to pony up any money. Am I right, sir?"

"You're 100% right, Joe," the assistant director said. "So tell us your plan,"

Joe went on to explain how the drone would be programmed to sniff out the cooking of meth and gave them the list of required chemicals. Some knew the list and others did not. It was quite eye opener, they said.

He then told the team that the drone would be in the air twenty hours a day for five full days. "After identifying the sites, the drone will be assigned to track the movement from one site at a time. In other words, as a car leaves the site, the drone will follow it overhead and report back the constant GPS coordinates. I believe that there will never be a direct route to the distributor but there will be many handoff stops along the way. That's why I also wanted a minimum of two teams at each site, one to leave to follow a vehicle, and another to stay in place to see who else shows up. In addition, whenever garbage is put out in cans or in black plastic bags, I want the teams to have the garbage picked up by their own garbage trucks, manned by law enforcement officers to avoid possible problems. The garbage truck is to be emptied at a site to be determined and the garbage bagged and tagged as evidence from a meth lab. A picture is to be taken by a team member for every step taken."

"Wow, Joe. I think you've done this before," one of the team members said.

"Probably no more than you have, but I'm extra careful in the planning because I've seen what happens when events go wrong. Have you ever had a machine gun go off in your direction, guys? It scares the living crap out of you."

Joe finished up by telling them that the drone would be in Nashville by Monday at the latest and he had to leave today for a memorial service.

They asked him who it was for but he was holding it very close to the vest and simply said, "A close friend. I'll be back Saturday to start the ball rolling."

He planned to meet Lacey Bradford's sister as soon as this meeting was over. The assistant director pointed at two individuals at the end of the table and said that they'd be going with him for the death announcement to the sister—a young lady, Faye Barlow, and an older man, John McCarthy, who were both members of the violent crimes unit, assigned to Nashville.

As Joe headed to his car, the other two headed for theirs and said they'd meet him out front and he could follow them to 1100 Fifty-Fourth Avenue North in the heart of West Nashville.

What was now marketed as "West Nashville—a Great Place to Live and Work" by the Nashville Chamber of Commerce was formerly known as "The Nations." When the old prison had been in operation, a lot of family members of the convicts moved to this area as well as the guards and their families. The nickname, "The Nations," actually came from the Chickasaw Nations of Native Americans who had lived there during the eighteenth century. The fact that many of the streets were named after states—California, Michigan—also added to the moniker.

Along with the majority of closed-in sections of Nashville and similar cities nationwide, "The Nations" underwent a long period of decline when relocation to suburban areas became popular in the 1950s. By the 1980s the area was a haven for crime and drug activity. In recent years, "The Nations" had begun to be cleaned up, with crime rates dropping to city average or below. New developments were built and professional rehabbing of some of the neighborhood's many vintage Craftsman and

Victorian homes took place. The area had benefited from its proximity to the fashionable Sylvan Park Neighborhood. However, it was still believed to be the home of a large number of small meth labs.

Joe pulled up in front of the house. It was a two-story, two-family residence on a side street that had seen better days. Like a lot of places, revitalization was going on all around this block, but just like back in Albany, gentrification only went so far and ended from one block to another. It was as if they had run out of money for the year. That was exactly what had happened in the south end of Albany and many other small cities as well.

Both Faye and John got out of their cars, all parked nose to tail, and fell in behind Joe as he pressed the doorbell to the first floor flat. A few rings later, a young lady peeked out behind the curtain in her living room window to see who it was. She held up her index finger to indicate that she'd be there in a minute.

She had a towel wrapped around her head and must have just washed her hair. "Hi, sorry. I was washing my hair. Can I help you?"

"Yes. Are you Casey Bradford? Are you Lacey's sister?"

"Yes, I'm Casey and yes, Lacey is my sister. Why?"

"May we step inside for a minute Ms. Bradford," Joe asked. "We've something to tell you."

"It's about Lacey, isn't it? What's she done,

now? I can't keep up."

Joe looked at her frankly. "Casey, I'm sorry to tell you that your sister, Lacey Bradford, is dead." He then grabbed her arm as she started to fall toward the floor.

"How? Why? What happened? She can't be dead. I just spoke to her a few weeks ago. She was doing fine," Casey said. "How?"

"Your sister was involved in the murder of a gentleman by the name of Tom Jones, back in Orlando. We don't know what her involvement was but we believe that she was murdered as well by a Jefferson Banks, who we believe stabbed your sister and left her body outside Chattanooga, Tennessee. We don't know why, but we think your sister got in well over her head with a two-time loser, well-known drug dealer, and now a murderer."

"Oh, my God. I told her about Banks but she wouldn't listen. She lived here with me right until she left with him to go to Orlando. He'd just gotten out of jail. I begged her not to go and not to get involved with him. Now, she's dead? I can't believe it—well, I guess I can, under the circumstances. She was the only family I had."

"We really are sorry for your loss. No one deserves what happened to her," Joe said. "Have you seen him or heard from him in the last week? We believe he's back in Nashville and we've got every law enforcement agency in Tennessee looking for him."

126

"A few days ago, I got a call and a hang up but didn't think about it at the time. Let me check my phone and see if I can find the number." She went to the living room, picked up the phone, and scrolled down for incoming calls. "Nope, the number seems to be blocked. It must be a cell number."

"That's probably the case," Joe agreed. "What can you tell us about Jefferson Banks? It might help us find him."

"He has a brother, Buddy Banks, who still lives in Nashville. Let me get you his address and phone number. Lacey left her address book here when she left for Orlando. She said she was never coming back and wouldn't need it anymore."

She went and got it from Lacey's old room. "Nothing was changed since she left. I thought she'd be coming back and left her room alone. Here is his phone number. He lives, or at least did, at 5300 California Avenue."

"We know where that is," Faye said.

"Buddy is older than Jeff by a few years, just like I'm two years older than Lacey," Casey said.

Joe had guessed about the same. "I understand Jeff dropped out of school at sixteen and was considered one of the best meth dealers in the area for his age. All that was true until he got picked up at twenty years old. Now at thirty, he's just served four years for the same offense and was given more time because it was his second felony for the same crime."

"He was also accused of manslaughter," she said. "But they could never prove it. He had enough witnesses that he wasn't there to choke a horse. All his meth friends lied for him, of course. Lacey met him when she was only seventeen. It was a party or something. He was twenty-four at the time and I was only nineteen. I told Lacey that he was bad news and as bad as his brother. She never listened. When he got out the last time, it was about six months later that she hooked back up with him. Then they headed for Orlando. He blew off his parole officer who came knocking at my door a few weeks later. I told the parole officer that I didn't have a clue where he was." She broke out in tears. "If I told the parole officer his whereabouts, Lacey would probably still be alive."

Joe felt bad for her but she was right. Lacey might still be alive if Casey had done the right thing. *Live and learn.* "Lacey's body will be released by the Tennessee Highway Patrol as soon as the autopsy is completed."

Casey thanked Joe.

He gave her all his phone numbers and email addresses and told her to please call if there was anything she could remember that might help them find her sister's murderer.

He didn't call him Jeff Banks. He called him her sister's murderer for a very specific reason. Both of the officers with him knew exactly what he'd just done, hoping she'd be mad enough to start helping.

She did hand him Lacey's address book and phone numbers. That was a start.

∽∾∽

They went back to their cars and Joe suggested that they head over to Buddy Banks's house immediately. It took less than five minutes. Joe went up the front steps very cautiously. He didn't have a warrant but he didn't expect Jefferson Banks to be there, either. Faye and John both took the back door. It was unlocked. Joe rang the bell to no avail. He banged on the door and on the windows. Nothing. No one was there, or if there was, he or she was not coming out. They needed a warrant to search the premises.

Joe went around back and told the officers not to go in. He didn't want to compromise the investigation.

He asked them to go back immediately and get a warrant. He'd stay out in front in case anyone came home. He had a few hours before his flight back to Orlando for the memorial service the next day. He was leaving tonight, Friday, at 5:15 p.m. from the Nashville Airport. He'd make a call now to see if he could get on as an air marshal, which was never a problem. He'd have to be there an hour before the flight in full dress, with his weapon and carry-on bag.

It seemed like a lifetime, sitting outside Buddy's house but Faye and John got back with the warrant in a little under an hour and a half. Joe was hungry but this had to be done first. His dress uniform was in the trunk so he could change at the police station before heading for his flight.

They went through the unlocked back door. Joe headed up the stairs with his gun drawn shouting, "Police, we've a warrant. Is anyone here? Please come out."

No one did. Faye and John went through the downstairs and brought back large leaf size bags in case they needed to take anything with them. There was a phone and they took it. There was no cell phone, no computer, and no records of any kind. However, Joe did notice a faint smell of ether coming from the closet in the bedroom. He piled the clothes into a bag and labeled it as evidence. These could be meth-cooking clothes or the smell could have been transferred once Buddy got home from his "job."

There wasn't anything else of value but, John said, "This would be good as any meth lab to keep under surveillance during the week."

"Agreed," Joe said.

They left to head back to the station. Joe thanked them, showered, and changed into his full military "air marshal" outfit. A few of the team members, walking by, asked him for his phone number. He laughed.

A few of the civilian female employees took a

second, noticeable glance as Joe walked out the door to head for the airport. One young lady went up to Faye and asked her who the young man was in full-dress uniform. Faye smiled and told her that he was probably "way too dangerous" for her. She meant it.

CHAPTER 14

It was around 4:00 p.m. as Joe got into his car. He downloaded the GPS directions from the police station to the Nashville International Airport. It said it was about twelve miles and fourteen minutes to the airport, taking TN-155E to I-40E. He headed out and pulled into the long-term parking lot in just about twenty minutes. He took the shuttle to the Southwest Airlines Terminal to catch Flight 2008, which was leaving at 5:15 p.m. He was able to bypass the long security lines as he flashed his badge and told the TSA agent that he was serving as a Federal Air Marshal on Flight 2008. He got to his terminal gate and checked in just before 4:45 p.m.

On the way, he stopped at a newspaper stand and got the local *Nashville City Paper*, and a travel guide to Nashville. Since he'd be in Nashville for a while, investigating the murder and meth operations, he wanted to know more about the city, not just the Chamber of Commerce hype. He wanted to compare Nashville to Orlando and see if there were any similarities.

When Joe had been back in Albany, submitting grants for the Coalition, the first research he'd have done would have been to go to the 2010 United States Census Bureau to get the behind the scenes data that gave him better information on what he'd be dealing with, and what the population looked like.

He checked in with the front desk outside Gate 3 and was told he could head to his seat before any of the regular passengers got on board. Southwest personnel were pushing a few wheelchair patrons down the aisle toward the plane. Joe had an overnight bag and his newspaper and guide in his hand. He dropped the bag and placed his hat in the carry-on bag and stowed that at the front of the plane, where the flight attendants kept their luggage. He was assigned an aisle seat by the wing section, where the emergency doors were located. He pulled out his iPad before leaving his bag, carried it with him, and got into his aisle seat. This Southwest flight had WiFi so Joe could do his online census data research from the air. There was a nominal fee but Joe didn't have to pay anything.

As the flight filled with passengers, Joe went into his Federal Air Marshal mode, watching the passengers move down the aisle one by one, loading their carry-on bags into the overhead compartments. If he'd gotten a quarter for every "excuse me," he could probably pay for a business class seat on his own. No one looked suspicious but no one ever did.

The plane took off right on time at 5:15 p.m. and was scheduled to land at 7:10 p.m. in Orlando. The Orlando International Airport was huge but Mark told him that he'd meet him at the Disney Magical Express Terminal, main terminal, B side, Level 1, right outside where the Walt Disney World buses took families to their resort hotels. There were several spots for police cars and for handicapped access. Mark could pull right in and wait for Joe's arrival.

After drink requests were filled and bags of snacks were passed out by the airline attendants, Joe settled in and turned on his iPad to make sure the airplane's Internet service worked. The last flight he was on from Albany to Fort Lauderdale, the Internet didn't work because of bad weather conditions. He found the Southwest Network System ID and got connected. No password was required. It was much different than trying to find out which Network Tom Jones had used at his condo complex. Joe immediately downloaded the 2010 census data for Nashville, Tennessee. He hadn't realized that Nashville was the capital of Tennessee. He always thought it was Memphis for some reason. He hadn't been in Nashville long enough to see any state government capital buildings. He'd put that on his checklist to see.

Memphis was the largest city with Nashville next and then Chattanooga. He knew it was called

Music City, as the heart of country music. He didn't know that it had a consolidated government of city and county and six smaller municipalities all rolled into one. The population of Nashville, itself, was around 600,000 people but the greater Nashville area, for the entire thirteen-county region, was over a million and a half people. He looked up the poverty index and, like most large cities, it hovered around 20% or over 300,000 people living in poverty in the region. That was a lot and a good reason for a high crime index. The United States' overall poverty rate was around 12% so Nashville was much higher, 75% higher. He checked the unemployment rate, the second largest factor for increased crime. It was 6.3% but was 8.3% only a year earlier in 2013. In real numbers, almost 100,000 people were still unemployed in the greater Nashville region and over 200,000 in the state of Tennessee. The largest surprise was a growing Hispanic population in Nashville. It was less than 1% in 1970 and, now in 2014, it stood at 10%, a significant increase. Joe was very interested in growing Hispanic populations because of his language expertise and fluency. He could always wind up here to address a growing Hispanic population just as well as Miami, which was settling into a fourth and fifth generations of Cuban-American citizens, who were now fully recognized into the middle class. If Nashville's Hispanic population was at 10%, Joe suspected it could be close to double that for the illegal Hispanic immigrant population.

Nashville was ranked the twenty-sixth largest city in the United States.

Joe went to the Orlando census data and saw very similar results. Orlando proper had only 238,300 people as per the 2010 census. However, the greater Orlando and Orange County area comprised of a large portion of central Florida, had a population over two million people, making it the twenty-sixth largest metro area in the United States but only seventy-seventh as a city. The poverty rate was identical to Nashville at 19%, meaning there were over 400,000 people who lived in poverty in the region. Orlando should have had a better unemployment rate due to the proximity to Walt Disney World, but it was 6.0% as well. Perhaps Disney jobs were similar to jobs in the music business in Nashville. Walt Disney World employed 51,000 people but had seasonality, as well, with ups and down in the total number employed in full time jobs. The biggest difference was a Hispanic population at 25% versus only 10% for Nashville. This would be a Hispanic destination city just, as Miami in the south would in the near future with Disney as an added attraction because it attracted people from all over the world.

After looking at both areas, Joe didn't believe there were significant differences that made crime in each city more or less representative of any ethnic group, except for the larger Orlando Latino population. However, previously, meth was considered a white population's drug of choice but as the numbers rolled out, it was become a non-discriminatory drug of choice. Once hooked, you were hooked regardless of ethnicity, social status, economic status, or even employment status. It was a young adult's choice, unfortunately, and growing out of proportion, just like heroin was now spiraling out of control in the greater Northeast.

Joe started to read the Nashville newspaper and the travel guide and made notations on the guide for places where he should visit while in Nashville. He could have kicked himself since he didn't do it in Orlando and missed a lot of areas that he'd have liked to see before going home after the investigation. Hell, he was only there for a few days, anyway. He never knew where he'd wind up and he didn't know if he'd get back to visit these places again, at least visit for enjoyment.

The overhead announcement came on with a dinging effect to ensure everyone's seat belt was securely fastened to his or her potential flotation device. The plane landed on time. Joe gathered his belongings and was the last to leave the plane as his job as Federal Air Marshal would only end as he stepped out the door. He gathered his carry-on bag from the front, thanked the crew, and headed toward Level 1 to meet Mark. To think it took him and Butler over eight hours to drive the 600-plus miles, and it only took two hours to fly. He was grateful for the change. It was only 7:10 p.m. He'd get some dinner, relax, spend time with Mark, and, hopefully, wake up refreshed the next day for the memorial service by the ocean. He'd be hopping back on the same flight to Nashville tomorrow night, Flight 1719, at 5:05 p.m., arriving in Nashville at 7:50 p.m.

Joe went from the A side, Level 2, down to the B side, Level 1 and found the Disney Magical Express Terminal. Crowded families waited in separate lines, depending on which resort hotel they'd be going to. The Orleans French Quarter and Riverside lines were crowded for after 7:00 p.m. Most families tried to arrive before noon so they could get to their rooms early and spend at least a half a day at the Magic Kingdom, the first stop, usually, for families with young kids. Their luggage would wind up in their room "magically" about three hours after they arrived. Even though most read the brochures on what to expect the first day upon arrival, many forgot to pack an overnight bag with clothes for the first afternoon. It was always hot and a change of clothes was always necessary. As soon as Joe went through the door, the heat and humidity hit him. He had two dress uniforms with him and he'd left one at the Embassy Suites with Mark so it could be laundered for the memorial service. It should be ready tonight. He'd hand them the one he had on to be laundered and pressed for his return trip to Nashville.

"Hey, Joe. How was your trip?" Mark asked as Joe opened the passenger door.

"The trip was fine but I'd have loved to have this memorial held at a later date. All this travel's getting to me."

"I hear you, Joe. I can't wait to get home to see Louise and the kids. It seems like forever since I saw them last. You know what I mean?"

"I sure do. I was supposed to fly to New York City to see Julie last weekend and this came up." *So much for a love life.*

"Get used to it if you get married."

"Not for a while, anyway. With our different schedules and, now, traveling, we don't see enough of each other to probably even be considered a couple, you know?" Joe sighed. "Let's get something to eat. All I had was barbeque up in Nashville. I want some Cuban food tonight. You must have found a spot by now. Do you want to invite Butler over and update him, as well? I'll tell him about our first 'drone' attempt over dry land and see what he says. After our first encounter, I wonder if he'll believe what's happening now? Is he coming tomorrow? Who's bringing Tom's girlfriend?"

"Christ, take a breath, Joe. Nice to see you, too," Mark said and smiled. "Let's go eat. Call Butler on the way. I'm sure he'd like to eat with us."

Mark had found a Cuban restaurant only a few blocks from the hotel, in the heart of downtown Orlando. Butler met them at the door. He'd just gotten done at the station. He was now on another case, since the Tom Jones murder seemed to be solved and he was forced to move on. "I worked all week and identified the Outlaws biker gang as probably the main distributor for meth in the Orlando area but I haven't picked up the delivery point, as of yet."

So knowing that it was the Outlaws didn't mean anything, if Butler couldn't find out where the meth pills were being delivered so they could be moved throughout the city.

"We've a pretty good plan in place to catch Tom and Lacey's murderer," Joe said. "And it could lead to the takedown of the distribution site that feeds the entire Southeastern Seaboard."

Joe was hoping that a raid on the distribution center, once found, would lead to some kind of records telling them who, where, and what was being transported to Orlando and other places. "Jim, if that happens, I want your chief on board, if anything comes down in Orlando."

"I'll meet with the chief on Monday," Butler said. "And I'll do a complete write up on where we are now and where the investigation is headed."

"Thanks. We look forward to reading it."

Butler also told them both that he felt great, never better in fact, and that he was back on speaking terms with his children. He said it would take a while to get back into the good graces of his estranged wife but he'd known, going in, that that would be the case. He was grateful to Joe and Mark for sticking with him and for putting in a good word with his chief. "I still don't want to be a cop after age fifty, two years from now, and I still want to pursue a career in security with Walt Disney World. My retirement pay and a full time position would help me take care of my wife, if we're still married or not. It's my fault. She deserved better and I still want to do the right thing." His kids would expect no less and he wanted a continued relationship with them, regardless of the outcome of his marriage.

After dinner, Joe and Mark headed back to the Embassy Suites Hotel. "Head home, after the memorial service, Mark," Joe said, "since I'll be going back to Nashville for the drone launch on Monday morning. I expect the human operatives to arrive Sunday night in a special van that they'll set up in the parking lot of the police station."

"Human operatives? They're called people, Joe."

"Yes, people. Okay?"

There was a West Nashville police precinct but that would make it too obvious, to those residing in the west end, that something was going on. The drone had to be netted and they needed room for it to land properly. The drone team could stay at the

Evergreen Motel and be out of the way. The drone would be airborne for twenty hours a day and the two operators could switch off and on, with Joe helping out as needed.

Mark would take the vehicle given to him by Frank and would be back by the end of the week. It would take about four hours, door to door. Mark missed his family and this would give him some time to catch up with his own duties and head over to the rear admiral's office in Miami to give him a detailed explanation of the investigation status.

Joe got a hold of Julie, finally. They spent a good hour on the phone, catching up, as well.

"I'm very happy with my progress and book sales to date," she said. "I'm especially pleased to be meeting young girls in the New York City charter schools who seemed to like what I've got to say. A few of the charters ordered my book for the freshman class of girls as part of their New York State English Common Core standards."

She was very pleased about that. "It could go a long way if several schools ordered the book as well, especially if it's used as part of the curriculum. If I've enough sales, I could give the book to my own Coral Shores High School freshman girls and actually be there as the model, day in and day out, when I get back to Key Largo."

"That's great. I'm very proud of you, Julie. I hope you're hanging in there. New York City can eat you alive if you let it. I know that for a fact."

Joe hung up on a good note and went to bed. It would be a long day on Saturday, with the memorial service and then flying back to Nashville in the evening.

❧❧❧

Joe and Mark got up early Saturday morning, around 6:30 a.m. The Embassy Suites had a full complimentary breakfast buffet for guests so they thought they'd take advantage of it. Joe and Mark's motto was: eat and sleep when you could because you never knew what the day would bring. They were in full-dress uniform. Joe had gotten his from the hotel cleaners late last night. The one the day before was wrinkled so he got that laundered as well. He didn't know when he'd get another chance, living out of a suitcase and all. Now, he'd be back to two uniforms, cleaned and pressed. Mark's uniform had only been used for the memorial service in Orlando at the beginning of the week, and only for an hour or so. He'd gotten back to the hotel and hung it up immediately, so he was good to go.

No matter where they went, Joe found it amazing the looks that they got from perfect strangers when in full-dress uniform. Many said thanks for their service, not knowing that they were in the Coast Guard and not the navy. There was always thanks for war veterans, but no one really understood the war on terror versus taking down drug dealers. Maybe it wasn't the same, but it sure felt the same.

At 8:00 a.m., they hopped into their car, with Mark driving. Mark checked out of the hotel and told them he'd be back the following week and for them to hold the same room if they could. He set the GPS for the Titusville Marina on North Washington Avenue in Titusville, about fifty miles away. Tom had kept his small boat at this marina for several years. The Titusville Marina was owned and operated by a veteran who gave veterans a 25% discount for slips and services. There were seventy slips and the marina was at 100% capacity. The marina was located on the Intracoastal Waterway in Titusville. With six acres of do-it-yourself dry yard, the marina was very popular among do-it-yourself boaters, which included Tom. Their lift could haul out boats to sixty-five feet in length, weighing up to thirty tons. Tom didn't have to worry about that. His twenty-foot fishing boat wouldn't make a dent on the marina's capacity. There was a nice restaurant attached to the marina. Claire said they'd meet them at the dock. Joe had called her on the way just to make sure that the memorial service was still on.

"We're picking up Gladys first and then heading out," Claire said.

Next, Joe had called Frank. "We're about five minutes away at Port Canaveral and we'll meet you at 9:30 a.m."

Butler called Joe on his cell. "I'm on my way to Titusville. I got a call early this morning from the Tennessee Highway Patrol Forensics Department. The only un-melted tire on Lacey's car matched the cast imprint made outside Chattanooga, where they'd found Tom's iPhone. This is the final piece of circumstantial evidence we needed to make the case. It would be nice to catch Jefferson Banks with the murder weapon with blood still on it, but that's wishful thinking."

"The weapon is probably long gone," Joe said.

Unlike the phone, that had a GPS tracking device, there was no such thing for the knife used to kill both Tom and Lacey.

Everyone met at the dock around 9:15 a.m. Joe and Mark joined Claire and her family, Gladys, Butler, and a full contingent from the Port Canaveral Coast Guard Station. An officer representing Jacksonville and the rear admiral's office was also there. That was a nice touch, Joe thought. A few of Tom's boating friends from the marina were at the ceremony, as well.

They all walked down the marina dock until they reached Tom's little fishing boat, tied to the end of the dock. It didn't even take up enough space to be called a slip.

Claire had a container that held about 40% of Tom's ashes. She had a few placed in a hermetically sealed vial that she wore around her neck. The rest of the ashes were in a burial container, back at her house, that would be placed at the Florida National Cemetery in a few months. There was no religious ceremony. Claire's Catholic priest had said the final prayers at the memorial service back in Orlando.

"Thank you, everyone, for coming," Claire said. "This isn't a burial or funeral service but a celebration of life for my father."

She asked if anyone wanted to speak and the two representatives from the Coast Guard headquarters gave a Coast Guard-tinted brotherhood speech about patriotism and service to your country. Frank told an amusing story about Tom, while he was going through the nightmare of Tom's boot camp. Everyone chuckled because they knew exactly what Tom was like.

Mark didn't like public speaking of any kind. "I'm proud to know Tom and I'm better for it," he said.

A few of Tom's boating friends chipped in a few tidbits about Tom with a few chuckles.

Claire turned to Joe. He stood closer to Claire and spoke to the group but looked directly at her. "Tom was like a father to me and, like my own father, Tom was also a pain in the ass."

Claire smiled. She'd guessed that this speech would be a little different.

Joe told her, and the assembled mourners, about various incidents since he was eighteen years old. He told them about the five-mile hike after they'd come in totally drunk the night before. "Tom had called it a refresher course."

Joe spoke for about ten minutes, which was a lot for him. He wound up by saying, "I loved your father very much and will miss him dearly. Whenever I'm feeling bad about his death, I'll remember what a pain in the ass he was, to ease the burden of knowing him."

Everyone had tears in their eyes from laughing and crying but Joe had lightened the mood so that it was indeed a joyful celebration of life. Claire then spread a few ashes over the waters near the dock. She handed the container to Joe who did the same. She invited everyone else to add a few to the water and they all said the *Our Father* prayer and watched Tom's ashes wash out to sea.

Claire invited everyone to the marina restaurant for a catered lunch. They all sat outside in the open air by the dock. Joe played with the kids so Brian and Claire could eat. Afterward, Joe grabbed a sandwich and a beer. He really wanted a beer after that. In fact, he had two, in full dress uniform. No one said a word.

Joe caught Claire's attention and they walked down the dock for a few minutes so he could bring her up to date. "I'm heading back to Nashville to meet the drone team, as I call it."

"Don't you mean the dream team?" she asked.

"Hardly," he said.

She smiled and told him it was a joke.

He laughed. "I'm way too serious and need to come down to earth. I'm going back with Jim Butler to continue discussing the case. I have to be at the Orlando airport by 4:00 p.m., or so, for my 5:05 p.m. flight as an air marshal, on Southwest Flight 1719 back to Nashville. I can't miss it or I won't get back until Sunday." He had a lot to do, starting early in the morning.

Mark headed home to Fort Lauderdale in the borrowed car. He'd be back later that week or early next week, depending on Joe's circumstances. "I'll return the vehicle then," he said to Frank.

"No problem, but if you break it, you bought it," Frank said.

Mark smiled. "It's only Joe who ruins vehicles, not me."

Butler pulled up by the restaurant to pick up Joe for the return trip to Orlando. Claire gave Joe a big hug and kiss. "Thank you for everything, Joe, especially for those very kind words about my father," she said, laughing. "It meant a lot and made me feel better about how he died. I'm still mad at him but I'll get over it."

"I meant every word of it, Claire," he said, smiling.

"I know you did," she said. "You're all a pain in the ass, but that's why I love you."

"Bye, Claire," Joe said.

❧❧❧

Butler and Joe made it back to Orlando by 2:30 p.m., giving Joe plenty of time to meet with the chief, who said he'd come in to be updated by Joe before he left. They went to his office and he was waiting for them. The chief looked at the way Butler and Joe now interacted and couldn't believe it was only days ago when they were on the verge of a fistfight. Joe went over every detail with the chief.

"Joe, I've never gotten this kind of cooperation from any federal officer before, and I appreciate how you went out of your way to get to this point," the chief said, handing over a forensics report on the Tom Jones murder case that had come in while Joe was in Nashville.

They set up a potential plan, if everything went well in Nashville, for taking down the meth distribution people. "If we get hold of any documentation at all, there will be a full heads-on assault in taking down the operation in Orlando, biker gang or not," Joe said.

Butler gave Joe a ride to the airport at 3:30 p.m. so he could grab a sandwich in the terminal and be on time for check-in. He dropped Joe back at the Disney terminal and Joe made it to the other side, A, and then the shuttle to the Southwest terminal. He showed his credentials and walked down to the gate and the waiting plane. He sat in the same seat as his previous flight, over the wing by the emergency door. This time, if there were no issues requiring his status as a federal air marshal, then after he read the forensics report he'd received in Orlando, he'd sleep until they landed at 7:50 p.m.

They arrived on time. Joe awakened to the bell to fasten their seat belts for landing. As he departed, he thanked the crew, once again, for their hospitality.

CHAPTER 15

As soon as Joe left the airport and picked up his car, he called Mark. It was a little after 7:30 p.m. when he got to his car. Something had been bothering him and he wanted Mark to work on it while he was home for the week in Fort Lauderdale. There was something about Jim Butler that just didn't seem to fit. Joe couldn't put his finger on it but he wanted to get Mark's opinion. Butler had kept nudging him for information all the way back from the memorial service.

"Mark? Hi, it's Joe. You got a minute?"

"Yes, Joe. I have a minute but the kids are heading to bed and I have to read to MJ. As you know, it's been a while."

"Yes, I know. Tell them I love them." Mark's kids were like Joe's own. Mark's daughter, Jennifer, was Joe's goddaughter.

"What's on your mind, Joe?"

"Give me your opinion of Jim Butler."

"What do you mean?"

"Is it my imagination, or does his turnaround from total prick to follower of Mother Theresa bother you at all?"

"I thought it was just me," Mark confessed. "After cursing us out and having his 'come to Jesus' meeting with the chief, I thought maybe he saw the light, but I don't know. Why?"

"I think it may be a loose end and here's why," Joe said. "I think he is over-cooperative and he popped up for both of Tom's memorial services. He seemed to ask a lot of questions on how we were proceeding, but his follow up to my questions seemed to be cursory at best. Do you know what I mean, Mark?"

"Yes, I do. However, he did give us information on biker gangs in Orlando and which one was dealing meth in a big way."

"We took that as gospel, though, didn't we? Maybe we should check that out for ourselves. Who really knows what gang is number one in the meth trade? It could be the Outlaws, or the Warlocks, or even Hell's Angels. He never gave us any written verification. It seems anecdotal at best. Could you ask Frank to check with the Jacksonville office and see who handles gang activity for north and central Florida for the Coast Guard?"

"I'll call him right after I hang up," Mark said.

"Good. I don't want to leave anything to chance, especially since we won't be in Orlando this week. Here's what's bothering me," Joe said. "First, I just found out that Butler's thumb print showed up in Tom's house on an end table. I thought it might be an accident and we'd use it to eliminate his prints as a suspect. However, I then remembered that when we entered together, he had on gloves just like the rest of us. Second, we never found the computer but we found the iPhone. What if the two went in separate directions? We need to check that out. Third, we should do a credit report on Butler and have Jack Forest do a full financial workup on him. We don't know a thing about him. Finally, how did he pick up Tom's murder investigation? Did he volunteer or was he the next man up in the rotation? Who do we ask that question?"

"You're right," Mark said. "We never did a thing to check him out and we should. I'll ask Jack to check out the financials and he can also go to the Orlando Police Department's web site and see if there was a rotation schedule with Butler on call for the next murder investigation. He didn't appear to be in good graces with the chief, especially as the chief told him that he could hit the road if he didn't cooperate. Your first thought's usually your best one, Joe."

"Thanks, Mark. Stay in touch. If you find anything, you can head back up and stay at the Port Canaveral facility with Frank or back to the hotel. It's up to you. I've a feeling we will need Frank, anyway. Can you call him and fill him in on everything going on?"

"Sure."

"Thanks." Joe suddenly remembered something.

"Oh, I almost forgot about how to handle the computer. Just like the iPhone, I think we can trace the computer if it was ever turned on after it left Tom's condo. Unlike the iPhone, Tom didn't need the GPS hookup since it was connected to the Internet supplied by the apartment complex. However, if someone took the computer and turned it on, regardless of where it was, or even if they couldn't get in without a password, downloads from Apple would come automatically, if it was turned on and connected to WiFi, anywhere. I gave you the list of serial numbers from his iPad, iPhone, and computer. You also have the passwords. It's the same passwords that were used for all three devices. The computer was a new thirteen-inch MacBook Pro. Call Apple on the 800 number and ask them if there were any automatic downloads since the day Tom died. If there were any downloads, it means that the computer was hooked up to the Internet and they should have the IP address the download was sent to, and the WiFi network connection would be identified as well. We can trace the computer that way, but only if it was turned on."

"Anything else, Joe?" Mark laughed. "Just kidding. Good luck this week in Nashville. You're there, right? You never told me."

"I just landed a few minutes ago and I'm in the car on the way to the Evergreen Motel."

On that note, they both hung up. Joe picked up dinner on the way. He had to contact the drone team and put together a "To Do List" for the next day, Sunday. It'd been a while since he made it to mass. When he got to the motel, he checked online for the mass schedule for Sunday morning. The Cathedral of the Incarnation was located in downtown at 2015 West End Avenue, Nashville. There was an 8:30 a.m. mass. He'd leave the motel at 7:00 a.m., stop at Dunkin' Donuts for his fix, and get to church on time. After that, at 3:00 p.m., he was meeting the drone team arriving from Dallas. Between mass and then, he had to make a stop at the FBI headquarters at 2868 Elm Hill Pike, then on to the Nashville Police Department's West Precinct on Charlotte Pike right afterward. Coordination was everything.

When he first thought about the drone that would be flying over "The Nations," he'd wanted the drone to land at the West Precinct but that was too obvious. Then in his divine wisdom—and now Joe laughed about it—he'd thought that placing it in the Tennessee Bureau of Investigation's downtown parking lot on Gass Boulevard would have been perfect. But now he realized that was just as stupid. How long would it take for the TV news trucks to pop by and ask what was going on? Immediately? That was really dumb. If he could swing it, and if the cost was right, there was a small airport only six miles away from the Evergreen Motel where they'd all be staying. It was perfect. It was well hidden and unnoticeable to the everyday drivers going by. It would be open today so he could stop by and see if he could set it up.

To cover their clandestine operation, Joe had learned from the drone team, they used the National Oceanic and Atmospheric Administration, NOAA, as their cover story and gave the National Climate Data Center as their billing address for doing research. It was located in the Federal Building on Patten Avenue in Asheville, North Carolina.

Any billing for rental of the airstrip would go through them. They couldn't call until Monday, anyway, when they'd be flying. However, they had to get the drone set up to fly and the netting in place to catch it, whenever it had to come down. It would be in the air for twenty hours at a time, so the downtime was minimal and not much of a distraction for airport users. Joe hoped that the meth distributors didn't use this small airport, but you never knew, and, hopefully, the NOAA cover story would be all they'd need. There would be a van, two staff, the drone, and the netting, and Joe popping in and out. Not much infrastructure to worry about.

He left a message for the rear admiral. Then he called Julie and talked for about a half an hour. Things were good but he felt that there was a growing distance between, them, not just geographic. He called Joan in Islamorada to catch her up as well. He told her they knew who the killer was, but now it was a matter of catching him.

After hanging up, he set the alarm for 6:15 a.m. and went to sleep.

ოოო

Joe got up on time and stopped at Dunkin' Donuts. He had his two donuts and large regular coffee and made mass right on time. It was a beautiful cathedral. His mother would have loved being here, attending mass, and sitting next to him. He'd kept up his Catholic faith because of his mother, and he couldn't see any harm in continuing. You never knew what life brought you and this gave him some peace in times like these that weren't only lonely but also dangerous as hell.

After mass, he went to FBI headquarters. They were already aware that he was in town and in charge of the investigation. The Sunday duty officer, the low man on the totem pole, was handed a written outline of where Joe was to date and what would be taking place in Nashville this week. Joe was also requesting assistance with the takedown when, and if, they found the distribution center. Joe didn't need help following the five soon to be identified meth lab's delivery people, but if he did, the agent said to give them a call. They worked well with the TBI and the meth team. The Nashville police were a different story.

The next stop was not quite as productive. The Nashville Police Department felt like they were the stepchild to the FBI, TBI, and Joe directly. He stopped at the West Precinct office on Charlotte Pike and caught Commander Felix Fernandez, who was doing his paperwork on Sunday to catch up. *Right up my alley. Maybe, I can have this conversation in Spanish.*

No such luck. Joe introduced himself but the commander wasn't happy. Someone must have pissed in his corn flakes that morning. At that point, Joe gave him less information rather than more. He told them there would undercover FBI special agents in ordinary rental cars, either older Ford Taurus models or Toyota Camry's for all of the following week. He told him this was a Homeland Security operation and the commander's officers weren't to interfere or there would be hell to pay. Joe was very easy going until he got a lot of crap for no reason. This was no exception.

He left and headed out to the airport. He probably should have gone there from the motel. It was so close. And he felt like he was on a merry-go-round. He met the airport director and told him that they needed a quick set up for this NOAA operation, scheduled for this week. It was an air-sampling audit of Nashville and it would be nice if he'd simply comply. He did. Joe gave him the billing information for the sub-division in Asheville, South Carolina. He got a hanger allocated for the van and the drone. It would have a large hanger door with a combination lock. It would also have bare sleeping accommodations with twin beds in an office for off duty. They could go back to the motel or simply stay there, taking turns spying in the sky.

Joe met the drone team at the motel when they pulled in a little after 3:00 p.m. Their trip was unglamorous, with a few stops along the way, and one overnight in Georgia. They said it would only take about an hour to set up the drone, the computer, and the netting, and they'd be good to go by Monday morning. The computer was programmed for the exact meth formula.

Joe told them about the pizza boxes added to the equation and they laughed. "You've a lot of balls talking to a rear admiral that way.

Joe chuckled. "Oh, well."

They headed out together, with the team following Joe, and were at the airport in less than fifteen minutes. They were lucky to get a facility outside town because Nashville traffic on a Monday morning would be bumper to bumper. Six hundred thousand people meant a lot of commuters heading to work, especially since it was the state capital of Tennessee. Joe knew about state capitals from working in Albany. I-787 S was a parking lot heading in to Albany on weekdays at 8:00 a.m. and the same at 4:00 p.m. heading home.

After the setup, Joe took them to the best barbeque restaurant in Nashville. They had a few beers, knowing how intense the next week would be. Joe stopped at two beers and drove them back to the motel. They had locked up the van and the drone in the hanger at the airport before heading to the restaurant, with Joe driving.

He dropped them off at the motel and went back to West Nashville to check on the surveillance team watching Buddy Banks's house. There was no activity and no suspicious characters driving by the house. Joe quickly stopped at Casey Bradford's house to see how she was doing. She was still in shock over her sister's murder. *Who wouldn't be?* he surmised.

"Call me at any time you need me and I'll drop everything to get Lacey's murderer, Casey."

This was becoming a meth investigation, but Tom and Lacey's murder investigations came first, in Joe's mind.

CHAPTER 16

It was now Tuesday. The drone had been flying since Monday morning at 7:00 a.m.

"The drone operated flawlessly and landed in the net after twenty hours in the air, at approximately 3:00 a.m., Tuesday morning," one of the technicians told Joe. "We worked on it for two hours and all systems were fine."

They liked the schedule of having the drone land in the middle of the night so they launched it back out at 7:00 a.m. on Tuesday morning.

The operators knew the drone would be up all day and late into the night, so they could hit their beds back at the motel at 7:30 p.m. on Monday night, after watching it for over twelve hours straight.

Joe took them back to the airport from the motel at 2:30 a.m. to get ready for the landing of the drone in the net. They'd been keeping track of all the data received, based on the inputted program. They had a state-of-the-art laptop linked to the main computer setup at the airport and, if there was an issue, an alarm would go off and they could make an adjustment right from the motel. It was very sophisticated, to say the least.

During the first few hours of Monday morning, they had found two meth houses, a block from each other. It was very clear and obvious. The next few passes, later that afternoon, brought into sniffing range eight more meth houses, all operating at different times during the day. They picked up another five from 11:00 p.m. until the drone landed at 3:00 a.m. on the dot.

What else is expected for $50,000.00 a day?

So during the first twenty hours, they'd found fifteen meth houses, fully operational. Joe was amazed. They placed the GPS coordinates of the meth labs onto a computerized city map of West Nashville that was printed out and blown up for the wall. They found that five of the meth houses were grouped together, within a block or two of each other. This probably meant that the daily meth pick up by the delivery guys for those five houses, could be done almost at once. It would be a full load for the surveillance squads, so they'd assigned at least three teams, of two officers each, to those five houses.

Joe then looked at the map, at all the pins marking the fifteen locations. In addition to the five houses bunched together, Joe picked out four meth labs that were far enough away from each other that suspicions wouldn't be raised if they saw a bunch of cars driving around their neighborhood.

These other four were probably independent of the five bunched together so they probably had other delivery teams in place, going to the same distributor by different routes. They'd watched nine of the fifteen houses found to be active meth labs.

Joe had known, by this point, that he needed seven teams for the five locations. Three to be located in the five-meth-house group and one team each at the other four isolated houses. He could always add any one of the six houses left over for a second wave. These houses also had to be watched for twenty-four hours straight. Joe figured that he actually would need twenty-one teams of two officers in each car, until they found out where the final handoff would wind up. The final handoff would then take them directly to the distribution site, hopefully. The problem was that they had to stay on top of each location, each pick up, and each hand-off before the final drop, and then follow up when the cash drop for payment was made to each house. They noticed that no money was exchanged during the pickup. They'd guessed that the meth labs didn't want to lose both the drugs and the cash at the same time if they were ever stopped. Whoever was in charge of this operation was no dummy. It was well planned and had the essence of a well-established delivery and distribution system. Someone had put a lot of thought into this.

With enough officers, and with the drone in the sky, Joe didn't believe that it would take more than the five days allocated by the rear admiral. They couldn't afford more than the $250,000.00 that it cost to fly the drone, fully staffed for the five days. They were lucky to get that for this experiment.

That's exactly what it is, an experiment that could prove very rewarding.

It could be the new way of tracking dope manufacturing, no matter what the substance. If it could be formulated, a drone could sniff it out, right to the GPS code. If they got the routes right, the drone could follow the identified cars and the men could watch the houses. If the distribution site came into view, the drone could take pictures of the center from all sides and take pictures of anyone going in and out of the facility. Pictures of the cars could lead to identifying the owners of the vehicles, which could help in understanding the dangers the officers faced. There was no doubt that whoever worked in the distribution center would have a long record of criminal convictions and would most likely be armed and dangerous. This was not a mom and pop operation by any stretch of the imagination.

Joe and the team would take their time. There was no rush. They all wanted to get it right. They wanted the murderer first and the take down second, at least that's what Joe wanted.

He held a team meeting back at the TBI headquarters. From the data they'd already received, they found out that the pickups for the five houses close together had one driver in one car. The pickups began at 7:30 a.m. and ended by 8:30 a.m. From there, the car left and met another vehicle at a local gas station. The handoff was made through the driver side window into the backseat of the other car. If they hadn't been watching closely, they probably wouldn't have even seen it happen. It was that quick. Starting at 9:30 a.m., another driver pulled up and stopped at each house, every ten minutes, and threw a bag on the front porch, as if he was delivering the morning newspaper.

The other four houses that were spread out had a completely different schedule. The first of the four isolated houses had a pick up starting around dusk. There was no set schedule that they could see or even mathematically calculate on the first day. There were four different drivers using four different vehicles, including two cars, a pickup, and a dump truck, with no follow up payment taking place. At that point, Joe knew that the best bet was to follow the set pattern of the first five houses that were located near each other and he assigned two more teams to those locations. He thought there was probably one boss for these five meth houses, and the other four that were isolated were separate operations.

Each surveillance team had taken pictures of the vehicles but it happened so quickly that there wasn't enough time to get a picture of any of the drivers and they only got two license plate numbers. They ran the license plate numbers and both pickup trucks were stolen. But they didn't want to stop anyone for a stolen vehicle at this point.

They'd had better success at the isolated houses and picked up three plate numbers and two pictures of guys getting out of their cars and looking around before heading out after the drop.

Joe assigned the drone to follow the isolated house pickups, one at a time, because they had enough surveillance officers on the other meth house drivers. The drone had full color pictures of each vehicle and license plates. They went to the Department of Motor Vehicle site and found out that two of the vehicles were registered to a corporation in Nashville. They'd check that out later. The other vehicle, a 2005 Ford Bronco, belonged to a Michael Johnson, residing on California Avenue in West Nashville. The driver's license matched the owner on the car registration. However, the driver's address and the registration for the vehicle were different. He'd probably moved and never updated his registration or license. Mr. Johnson was thirty-one years old and had two minor convictions. One was for DWI and the other for possession of meth. *Bingo*. Mr. Johnson was on the TBI meth web site in all his glory. Joe took the one team off at the house where they found Johnson and had that team pull surveillance on Mr. Johnson's residence. They had to check both addresses to see if, in fact, he lived at either one.

They'd also follow him 24/7 just in case.

It seemed like the plan was running smoothly, with a few glitches here and there, but it was under control at this point. It was Tuesday evening, and the drone was flying for its second day. Joe went back to West Nashville from the team meeting to check on Buddy Banks's house. He just wanted to go through the rooms again to see if he could find any connection to Buddy's brother, Jefferson Banks. Hell, they didn't have any proof that Buddy was even involved in the meth business unless they caught him red-handed or standing next to his brother. *Wouldn't that be nice?*

❧❧❧

Joe pulled up in back of the police surveillance vehicle and popped into the backseat. He was old friends with the team by now. He'd stopped at Dunkin' Donuts and refueled them. They were tired but grateful. After they ate, they all got out of the vehicle and went to the back door. They'd hoped that the backdoor, preciously left unlocked, was still unlocked. It was. Joe went in first with his gun drawn. One detective was at the front of the building and the other right behind Joe. Joe shouted that they were the police and had a warrant to search the house. No one answered. They went from room to room. The house was empty.

Joe knew what meth smelled like. So did the

167

other officers. He went back to the largest bedroom's closet and started to sniff the shirts and pants that were on hangers. He picked up an ether smell, which by itself wasn't evidence of meth, but it was the most prominent smell of the chemical grouping. They all had on gloves and Joe took a few shirts and pants and placed the clothes into an evidence bag for further analysis. He knew that the smell and chemical residue never really came out of the cloth. He was hoping to identify it as meth so if they found Buddy, they could bring him in on suspicion of conspiracy to sell drugs. That was the easiest way to get someone to talk. A conspiracy charge could be leveled on just about anything you needed. Joe handed the bag to the officers who were being relieved by the next shift. They'd bring it in for analysis. By itself, it didn't mean much, but it kept them moving in the right direction. Hopefully, all the evidence would add up to an arrest and someone spilling the beans on Jefferson Banks's whereabouts and possibly where the distribution center was located.

Joe finally had time to look at Lacey's phone directory and address book that he'd gotten from Casey. Most of the numbers were for her high school girlfriends from five years ago. Under "B," was listed the phone number and address of both Buddy and Jefferson, both at Buddy's address. That was nothing new. The phone number was the landline that they found at Buddy's house. It was very clear that criminals didn't go to the local cell phone store and get the latest model. It was equally clear that 100% of the cell phones used were burner phones—prepaid phones with no record of owner-ship. Every terrorist or drug dealer that Joe had en-countered previously had a burner phone. Every phone they found that was sold out of the local cor-ner store was paid for with cash. *Wow, what a con-cept.*

He'd go back and visit Casey one more time be-fore the end of the week. He'd also make sure that the teams drove by her house every few hours to make sure she was safe.

The more he thought about it, Joe was never sold on the fact that Lacey was in on Tom Jones's murder. He couldn't envision how a young girl, twenty-three years old, could be in on the planning of an execution of someone she didn't even know. There was no doubt that she loved Jefferson Banks, in spite of his record. However, Joe didn't think she believed, in her heart, that he was a criminal who'd wind up murdering her on the side of the road in rural Tennessee.

Joe would bet that she was packing while Banks and someone else killed Tom. He bet that she thought she was returning home to get married to Banks. But that left Joe's premise that Tom would never open a door to a man he didn't know, want-ing. Especially, Joe thought, that would never hap-pen after all his training and the training that he gave to Joe, and all the others who went before and after him.

There had to be a good reason why he opened the door to his killers. Unless it was for a pretty girl, the only other reason Tom would open that door would be for some kind of authority figure, or for someone he knew. Joe doubted that someone he knew would ever kill Tom. He was a pain in the ass, but no friend or acquaintance would do what he or she did to Tom. At least that's what Joe thought.

CHAPTER 17

It was Wednesday morning, early, around 7:00 a.m. Joe and the crew had been at the airport once again at 2:30 a.m., getting ready for the drone to land in the net at 3:00 a.m. Everything continued to go smoothly. The drone had picked up another three meth houses on the way back to the airport. They flew it from a different direction so as not to confuse the test sample of the fifteen meth houses already found.

Christ, every time we send up the drone we pick up more labs.

They decided to place the new-found houses on the back burner with the other six. For today only, they'd continue to concentrate on the five clustered together and three of the other four houses that were isolated by themselves. They didn't need to follow one of the houses after picking up the trail of Michael Johnson. They were now following his vehicle and knew the times he went to the one house. The drone would follow him from that point in time until he stopped and parked his car. The surveillance vehicles would take care of the rest for the day. It was now time to concentrate on getting to the end distribution center. They also had a team looking to find Johnson's real address with the driver's license and car registration addresses not matching. They should have that information soon and be able head out to the right house.

Joe's cell phone began to vibrate. They were just about to re-launch the drone once again after reprogramming what the team wanted to cover for the day. Joe kept his cell on vibrate because he didn't want the team disturbed while launching a multi-million-dollar, high-tech drone. One false step and a drone could fall from the sky, virtually anywhere, and at any time.

Joe looked down at his iPhone and saw that it was his brother calling him. *What does he want at 7:00 a.m.?*

"Pete, can I call you right back in five minutes? I'm in the middle of a critical operation."

"Sure Joe, but don't forget. Call me as soon as you can. It's about Dad."

"Will do. Thanks, Pete."

The drone was launched again successfully and Joe and the two technicians breathed a sigh of relief. The drone took off like a bat out of hell, going straight up and leveling off. It turned and then took off back toward west Nashville.

Joe picked up his cell and hit redial. Pete picked up immediately. "Hi, Pete. What's up? Why are you calling so early?"

"Joe, it's Dad. He had a heart attack last night and we rushed him to Samaritan Hospital. They took one look at him in the emergency room and rushed him to Albany Medical Center. They said it was due to complications from his concussion from the break in at his house. Evidently, his brain and heart weren't in sync."

"Pete, is he alive?" Joe asked.

"Yes, we got to him just in time. However, he needs a triple bypass tomorrow morning at 7:30 a.m. at Albany Med. Can you get home? In addition to the complications from the concussion, Mom feeding him steak and eggs for breakfast for all those many years took its toll as well. He had major blockage in his heart, as well, and the concussion exasperated it."

"Honestly, Pete, I don't know if I can make it in time. I'm in Nashville in charge of a critical investigation. I don't even know if I can get a flight out of here in time. I told you about Tom Jones's murder. We're on the verge of catching his killer and shutting down a major meth distributor at the same time. I can't say more about it over the phone, but I'll fill you in later."

"I understand, Joe, but after Mom's death, I know you felt bad about not being here for her. I know how you felt when Dad called you and told you she'd died. You were in a critical investigation then as well. Sorry, Joe. That's just the way it is."

"Let me make some calls and see what I can do.

You know I want to be there, Pete."

"I do, Joe but this is a one-shot deal. If you can get home tonight, we can see him in the hospital before his operation tomorrow morning. It will be successful, or not, and in either case, not to be blunt, I can handle it afterward. I think you know that now. Don't you?"

"I'm glad you didn't ask me that last year," Joe said with a smile. "I'll do everything I can to get home, but I have to be cleared by my rear admiral down in Miami and that may take some time."

"Call me as soon as you know. If you're coming, I'll pick you up at the airport and we can head right to Albany Med. I hope you can make it, Joe."

"Me. too."

Joe turned to his team members and told them exactly what was going on. Both said to do everything he could to get home and that they could handle it from there.

"I'll ask Mark to come to Nashville and he can do just as well as I can in moving the pieces around to get the end results. We've worked together since I was eighteen and I trust Mark with my life. He would never let me down."

Joe called Mark and got him right before he was leaving his house for an 8:00 a.m. meeting. "I got back information on Jim Butler and doesn't look good for him," Mark said. "I'll call you after you get my flight arranged and I'll get a flight as soon as I can out of Fort Lauderdale. Unfortunately, there're no direct flights from Fort Lauderdale to Nashville or for that matter from Nashville to Albany."

"I'm calling the rear admiral immediately after I hang up and I'll call you right back if it's go." He'd then call his brother back.

Joe dialed the rear admiral's office. It was only 7:30 a.m. so he wasn't sure if anyone was even in at that time. He was surprised when Rear Admiral, Jake Barnes picked up his own phone. "Hi, Joe, what's up?"

Joe proceeded to tell him where the investigation stood at that very moment. He went on to tell him about his father and then asked permission to leave for Albany to get there before tomorrow morning's operation. "My mother died while I was on an investigation a few years ago, toward the end of my Coast Guard career," Joe added, "and I don't want that to happen again."

It was cheesy but effective. "Give me ten minutes," the rear admiral said,

He called Joe back and told him to call Mark and tell him to head to the Fort Lauderdale International Airport to the corporate private jet offices and runway for 2:00 p.m. A US Navy corporate jet would pick Mark up to go to Nashville. He needed to bring all his credentials to manage the Nashville operation and take Joe's place until Monday morning.

"Joe, go to the Berry Field Air National Guard

Base and meet the jet at 4:00 p.m.," the rear admiral said. "Berry Field is located in the military enclave of the Nashville International Airport. Park your car right in front of the air national guard building. Don't forget to lock it and give the keys to Mark upon his arrival. The plane will leave immediately upon arrival, after Mark gets off, and you'll head to Albany. Tell your brother to pick you up at the headquarters of the New York Air National Guard, located at the north end of the Albany International Airport, at 6:30 p.m. You'll be transported by shuttle to the office building from the landing strip."

Joe was speechless. He couldn't believe what the rear admiral had done for him and Mark in only ten minutes. Joe guessed that he'd meant what he'd said, when he'd told Joe, "When one of us is suffering, Joe, we all are suffering."

The actual headquarters element of the New York Air National Guard was located in Latham at the Division of Military and Naval Affairs Building, which was connected to the airport. The staff there included both full-time employees and traditional guard members. JFHQ-AIR, as it was known, was responsible for establishing policy and monitoring operations of five flying units and four geographically separated support units. The NYANG was a diverse organization with a total strength of more than 6,000 people. The NYANG had air bases on Long Island, in the Hudson Valley, the Capital Region, Syracuse and the Niagara Frontier.

Then out of the clear blue sky, the rear admiral said, "Joe, by the way, isn't your girlfriend in New York City right now doing publicity for her new book?"

"Yes, she is, sir. How did you know that?"

"There's very little I don't know, Joe, so leave it at that. If you want to, and if your father is all right after the operation, I want you to hop on a train to New York City and spend some time with Julie before she forgets who you are. Do you hear me? You can head back late Sunday afternoon and still be in Nashville to take back over your investigation. I might add, Joe, that you're doing a remarkable job."

How did he know her name? "Thank you, sir, for your kindness. I won't let you down."

"No, Joe, you won't. We aren't all hopeless, uncaring bastards you know, just some of the time. Probably only the time that you actually see us."

"Thank you, sir." With that, Joe called Mark right back and told him what was happening.

"I'll call from the airport and let you know exactly what they found out about Jim Butler and the lost computer," Mark said. "We really lucked out but you were right on top of it as well. When something doesn't pass the smell test, something's wrong."

Joe called his brother back. "I'll be at the New

York Air National Guard Building in Latham at 6:30 p.m."

Pete laughed. "What took you so long, Joe?"

❧❧❧

The two technicians stayed in the hanger and Joe headed out to talk to the TBI team to let them know that Mark was coming and that he was headed to Albany until Sunday night when he'd be back. He called Joan Talbot and told her about his father and that he was headed to Albany and that Mark would be filling in for him in Nashville.

He called Julie on her cell and she picked up while walking to the subway to head for the South Bronx Girls Charter High School. He told her about his father and that he was headed home. "I got permission, and I don't even know how. I can head to New York City late Friday afternoon, and stay with you until my flight leaves from JFK to Nashville, if my father is okay, of course."

"I'm thrilled to death, Joe. I can't wait to see you. I'd even meet you in Troy, if you want."

"That wouldn't be practical and I can leave at any hour on Sunday from JFK and still make it back to Nashville by Sunday evening. Before calling you, I looked at the JFK to Nashville schedule and could take a direct flight at 4:40 p.m. and land in Nashville at 6:10 p.m. I have to fly on a commercial flight because there are no air national guard facilities in New York City."

During the call, near the end, Julie said, "Joe, I love you and I can't wait to see you. I'm very sorry about your father, but it's the right decision to go home to see him before his major operation." She knew how he felt when his mother died and he wasn't there to say goodbye.

Both she and Tillie went to Troy for the funeral. It was both Julie and Tillie's first ever plane ride. Julie had only been on a plane that one time before she headed to Brown University, but now it was old hat. "How did Tom's memorial services go and how is the investigation going?" she asked.

He told her what he could, but not all of it. After what she went through with Tillie with having her father mysteriously come back to life, after being presumed dead for over seventeen years, he wanted to keep future dangerous situations away from her for as long as he could. He'd tell her more over the weekend.

ତଃତଃ

Joe took a breather and called Mark back before he left for the airport.

"Jack Forest, our forensic friend and resident genius up in Virginia, took apart Jim Butler's life in less than a day," Mark told Joe. "Butler is forty-eight years old and is separated from his wife. They've got two grown children. He's been a cop with the Orlando Police Department for over twenty-five years. At one time, he was considered one of the best investigative detectives on the force.

"Anecdotally, Jack learned that Butler has been struggling with alcohol for at least the last five years and that it led to the separation with his wife. Butler's telling us about his kids not talking to him was probably true. It also looks like he has short timer's disease and is probably going to be eased out within the next few years."

"How did Jack find this out?" Joe asked.

"He pulled an online file from the Orlando Police Department's personnel files and Butler's jacket was not clean. Hang on, I need Jack's notes," Mark said. When he came back to the phone, he continued. "His finances don't reflect the pay grade of an Orlando detective at $65,000.00 per year, plus benefits, Joe. He has accounts at four separate banks. The first bank, his main bank, is used for the automatic deposit of his paychecks into a checking account. In addition, he has a small savings account with a little over $8,000.00 in it. Jack checked his OPD retirement account and Jim could retire anytime he wanted and would receive approximately 60% of his last five years' salary. With overtime, he averaged about $85,000.00 a year, so he'd receive around $51,000.00 a year to be split equally with his wife if they divorced or only $25,500.00 each. He wouldn't get social security until age sixty-two. So he'd need to go work for Walt Disney

World if he left the force and retired. He has three other savings accounts that are held at three separate banks. There was a cash deposit into each account of $1,000.00 weekly for the last eighteen months. Every four weeks, two accounts had withdrawals of $4,000.00 each, which was subsequently deposited into the third savings account, in three separate deposits to keep the cash deposit below the government notification limit. Then, the following day, a $12,000.00 wire transfer was made from that savings account to a numbered account in the Cayman National Bank, leaving a balance of only a $1,000.00 in the stateside account. Jack has all the wiring instructions he needs to transfer the money out of the Cayman Bank to wherever they wanted it. In total, over the last eighteen months, $234,000.00 had been transferred to the Cayman Bank."

"Wow," Joe said. "Shit, like wow."

"I know," Mark said. "Now some other good news. I called Apple just like you did for the iPhone to get the GPS coordinates. I went through the password protocol, just like you did, and I asked if there had been any downloads of new software applications. I said I'd been away and wanted to make sure my computer was updated. I told them I left my computer on at home and I left it connected to the Internet in case there were any updates. Tom had a thirteen-inch MacBook Pro, state-of-the-art computer with retina display. That machine, as soon as it was turned on and hooked up to the Internet, automatically downloaded the newest version of Maverick OSX 10.9.3, iTunes 11.2.1, Safari 7.0.4, and Digital Camera RAW 5.05. The downloaded software took place later the same night that Tom was found murdered, specifically at 8:02 p.m. There must have been two intruders into Tom's home. I don't believe that Lacey was one of those intruders.

"I think that the iPhone went north to Tennessee with Jefferson Banks and the Apple notebook computer was taken by someone else. It popped up at a network identified as 'DD5422.' The computer was hooked up to the Internet so we don't believe that there was any password protection. As you know, you mostly put in passwords for your cell phone and iPad, but if you leave your computer hooked up to the internet at home, and you use it a lot, it's a pain in the ass to keep entering the password. So 90% of the population, for what it's worth, don't use a password."

Joe agreed with Mark's analysis. "That was a mouthful," he said. "Take a breath. So in addition to Jim Butler's being a crook, it seems, you now found the computer. Maybe not found it, but found out where it went."

"Yes, that's what I'm saying. I know exactly where the computer was when it was turned on. I've no idea where it is now, but this is a very good start."

"Did you find out what the network 'DD5422' represents? I know that in Tom's apartment complex, the last name of the condo renter was the WiFi network address identifier."

"Yes, Joe, I found out that DD stood for Dunkin' Donuts and 5422 stood for the Dunkin' Donuts WiFi at 5422 North Orange Blossom Terrace in Orlando. I've the phone number as well. In addition, Frank believes that Butler lied about the Outlaw Motorcycle Gang being the major meth distributor in the region. He asked the Coast Guard Gang Prevention Team in the Jacksonville Office to investigate and they told him that it was the Warlocks who were dealing meth, to the best of their knowledge. By the way, the Warlock's clubhouse is located at 5600 Fourth Street in Orlando, at the end of a dead end street. I went online to Google Earth and printed out a picture of the clubhouse. They aren't living large, by any means. Out of curiosity, we went on to the Dunkin' Donut locator site and put the Warlock's address in and it's exactly six tenths of a mile from the Dunkin' Donuts WiFi where Tom's computer was fired up, after he'd been dead for several hours."

"Please thank Jack and Frank for me, Mark. What would I do without you guys? Now, since you're covering me in Nashville, can we ask Frank in Port Canaveral to go to the Dunkin' Donuts location in Orlando and get the videos for that exact download time? If we can see who was in Dunkin'

Donuts store at 8:02 p.m., maybe we found the second killer that helped Jefferson Banks."

"I knew you would ask so I called the rear admiral's office and got permission for Frank to head to Dunkin' Donuts tomorrow and do exactly that. He'll get that video, just short of arresting anyone in the building, from that day forward. In fact, from Google Earth, it looks like the parking lot was well lit and maybe we could get pictures of the cars in the lot. If we get any pictures in the shop, we can send the pictures to Jack and he can use his facial recognition software and see if we can get names and addresses. If someone was in Dunkin' Donuts at that time, they were probably a regular."

"I guess I'll see you around 4:00 p.m. in Nashville," Joe said with a grin. "Remind me to give you the keys to the car. It's all the GPS setup you'll need to get back and forth."

"See you then, Joe. I hope your father makes it."

Louise gave Mark a ride to the airport in Fort Lauderdale. Mark would have to get Frank's car back to him somehow up in Port Canaveral. For now, it had to sit in Mark's driveway. Mark made a note to remind Joe to give him the keys to the government car when he landed. As Joe had said, all the GPS coordinates that he'd need would be stored in the car, and it would make it easier for Mark to get back and forth.

CHAPTER 18

The Nashville International Airport, BNA, ranked as the thirty-fourth busiest airport in the United States, in terms of passengers, with 10,351,709 passengers flying through the airport in 2013, making it the airport's busiest year on record. BNA had added fourteen new nonstop flights in the past year. None of the new flights went to Albany, New York. BNA stood for the Nashville Berry Field Military Base attached to the airport. Without the navy jet coming to pick up Joe, he'd have never made the trip in time to see his father, before the operation.

The airport was located in the southeastern portion of Nashville, not that far for Joe to travel. It was less than fifteen minutes. He dropped his car in front of the air national guard headquarters, got directions to the terminal, and watched as the navy plane landed exactly at 4:00 p.m. The plane rolled up to where Joe was standing, next to the refueling station. The crew refueled the plane so they wouldn't have to stop in Albany for service.

As soon as the stairs popped open, Joe saw

Mark walk down to the runway. "How was your flight?" he asked.

"Unexpected, to say the least. How is your father? Did you hear anything new?"

"Not until I get to Albany and meet my brother. Pete said he was stable and they were monitoring him carefully. If he had to go in earlier, at least I'll be there at the hospital by 7:00 p.m., tonight. I hope nothing happens in the meantime. I do want to see him and talk to him. There will be no repeat of my mom if I can help it."

"I hear you, Joe. This investigation will be in good hands. I already called them at the hanger and told them that I'd be there before 5:00 p.m. and we will go out to dinner. I'm meeting the TBI team at 8:00 p.m. at their offices. I called Frank and he knows exactly what's to be done tomorrow. He said he'd get the videos and pull a full surveillance once they've identified who has the computer. He's optimistic and I want you to stay that way too. We got this, Joe."

"Thanks, Mark. I know I can count on you. My trust issues are getting better but not all there yet, as you so well know."

"Too bad your anal-retentive issues aren't getting better," Mark said with a smile.

Joe handed over the car keys. "I'm working on it. Doesn't seem to help much though. Oh, well."

With that, Mark gave Joe a one-armed hug and headed to the car. Joe hopped on the plane as soon as it refueled and they taxied down the runway with a green light to head for Albany. They'd been on the ground for less than twenty minutes. Joe hoped that this operation in Nashville and his father's real operation both went smoothly.

☙☙☙

Once in the air, Joe felt better about everything. Hopefully, he'd make it on time to see his father. He'd meet Julie down in New York City later on Friday and make up for lost time, if that was possible. He really hadn't seen much of her since she headed out for her book tour and ongoing discussions with Brown University, her new agent, her publisher, and her editor. They seemed to have come first. Joe knew it had to be this way. He'd never stand in her way, not after everything that had happened to her since early childhood.

Knowing that they were now a couple, after being her big brother for all those many years, was not easy for him. In the back of his mind, even though she was now a twenty-four-year-old published author and a beautiful woman, he still saw that ten-year-old girl who went up to him those many years ago after his first career day speech for the Coast Guard. He'd just turned nineteen years old at the time, and was a first year seaman, E-2, long on attitude but very short on experience.

Now, only a short while ago, with her asking

him if he loved her or not, that day in an Islamorada luncheonette, his life had changed forever. Now, after almost six months, he wondered if she still meant it, especially after being away in the real world. He wondered if she was having any doubts. She'd never been anywhere before college and now she was running around New York City, staying in the publisher's accommodations in the middle of the city. Did she really know what love was? At thirty-three years old, he'd already gone through those first stages of love, or so he thought, first with Jennifer Alvarez in Miami. Then, when Mary Lynch came along up in Albany, he thought it was love, as well. He was very sadly mistaken in both cases and didn't want to misjudge this relationship, too. Joe had loved Julie forever, or so it seemed. He wanted this to work. She was family.

ℰℬℰℬ

During the flight, Joe broke out his iPad and did FaceTime with Frank. Joe just couldn't sit still. He wasn't sure if it was his trust issues, but he knew he'd feel better if he were assured that they agreed on one plan. Then, as long as his iPad was open, he reconfirmed his Sunday direct flight from JFK to Nashville, scheduled to leave JFK at 4:40 p.m. and land in Nashville at 6:10 p.m. He'd print out the ticket tonight when he got home to his father's house.

Joe landed at the Albany International Airport a little after 6:15 p.m. There was some bad weather out of the Washington D.C. and Baltimore areas. They weren't prevented from landing but the bumpiness had slowed them down. They landed right at the New York Air National Guard Terminal at the north end of the airport. Joe thanked the crew, got his bag, hopped into a golf cart, and headed for the building where his brother would meet him. It was still a military facility so Joe had to check in and show all his identification, including his Coast Guard, FBI, and Homeland Security credentials.

He shook the hand of the officer in charge and thanked him as well. As he went through the front door, his brother's car was idling at the curb. You couldn't miss that this was a military facility with a tank and a helicopter turned into statuary on the front lawn. They pulled up at the guard hut and Joe gave the guard his identification one more time. If anyone thought that 9/11 wasn't an eye opener, they were delusional.

Joe and Pete never hugged. In fact, they really never got along until earlier this year. Instead, Pete shook Joe's hand. "Good to see you, Joe."

Joe did likewise. Pete was the older brother by two years, but you would have never known it until everything went south last year when their father was almost killed in a home invasion. He was rushed to the hospital in critical condition and it'd been a long time for his recovery. He was put into an induced coma to relieve the pressure on his brain. His cognitive skills finally came back after many months. Their father was back to work part time with Pete in charge for the first time.

The change agreed with Pete and Joe saw a lot of personal growth in Pete's attitudes and life. Joe hated to think that his father's injuries were the best thing to happen to Pete, but it had probably turned his life around. When Joe came home after returning to the Coast Guard, the change in Pete was remarkable. He'd even started dating and Joe met Pete's girlfriend, Tanya Fields, on his last trip. Tanya was a year in between Pete and Joe in school and went to Lansingburgh High School where Pete graduated. Joe went to Catholic High, which had become a bone of contention from the start for Pete. Joe was the better athlete and student, while Pete just went along because he knew he'd be working for his father for the rest of his life.

Joe had had to get out, which made the situation even worse. When he joined the Coast Guard, at eighteen years old and gave up his full scholarship at MIT, the silence was deafening.

Pete and Joe got along a lot better now, due to a long sit down and better understanding of their relationship, after their father was attacked. The attack shook Pete up enough to change his life and he recommitted himself to the business his father had started. He handled all the jobs under contract to completion, understood what had to be done, and did it. Joe was pleased when Pete started dating Tanya. She was a nice woman.

They'd known each other for years, but Pete never attempted to ask her out. One day, they were at the same wedding, not too long ago, and she went over to him and asked him to dance.

"Why have you never asked me out?" she'd asked him. Pete felt quite sheepish when she told him she liked him and would like to go out on a date. "I've never done this before, but decided to give it a try."

Pete laughed when he told the story to Joe and Joe said that he'd received the same message from Julie. They both laughed at how truly dumb they really were when it came to women.

෴

It was now Wednesday night and Pete told Joe that he wanted to take him out on the town with him and Tanya, the following night, if the operation was successful.

"Fine," Joe said. He had nothing better to do before taking the train Friday afternoon out of Rensselaer to meet Julie in New York City. He needed a good drunken time, he thought, and it had been forever. At least, he could sleep a little later Friday and help his hangover. He planned a hangover, just like he planned everything else.

Pete headed north on Wade Road to Route 2 to pick up the Northway I-87 S to Albany Medical Center. Traffic had slowed down since the Albany government worker traffic eased after 6:00 p.m. Pete got on the ramp for I-90 E and got off on the third exit ramp toward Albany Medical Center.

Albany Medical Center had taken over several square blocks in the last ten years, making it a city unto itself. There was a new parking garage across the street from the main entrance with an overhead walkway into the hospital. They headed to the surgical wing, which was stuck in the back of the large complex. A new multimillion-dollar surgical wing was now being built but wouldn't be ready until next year. It seemed liked they walked for miles but Pete had been there earlier in the day and he had the route down pat.

They walked up to the nurses' station and checked in to see their father. The nurse wasn't going to let them in because it was after 7:00 p.m. and their father was being prepped for early morning surgery.

"I just flew in on a navy jet and I have to get back as soon as I can. Can I please see my father?"

She was still reluctant to let them in until Joe showed her his Homeland Security, FBI, and Coast Guard official credentials. He was only dressed in jeans and a Yankee T-shirt. Pete was dressed in his every day work clothes.

She looked at Joe and probably thought "You

can't judge a book by its cover." She pointed her index finger at Room 707 at the end of the hall. As they both thanked her, Pete could hardly contain himself. "Can I see what the hell you just showed her? What was that you flashed?"

Joe popped open his wallet with the three credentials and Pete stared. "Are you shitting me? I never knew any of this. When did this happen?"

"About ten years ago, Pete, you dumb shit. You never asked me, even once, what I did, so I never told you. Over a few beers, I'll tell you about Tom's murder investigation and the biggest meth operation takedown in the history of the Southeastern Seaboard. Are you interested?"

"Of course, Joe. I'm always interested in what my little brother does with his life," Pete said as he grinned from ear to ear.

"I liked you better when you were surly and uncooperative."

"Sure, Joe. Now please be on your best behavior. I have to set the example here as your big brother. We don't want to upset our father on the eve of his pending heart operation, now do we?"

"Fuck you, Pete."

"Now that's better. Isn't it, Joe?"

They both had big grins on their faces as they entered their father's hospital room.

"Hi, Dad," Joe said.

"How did you get here? I didn't know you were coming."

"I didn't either until this morning. Mark and I had our own personal navy jet escort service, first to Nashville for Mark and then to Albany for me."

"Really? That's kind of neat. I didn't know that my youngest son had that kind of pull. Tell me about it."

Joe did. He told him about the trip. He told him about the investigation into Tom Jones's murder, and how they'd be taking down a major meth distributor when he got back to Nashville.

"Pete, did you know any of this about Joe?" Dad asked.

"I do now. He just flashed me his badges on the way in." Then Pete started quoting the movie *Blazing Saddles*. "Badges? We don't need no stinking badges."

He laughed his ass off at Joe until tears were streaming down his face. Their father smiled and started quoting from his favorite movie of all time, the 1990 *Goodfellows*. "I mean funny like I'm a clown, I amuse you? I make you laugh? I'm here to fuckin' amuse you? What do you mean funny? Funny how? How am I funny?"

Joe and Pete were now almost rolling on the floor, laughing, as the nurse came in. She wanted to know what was going on.

Joe looked at her. "Where's your badge, you need a badge."

Their father laughed so hard he started choking. The nurse told them all that he'd be dead before he even got to the operation, if they didn't stop. Chastised, like three schoolboys, they said they were sorry and it wouldn't happen again. As she left the room, they started up again and couldn't seem to stop.

Pete and Joe stayed for about forty-five minutes and then they had to leave to get Joe home and unpacked.

"You're full of crap and have one on me as well," their father said.

Both boys kissed him and told him they loved him and would be there before he went in to surgery, if they were sober enough to drive.

With a smile, their father told them to get their asses back on time. "Make sure Tanya comes. I'll know if she's here or not," he said.

Joe turned to Pete. "Well that was fun."

"Yeah, until someone shoots an eye out."

"Stop before I piss in my pants, Pete. *A Christmas Story*, really?"

They meandered back to the parking garage and decided to go to the Recovery Room Sports Bar on Hoosick Street in Troy. It was attached to the new Hilton Gardens Hotel and had over forty large-screen televisions and the best wings in town, next to the Ale House. The bar had thirty craft beers on tap and they could take the back way home through Frear Park and down to the Burgh, if they'd a few too many. Better yet, if more than a few, Tanya said she'd pick them up at 11:00 p.m. They just needed to call her before 10:30 p.m.

"Pete, you know you really lucked out with Tanya, don't you?" Joe said.

Pete just smiled at him and didn't say a word.

They headed north on I-787 and made it in fifteen minutes when they pulled into the parking lot. This was Joe's first time in the restaurant. *What a change for Troy and Hoosick Street*, he thought as he looked around.

As they walked in, three of their old friends were sitting at the bar. Among the three were Cathy Wells and her never-leave-her-side best friend, Molly. *Just what I needed*, thought Joe. He'd stopped going to McGuire's in downtown Troy because he'd dated Cathy when he bartended there, but Molly was relentless in trying to make him her full-time boyfriend. He thought Cathy was nice but Molly tipped the scales to celibacy when it came to Cathy. At that time, he'd had to call to see if either one was at McGuire's before he'd even enter the bar.

"Hi, Joe. Hi, Pete. How are you two?" Cathy said.

"Good, Cathy. Hi, Molly. How are you all doing?"

They asked Joe what he was doing home, if he was on leave from the Coast Guard.

"No, I'm home on an emergency compassionate leave due to my father's operation tomorrow."

He sidestepped a few choice comments from

Molly and smiled at Cathy. He gave her a hug and he and Pete took a booth in the back. They had a few beers, ate a few wings, and watched the end of a Yankee's game. This was Jeter's final season and Joe missed seeing him play while living down in Florida. You could go to a sports bar in Miami and see the Yankees on the satellite television, but with Joe's schedule, and staying in Islamorada, it just wasn't very convenient.

Jeter got up the next inning and promptly got a single on the first pitch. It was the fifth inning and they were down 5-0 to Toronto. So much for the millions the Yankees spent to revitalize the team. At least A-Rod was suspended for a full season so they didn't have to watch his antics tonight. Joe had missed Andy Pettitte's retirement at the end of last season. Joe idolized Pettitte and had copied his left-handed pitching moves down to a science.

Joe's pickoff move to first base came from years of watching Pettitte, as Joe grew up and started pitching himself. When Pettitte announced that he was retiring, Joe saw his last game on television back in Miami, but it wasn't the same as being back in Upstate New York, watching it with his brother. It was the best game Pettitte had pitched in the last fifteen years.

Damn, Joe thought. When Pettitte was done, he'd allowed only one run and five hits over 116 pitches in a 2-1 homecoming victory over his former team, the Astros. Pettitte walked away with

256 victories, 18 non-losing seasons in 18 attempts, five World Series titles, and the most postseason victories, 19, of all time.

Joe clinked his glass with his brother and toasted Andy Pettitte. The Yankees would never be the same without Pettitte, Jeter, and Mariano Rivera.

They only had two beers with dinner and Joe was getting tired. He'd been up since 2:00 a.m. the previous morning, over twenty hours straight. He felt like the drone, flying around Nashville for the same length of time before landing. Pete quickly called Tanya and said they were heading home. She was staying over at his house because she wanted to be with them early the next day for the operation. As they walked in, Tanya gave Joe a big hug. "Thanks for coming, Joe."

He smiled. "Thanks for being here for us, especially for Pete."

She knew what he meant. Joe had been so independent for so long that it had completely contrasted with his brother's actions until just recently.

Joe took a quick shower and headed to his old room on the second floor. It was a four-bedroom house and nothing had changed in Joe's thirty-three years.

It was like he was back home for good. It was a good feeling, but Joe knew it wouldn't last past tomorrow.

ɔͻ

The alarm seemed to go off fifteen seconds after his head hit the pillow. It was 5:00 a.m. and he'd slept right through since 11:00 p.m. That was six hours more than he thought he'd get. He hit the shower. So did Pete and Tanya. Then she made coffee and buttered English muffins.

They were out the door by 5:30 a.m. and headed toward Albany Med. Joe could do this trip in his sleep after working all those years in downtown Albany at the Albany Coalition for Families. His old friend, Dan Simmons, was still the new president and his old girlfriend, Mary Lynch, was still the controller. He spoke to Dan on the phone at least once a month to stay in touch. Joe didn't want to call him on this trip because he really didn't have any time and, what time he had, he wanted to spend with his father and brother. They got to the parking garage and headed toward the surgical wing.

It was 6:00 a.m. they went into their father's room with Tanya right by their side. John Traynor's eyes lit up when he saw her. He opened his arms for her and gave her a big kiss. "Thanks for coming, Tanya."

She did the same. It was remarkable how well she got along with their father after such a short time of being in Pete's life.

It didn't seem to matter to John. It was the here and now that meant everything to him.

They stepped out into the hall while the final pre-op prep took place. Their father's cardiologist stopped in the hall to see them and explain exactly what was to be done, during the surgery. "The triple bypass would normally take three to six hours in duration but because you father was having concussion issues interfering with his regular heartbeat, I'll also install a pacemaker at the same time. John has two distinct separate issues that will be corrected this morning."

He explained that coronary bypass surgery was a medical process that allowed blood to flow directly to the heart, even though the patient had blocked arteries. "The surgery uses a blood vessel from the arm, chest, abdomen, or leg and connects it to other arteries in the heart area. This ensures the blood bypasses the blocked or diseased area of your father's heart. Coronary bypass surgery is one of several ways to treat heart disease. It could also be called coronary artery bypass graft, CABG—or cabbage—surgery, since the process of connecting the alternate artery is called grafting," he explained.

"There are an estimated 800,000 CABGs performed throughout the world every year. The grafts, if successful, tended to last ten to fifteen years. Your father is a very lucky man. The surgery usually takes between three and six hours to complete. Typically, the surgeons will fix from two to four coronary arteries. This number depends on how severe blockages are and where they in John's heart," he continued. "John will be rendered unconscious by the anesthetist and then the mechanical ventilation begins. I'll make an incision in the chest, down the center along the breastbone. The rib cage will be spread open and the heart will be exposed. The surgical team temporarily stops the heart and a heart-lung machine controls the blood circulation to his body for the duration of the surgery. The healthy veins are grafted and the blood flow will be diverted around the problematic part of the diseased artery. The process will be repeated until all possible blockages are diverted," the doctor said.

"After all the grafts have been completed, the heart-lung machine will be turned off and the heart will begin to beat again. The chest will be sealed up, but before that, John will have a pacemaker put in place for an added measure. Your father will then be taken to the intensive care unit for one to two days of close monitoring. After it has been determined that there are no immediate complications, he will be transferred to the nurse's unit, where he will remain for the next three to five days."

As their father was being wheeled away, the doctor said. "John's full recovery from the surgery will take about eight weeks, but everybody heals differently and only I, as the doctor, am the best judge of when everything can resume as normal.

"Since this surgery is not a cure-all, there will be many recommendations for changes in his lifestyle after the surgery. For example, quitting smoking, eating a heart-healthy diet, controlling stress, exercising regularly and treating high cholesterol."

Pete would have plenty to do taking care of their father, Joe thought. No more steak and eggs, no more climbing ladders and working twelve-hour days. Joe wouldn't be there. At least he was there for this operation. He would try to come home several times a year if he could. He would have to push himself because he was his own worst enemy when it came to making time for family functions. He vowed he would do better.

John had never gone to a doctor until the time of the break-in. The concussion actually highlighted some other problems that he'd had that would have killed him eventually if left untreated.

Tanya, Pete, and Joe had nothing to do for the next several hours. Tanya had brought her Kindle and she started reading. Joe paced the halls as usual. Finally, Pete broke up the monotony by saying, "We're going to breakfast in the cafeteria".

The cafeteria for Albany Med, that fed thousands of people a day, looked like a food court at a major mall. They had every food station imaginable. Since it was only going onto 9:00 a.m., they all decided to have breakfast. Tanya got a coffee and Danish. Pete and Joe got a full breakfast, including bacon, eggs, home fries, toast, and coffee. Joe loved hospital food prices. The three breakfasts were under $20.00.

Joe remembered all that time he spent in the

Mariner Hospital down in the Keys when Tillie, Julie's grandmother, was in a coma. They must have eaten there every other night, it seemed, for over a month. At least he didn't go broke. Joe looked into his wallet and remembered he had to get cash from the ATM in the cafeteria for his trip to New York City. He'd lived forever on the government Visa credit card and his own debit card that was connected to his checking account. His paycheck was dumped into the account every month, but Joe never seemed to spend any money living at the Islamorada Coast Guard facility. He'd gone from completely broke and owing over $20,000.00 in student loans, a few years ago, to now having over $30,000.00 in his account. He needed to do something with it to make it grow. He thought, maybe he and Julie, if and when they got married, would need money for a down payment on a house. But where would they buy one? Miami? Key Largo? New York City? Definitely not back in Troy. They had a lot to discuss, maybe not this weekend, but soon.

The operation ended at 12:30 p.m. It took almost five and a half hours so they were worried. The doctor finally came out. "Everything's fine and the bypass was done in three hours, but the pacemaker had to be programmed a little differently for now because it was in combination with the surgery. It took a while to get his heart back in rhythm, but everything is fine. He only had two blockages and that was a very good sign. We also checked his concussion symptoms and we're relieved to find no major continuing issues. He'll be in the hospital for less than a week and then he will be good to go."

The doctor did explain that John had to make some serious life altering changes to keep himself healthy. They agreed, shook the doctor's hand, and left for home. Joe needed to print out his train ticket before he forgot. He did it and put it in the side pocket of his carry-on bag. Their father wouldn't be awake for another several hours so they'd go back before their planned night of celebration.

With Tanya at their side, Joe didn't believe that a "wild time" would be had by all. Hell, he was looking more forward to the weekend with Julie than anything else. *Sex, yes sex.* He had to remind himself about sex. It was like he was in combat, waiting to get home. Unfortunately, his combat kept him away from Julie even if it was stateside and fighting with his own citizen criminals in Nashville and points south.

They went home to change to go out that night and then went back to the hospital. Their father was awake and very glad to see them, and especially to be alive. The doctor had told him how lucky he was and what he needed to do to keep up his health.

"I saw Jesus on the highway and he was talking to me personally," John told the boys.

He smiled and was relieved. You could see it on

his face. Joe guessed that his dad had seen the light. Joe would see him one last time on Friday before leaving by train for New York City.

They headed back out and Pete actually had a list of bars that he wanted to go to with Tanya as their designated driver. *Boy, she must really be in love with Pete or just plain crazy.*

As suspected, Pete's definition of debauchery and good times was a lot milder than Joe had discovered while in the service. Nevertheless, he enjoyed himself immensely. He really liked Tanya and felt that Pete was a lucky man. Joe wondered if his anal-retentive nature was rubbing off on Pete. They hit the Recovery Room Sports Bar, first. Then to Jack's on State Street, in downtown. Then over to North Pearl and hit four bars in a row. Finally, they ended up in Troy and ate at the Dinosaur BBQ, on to the Ale House on River Street, ending up at Pete's favorite, The Burgh Grill on One-Hundred-Fourteenth Street, right around the corner from their house.

Pete had stated that he could actually crawl home if needed. He'd done so on many an occasion but not since dating Tanya. They were exhausted and headed home to bed by midnight. Joe knew he would feel the pain in the morning. He profusely thanked Tanya for her support, for loving Pete, and for helping him find the bathroom and bed.

They got up around 11:00 a.m. Joe felt like the Russians were trampling across his tongue and that he'd swallowed a wool sweater. Pete wasn't much better.

Tanya was a breath of fresh air. "Two glasses of white wine over seven hours really didn't affect me that much," she said.

Pete said she was being very polite because she could drink him under the table, depending on the occasion. She made breakfast for the boys. She laundered Joe's clothes that were on the floor, and she could smell dirty socks in his bag.

By 1:00 p.m. they headed out to the hospital. Joe had to be at the Rensselaer Train Station for a train leaving at 4:10 p.m., with a reserved seat, getting into New York City for 6:50 p.m. He was meeting Julie at Tracks Raw Bar and Grill at 1 Penn Plaza, right in Penn Plaza, when he arrived.

The station was located in the underground levels of Pennsylvania Plaza, an urban complex between Seventh Avenue and Eighth Avenue and between Thirty-First and Thirty-Third Streets in Midtown Manhattan. It was also located underneath Madison Square Garden and lay in proximity to other Manhattan landmarks, including the Empire State Building, and Macy's at Herald Square. Julie's publisher's apartment was only a few blocks from Penn Station, right in the heart of the city, and only a few blocks from her publisher's office.

Joe said his goodbyes to his father and was pretty sure, as sure as he could be, that his father would fully recover and was in Pete's good hands. This short stay probably brought the family together better than anything else since Joe's mother died. They dropped him off at 3:30 p.m. right across the river in the City of Rensselaer, which now housed the Rensselaer Train Station, a mausoleum, costing over forty million dollars. It was built because they could. No other reason. It sat in the middle of the most needy small city in the State of New York.

Joe gave Tanya, and for the first time for Pete, a hug and a kiss and told them he loved them and would miss them. He took his bag and went through the front door. He turned around, waved, and wondered if he would ever see them again.

In every investigation he'd ever been in, someone had been hurt, or worse. He was lucky that he'd only been shot in the arm in the Mexican Mafia takedown. It could have been much, much worse. Only inches often separated life from death.

CHAPTER 19

Joe loved traveling by train. He'd only been to New York City three times in his life by himself. His father and mother took both him and Pete to Yankee Stadium a few times at the end of the season for the little league annual bus trip. He hadn't been to the new stadium that opened in 2009, the year the Yankees won their last World Series championship. Joe had taken the train to New York City for a job interview after he graduated from Rensselaer but he didn't really like the feel of a city that big. He felt lost.

He was offered a position at a major investment house because of his bilingual ability coupled with his MBA. He turned it down when he accepted the offer from the Albany Coalition for Families. He took Mary, his girlfriend at the time, for a trip to New York City by train to stay the weekend and see a new Broadway play. That was fun, more fun than their overall relationship, which ended on a down note. He could barely even remember the third trip.

The *Empire Route* left the Rensselaer Station

right on time at 4:10 p.m. and would arrive at 6:50 p.m. He would head to the restaurant to meet Julie right in Penn Plaza, above Penn Station, as soon as he arrived.

WiFi had finally come to Amtrak so he pulled out his iPad and started to send emails to Mark and Frank to see what had transpired. He had over twenty emails that he hadn't even looked at since he arrived in Albany. Evidently, both Mark and Frank were making good progress.

In three days, it looked like Mark and his team were honing in on the meth distribution center. Frank went to the Dunkin' Donuts and got the videos for the day Tom's computer received downloads from Apple at 8:02 p.m. He sent the videos directly to Jack, who said they would be hearing from him by Sunday, at the latest. Frank got pictures, both inside and outside the store, in jpeg. He looked at the pictures but he was waiting for Jack to send precise clear pictures back. If the pictures were clear, Jack could use his facial recognition software to see if he could identify the individual with the computer. From the outside, he could only see the person receiving the computer but not the one handing it over. There were clear pictures of the man's hands and wrists giving the computer to the other person, but every other feature was in the shadows or blacked out completely since the camera didn't fully see that part of the parking lot. Frank told Joe, in the email, that he would call him as soon as he got word.

The two-hour-and-forty-minute trip to New York City went effortlessly. Joe sat on the Hudson River side, the right side, heading south. About one hundred miles into the one-hundred-and-fifty mile trip, Joe could see West Point as the river curved and headed to New York City. From there, they'd make a few stops at Croton-on-Hudson and Tarrytown, just before hitting the city.

Joe always knew when New York City came in to view. Instead of bucolic pastures and sailboats, both sides of the tracks were lined with cement canyons, welcoming them to New York with large illustrated graffiti scenes. Along with the artistic personal graffiti billboards were burnt out cars, up on blocks with the tires gone. Garbage just seemed to float in the air like snowflakes. He could tell that he was in The Bronx and saw Yankee Stadium from the left side of the train just looming over the borough. Joe remembered the five boroughs: Kings—Manhattan; Queens; Richmond—Staten Island; The Bronx; and Brooklyn.

At Saint Augustine's School, he had to do a paper on the history of the Irish in New York State and in New York City. The Irish took two separate routes to get to New York. Not everyone who came to New York from Ireland came through Ellis Island. A majority came through Montreal and walked across the border, populating all of Upstate New York and Vermont, and then migrated to the

Boston area. During the potato famine it was ten times cheaper to take a ship to Montreal rather than New York because the British didn't want the Irish to wind up in New York City.

The train slowly moved through Penn Station and stopped at the final destination ramp. Joe had placed his iPad in his bag that was sitting right next to him. There was hardly anyone on the late night train heading to New York City. It was a madhouse going up to Rensselaer on Friday and Sunday nights, but Joe would miss the privilege of that trek. As he got off the train, he got his bearings and headed upstairs toward Penn Plaza.

In five minutes, he was almost at the front door. Julie was patiently waiting for him. He grabbed her and hugged her as hard as he could. He planted so many kisses on her that she laughed.

"Joe, stop." She placed both her hands on his face and gave him the biggest kiss on the lips that he'd ever gotten. Most people in New York City wouldn't even bat an eye at this, but many of them stared at the two of them and smiled.

Joe and Julie heard an older couple's comments of "Oh, to be in love again."

They smiled at each other. Julie took Joe's hand and they entered the restaurant. The last thing Joe had on his mind was eating, but he didn't want to be overly obvious when meeting Julie.

As they waited for their 7:30 p.m. reservation, Julie asked, "How was your trip?"

"The train trip was fine. I arrived in Albany in a navy jet, just me and the flight crew, after they dropped Mark off in Nashville."

"How impressive, Joe," Julie said. "You must have some pull."

"Right place, right time, that's all."

Their table was ready and they ordered. Joe was famished, like always. He'd gone to the bar car on the train and gotten a Pepsi and a bag of chips. He'd sat and read the *New York Post* for a while. He'd wanted a beer but he didn't want "beer breath" for when he met Julie. He was glad he'd had the Pepsi.

Joe had a dozen fresh oysters and a bowl of Manhattan clam chowder. Manhattan style wasn't a "chowda" at all, so he'd been told, since it didn't have either milk or cream in it. Julie'd picked that up at Brown University. She had lobster, a fresh Main lobster flown in that day. Both only ate Florida seafood, now, so this was a real treat for her. They finished up talking and eating and Joe got the bill. It was around 9:00 p.m. Julie was full of questions and so was Joe, so they decided to head to Julie's apartment which was only four blocks away, near Fifth Avenue.

"My publisher has several small, one-bedroom apartments near their offices for authors coming into see them from out of town." Julie had already been there for two weeks and had two weeks more to go before heading back to Key Largo and her fall duties, working for the Monroe County School District.

They walked out of the restaurant. Joe had just dropped $120.00 on dinner, including tip. *Welcome to New York City*. Hand in hand, they walked down the street, headed toward the apartment. She turned and kissed Joe at each crosswalk. He did the same.

"I love you, Joe."

"I love you, too," he said.

As they arrived at her building, she looked up and pointed to her apartment on the tenth floor. "An apartment, like the one I'm in, 750 square feet, sold for almost two million dollars."

In Key Largo, which wasn't cheap, it would be less than three hundred thousand dollars. A doorman opened the double doors as they entered and he greeted Julie. "Good evening, Ms. Chapman. How are you?"

"Great, Sam, I'd like to introduce you to my fiancé, Joe Traynor," she added.

Fiancé? It sounded good to him.

"Pleasure to meet you, Mr. Traynor," Sam said politely.

"Joe, please."

"Joe is here visiting for the weekend and has to go back to the Coast Guard in Florida late Sunday, Sam."

"I hope you enjoy yourself, Joe. It was pleasure meeting you."

Joe signed in, followed by Julie, and they headed to the tenth floor by elevator. As soon as the door opened on her floor, Julie ran to the apartment and opened the door. She waved for Joe to hurry up and he did, carrying his bag over his shoulder. Julie quickly closed the door and grabbed Joe by the face. She kissed him, grabbed his arm, and pulled him toward the bedroom down the hall. She started to undress him and he grinned from ear to ear. He followed suit, with all their clothes hitting the floor at the same time, as they both dove onto the bed. Their pent-up desires culminated together in less than ten minutes.

଼ୡଔୡଔ

Julie looked Joe in the eyes. "I love you so much."

"You've no idea how much I missed you," he said.

Julie laughed. "I'm starting to get a pretty good idea."

"It shows, huh?"

He could barely contain himself. He was ready again and he couldn't believe it. He rolled on top of her and began more gently this time, in rhythm. They explored each other as if it was the first time. It was the first time in a long time and they wanted to catch up quickly, both coming, once again, at the same time.

It was now almost 10:30 p.m. Joe smiled at her. God, she was beautiful. When he saw the rear admiral again, he'd plant a big kiss on his forehead for telling him to do this. Like Joe needed encouragement. He did get caught up in his work and this just reminded him what he was working for.

Julie hopped out of bed, naked and unashamed, and headed for the bathroom. She turned on the shower. "Wash my back, Joe."

He never neglected his duties and volunteered. "At your service."

Once in the shower, he washed every part of her and kissed the just washed spots accordingly. Her moans told him that his concentration on one particular area proved effective. Then it was her turn and she stopped to wash a very noticeable erection that had caught her attention. Her drying methods for that particular body part made him shiver like never before. He could barely stand in the shower. He smiled at her and asked for mercy.

They toweled each other off and went back to bed. Arm in arm, they fell fast asleep. Joe woke up around 5:00 a.m. like always. It couldn't be helped, after fifteen years. He went to the bathroom and snuck back into bed, putting his hand over her breast, looking to see if she was awake. She was awake all right. She turned over, rolled on top of him, and gently began to pump, once again moaning with great delight as they both came together.

"Good morning, Joe. How was that wakeup call?"

"The best I ever had," he said.

"Best lay, or best wakeup call?" Julie asked.

"Best of both worlds," he said, grinning.

Julie rolled off the bed, put on a robe, and went into the kitchen to make coffee and breakfast.

Joe came out with his jeans on. "Have you seen my underwear?"

"I think I ate them last night," she said and smiled.

He did as well. "What do you want to do today?" he asked. "I don't have to leave until tomorrow afternoon. You're coming home in two weeks. Right?"

"Yes, I'm coming home the week after next and I'm done with New York City until my next book is due, early next year. Thank God. As to your second question, if you don't mind, I made plans for just the two of us until you leave."

"Are you going to tell me?" he said.

"This morning, I'm making you a big breakfast. At 10:00 a.m. I have to drop off a new manuscript at the publishers and have a quick chat with my editor, who'll be coming in just for that. Then we're taking the subway to The Bronx. I've got two tickets for the Yankees and Toronto game, starting at 1:05 p.m. We will be seated along the right field line, about hundred feet from first base, from what

216

I've been told. From there, after the game, we will be coming home and making love three more times and then heading for a carriage ride in Central Park. From there, we will be going to dinner and a jazz club, right around the corner from here. Tomorrow, we will go to mass at 10:15 a.m. at St. Patrick's Cathedral, head back here for another quickie, and then I hired a town car for 2:00 p.m. to take both of us to JFK for your 4:00 p.m. flight to Nashville. If the windows are tinted, I'll let you ravish me one more time before your flight. I've got all this written down in a timeline for you, Joe." She laughed so hard she nearly rolled around the kitchen floor. "Do you think your anal-retentive nature has rubbed off on me or what?"

"All I can say is thank you, thank you, thank you. If I die and go to heaven, I'd ask for the Irish wing of heaven, which would only consist of your outline of beer, sex, Yankees, sex, beer, and more sex. Yes, I already have died and gone to heaven."

"Well then, let's get a move on, buddy. Time is money, you know, here in New York City." She opened the refrigerator, scrambled some eggs, made toast, and popped the precooked bacon into the microwave. It was a trick Joe had shown her years ago. Cook all the bacon at one time, keep it in a plastic bag in the refrigerator, and then pop in several slices into the microwave for thirty seconds and you have perfect bacon every time, with no fuss or muss.

217

They ate, dressed, and headed for the publisher's office.

⋐⋗⋐⋗

The publisher was two blocks from her apartment. They rode the elevator up to the forty-second floor and Julie introduced Joe. "I'd like you to meet Joe Traynor."

"Nice to meet you, Joe," Julie's publisher said. "Julie has told us so much about you, I feel like I know you already."

"Nice to meet you, too," Joe said.

He went over and sat in the waiting room to wait for Julie. This was not his world and he felt uncomfortable. He didn't want to explain why he was back in the Coast Guard or what he was now doing. It was better left unsaid.

Julie went into her publisher's office and handed her the updated manuscript for her second book then had some small talk for several minutes.

"Julie, he's a cutie, isn't he? No wonder you've been keeping him under wraps. Where's his uniform. I love a man in uniform," she said.

Julie began to blush. "He looks a lot better out of his uniform, too."

The publisher laughed and winked at her. "Have a great weekend," she said. "I'm sure you will."

She wanted to know all about Joe but Julie told her it would have to be another time because they were headed to the game. Julie had already asked her about the use of town car for Sunday's trip to JFK and it was all arranged. Joe was very impressed on how Julie was treated by these New Yorkers. Evidently, she fit in fine with her Brown master's degree and her writing skills.

Joe guessed that they had big things planned for Julie down the road. He hoped that he would be a positive in her life and never stand in her way. During her childhood, although loving with her grandmother raising her all those years, she'd missed having a mother and a father and the money to do the little things that most kids expected while growing up. Julie never expected anything but love from her grandmother and got that in spades.

They took the subway, getting off at the Yankee Stadium stop. They had to go to "Will Call" for her tickets. She wouldn't say how she got the seats but Joe knew where they'd be sitting for the game and it must have cost an arm and a leg. Before the game, Julie had also set it up for a quick trip to Monument Park in center field where all the Yankee greats were enshrined. She took a picture of Joe next to the Mickey Mantle plaque to send to his father. Joe had called him at the hospital in the morning and spoken to him. He told his dad that Julie was treating him to the game so his father said, "Marry her on the spot and send the picture of the 'Mick' to me."

Julie overheard the conversation and smiled.

219

"Tell him I'll get the pictures to him by the end of week." She knew once Joe got back to Nashville, he wouldn't have time for anything. "Your father has good taste, doesn't he?"

"Enough," he said and laughed.

They got to their seats about a half hour before game time. Joe bought Julie a coke and a hot dog. He got a beer and a hot dog. "That was the fastest $30.00 I ever spent."

Jeter was playing today in the new Yankee Stadium. It was Joe's first time in the new stadium and Julie's first time ever at a major league game. Before leaving for the game, Joe just wanted to see how Jeter was doing during his last year as a Yankee before retiring. He'd announced his retirement before the season began and he was just starting to hit his stride after missing all of last year with a broken ankle. His fielding was down. He couldn't make the patented "Jeter throw" from near left field to first base anymore but he was making the routine plays as usual. His hitting was way down around .250 to .260 but he had recently brought it up to a respectable .270 after a few multi-hit games.

What a remarkable career, Joe mused. If his Coast Guard career could be half as good as Jeter's baseball career, Joe would be more than satisfied. Playing for twenty years for the same team, especially as a shortstop and captain of the team, was unheard of.

Jeter got kudos from every team in the league as

he was going through his final at bats at other stadiums. Jeter's best year was in 1999, when he was 25 years old. Just the other day, the night before his operation, Joe's father was talking about Jeter versus Mickey Mantle, Joe's father's favorite Yankee. "Mickey Mantle's best year was in 1956 at age 25, as well. How can you compare either player? You can't because they were so different but so great in their own way."

"During Jeter's twenty-fifth birthday, he hit for .349, had 24 homeruns with 102 RBI's," Joe said. "With an on-base percentage of .438. He came in as runner-up in the MVP balloting and that was a tragedy. They won the World Series as well that year."

"Mickey Mantle, at age 25, had even better numbers, if it can be believed," Joe's father had said. "He batted .353, had 120 RBI's, and 52 homeruns, with no one else even coming close. They too won the World Series and 'The Mick' was MVP that year. He also won the Triple Crown, the most prestigious award in baseball. He was almost overshadowed by Don Larsen's perfect game in the World Series that year, with winning game five, 2-0 over the dreaded Dodgers."

The Yankees won today over Toronto.

It's too bad Andy Pettitte retired, Joe thought. *He's my favorite pitcher of all time.* Jeter was 2-4 and drove in a run, but had a throwing error. He wasn't the same. The nice thing about being a math wiz, and all, was that Joe calculated that Jeter would end up with a .310 lifetime batting average. If he went zero for the next 420 at bats, he would still wind up at a .300 lifetime batting average. "The Mick" didn't finish out his last season, at age 37, stricken with bad legs. If he hadn't played at all his last year, he would have wound up with a .3016 lifetime batting average.

"'The Mick' wouldn't even care about that," Joe said. "He'd have played until he dropped. He only hit .237 in 1968, which dropped his average to .298 lifetime, short of .300 by only 56 hits, in over 8,000 at bats. He did hit 18 homeruns that year and put him in sixteenth place on the all-time list. If he hadn't played at all the last year, he would have dropped to twenty-first. So as a homerun hitter, 'The Mick' was probably pretty happy, anyway." Joe knew his father idolized Mickey Mantle.

"Statistics, huh, Joe?" Julie said. "Can't you just enjoy the game?"

"Not really. No," he said. "Baseball is nothing but statistics. Without it, the game would be meaningless to me. Stats are everything."

"Well, you got your fill of stats, today and the Yankees won. You also saw Jeter. Sounds like a pretty good day to me," Julie said.

"So far, it's been great."

"Wait until we get back to the apartment. I've a few stats of my own to show you," Julie said and snickered.

"Stats, huh? Okay."

Joe and Julie headed back to her apartment. Joe was thrilled with the day and couldn't stop talking about the game. Julie finally experienced what Joe felt about baseball and the Yankees. Until then, she'd never understood what it meant to him.

⁓⁓⁓

They got home at 5:00 p.m. on the dot. Julie wasn't kidding. Her checklist was very accurate. After the third turn at lovemaking, they dressed for the carriage ride in Central Park. It got breezy and colder at night so Joe took a jacket and Julie had a shawl over her shoulders. They walked the six long blocks to Central Park and took a long ride.

Julie paid for the trip and, when Joe went to pay, she shook her head. "I'm a big girl now, Joe. I pay my own way from now on."

"Yes, ma'am," he said and smiled. God she was beautiful. He didn't want to think about how horny she was too, but he couldn't help himself. He smiled and told her he was having the time of his life, and he meant it. After the ride, they had a young couple, in line for the next one, take their picture sitting in the carriage. Julie got out, patted the horse on the neck, and they went to her new favorite Italian restaurant. It was a little hole-in-the-wall place. When she walked in with Joe, they greeted her by name.

"Julie, welcome," the hostess said.

Joe was impressed.

"I'm so busy most of the time that I eat here at least four nights a week, usually after 9:00 p.m. and it interferes with my once very thin figure," Julie said.

"I think your figure is just fine." He thought she'd filled out very nicely.

After dinner, and goodbyes, they went for a drink down the street at a local jazz bar. After two drinks each, and another fifty bucks, they went back to her apartment. They were beat. They hit the head, brushed their teeth, and fell asleep in each other's arms in a matter of minutes.

 భళఫ

After the last few days, Joe would normally miss going to mass but neither of them had ever been to Saint Patrick's Cathedral. There was a 10:15 a.m. mass that featured Saint Patrick's well-known choir. The cathedral was located at 460 Madison Avenue, not that far from Julie's place, but they decided to take a taxi so they'd have more time to look around the cathedral before mass. They ate a quick breakfast of bacon and English muffins, washed down with a couple cups of coffee. They caught a cab right outside her building and were there by 9:30 a.m. Between when the 9:00 a.m. mass ended and the 10:15 a.m. one began, short tours could be taken with a quick trip to the gift shop. Joe wanted to buy a Rosary for Tillie, and Julie wanted one as well.

"I want a booklet on the history of the cathedral," Julie said.

They went to mass and communion and left the church by 11:30 a.m. Julie wanted to take Joe for lunch before the town car came to pick them up. Joe was surprised when Julie said, "I'd love to get married in Saint Patrick's Cathedral."

He was kind of floored at her last comment and turned to her as they were leaving. "Julie, I love you more than words can say. Will you marry me?"

"Yes," she said. She had tears streaming down her cheeks. "Does this mean I can officially call you my fiancé to everyone now, not just the doorman?"

He laughed. "I love you so much. You know that, right?"

"Of course, let's go to lunch," she said. "We have to stay on schedule, you know."

She laughed and grabbed Joe's hand. He was embarrassed because he didn't have a ring picked out. He always wanted them to go together to select one when the time was right. This was totally unexpected but he wouldn't change a thing. An engagement and wedding ring was a lifetime keepsake. *What the hell do I know about diamond rings and settings?* He knew it would cost him around $10,000.00 to $15,000.00 for one he'd seen in Miami. But he would wait for her decision.

After lunch, they headed home. Julie checked her list and smiled. "Quickie? When I drop you off at the airport, my list will have been completed."

ɔɛ

They hopped in the town car and got to the airport in about an hour. It gave him an hour and a half to check in and go through security. He wasn't going as an air marshal, so he would have to stand in line. The windows in the car were blacked out but Joe just wanted to hug her to death. From the look in her eyes, she felt the same.

"This was the best weekend of my life," he said.

"Mine, too."

"I hope that the investigation will end in a few weeks just in time for when you get back to Key Largo. The final memorial service for Tom will be in a few months, after everything has been settled. It's a long drive to the Florida National Cemetery but we'll make a weekend of it."

They both got out of the car. Joe held her in his arms one more time. "I love you, Julie Chapman."

"I love you more than I ever realized, especially since this has been our first real weekend away together outside of the Keys," she told him.

Joe turned and started to walk away. He blew her a kiss and she did the same. He went through the doors and his heart sank. He didn't want to leave her but he had to. In a few weeks, they'd be back together again. They'd be together for life. *Fiancé*. He couldn't believe his good fortune. He would never forget this weekend, that was for sure.

CHAPTER 20

Joe's 4:40 p.m. flight, from JFK to Nashville, landing at 6:10 p.m., was right on schedule. By the time they boarded and taxied up the runway, it almost seemed like they had already landed.

Once in Nashville, Joe came up the ramp from the plane to the gate. Mark was standing there waiting for him. Joe nodded and they left the airport, heading for the car, parked in the police parking spot, right outside the main entrance. *It's good to be the police, or whatever we are, but no one's going to say anything, anyway, with government plates on the car.*

Once in the car, both being of very few words, Mark asked, "How was your trip?"

Joe smiled. "If I said great, you'd say I was a liar, but it went great. Dad's doing okay. He went through the surgery with flying colors. He had two blockages that they fixed and they threw in a pacemaker at no extra charge."

"It's good to be the king, huh?"

"Something like that. Pete and I reconnected. Tanya's great and is really good for Pete. I think

228

with Pete and Tanya working together, our father will do fine once he's home. We actually had a good visit before and after the operation. The trip to New York City was really good. By the way, would you mind being in our wedding?"

"When the hell did that happen?"

"About seven hours ago on the front steps of Saint Patrick's Cathedral in New York City. She half-spoke out loud about getting married in Saint Patrick's because it was so beautiful and I jumped in and popped the question—*Will you marry me?* She simply said 'yes' and then said, 'Let's go to lunch.' I wanted to pick out a ring together so it was kind of cheesy not handing her a ring with the proposal but she just didn't care. It was simply the best weekend of my life, following the successful operation on my father." Joe paused for a breath and sighed. "Now back to the crap storm."

"Well, congratulations. Can I call Louise right now and tell her? We had a bet that it would happen. She said this weekend and I told her she was crazy. I guess she knew more than me or you."

"Go ahead and call her but I'll bet Julie has already called her to tell her along with her friend, Maddy Malone, up in Reading, Massachusetts. Did you know that when you and the family came down to Key Largo for the cookout, and I showed you the cash with the Cyrillic strap, that Louise asked Julie if I even knew that she was in love with me? Louise knew then. How? How can women know these things? I never even approached the subject until that day in Islamorada at lunch when Julie asked me if I loved her, and I foolishly said 'Yes, I love both you and Tillie.' She said that's not what she meant and I should have known better. I swear to God I didn't know it until that day. As a matter of fact, when you and I were walking in the door that day, they were laughing because Louise asked Julie if all four of you could be in the wedding. Julie swore at her in jest."

"I knew all that, after the fact," Mark told him with a chuckle. "Louise told me the whole story on the way back to our house that night. The kids were fast asleep, otherwise they'd have spilled it. They have big ears and bigger mouths. I'm calling her right now."

Mark called Louise and she said that she expected his call as soon as Joe landed. Julie had already called her, half of Key Largo, and her friend Maddy.

"All four of us are in the wedding," Louise said.

After Mark hung up, Joe asked, "Did she tell you a date? It would be nice to know so I can save up."

"Let me give you some older brotherly advice," Mark said. "Don't say a word except for 'yes, dear.' Go along with everything she wants and your life will be wonderful. If not, it can be a living hell. I took my 'to do list' and did everything on it, and I got enough brownie points to last a lifetime."

"Sounds good to me. Can we drop my pending marriage now so can you tell me what's going on?"

"We pinpointed the exact location of the distribution center. We don't believe they knew they were being followed at any time during the week. No one screwed up," Mark said. "It took right up until late Friday night around 2:00 a.m. until the final hand off took place. Afterward, we found out that they only went to the distribution center once a week and we'd gotten lucky," Mark said.

"Mr. Michael Johnson, residing on California Avenue, was picked up delivering a whole lot of meth pills. None of the pills had the 'TN.' That's what they did at the center before distribution. Johnson was the individual discovered by the drone at the beginning of the week. Targeting the weakest link in the chain seemed to work again. With a quick look into the bag, we saw there were enough unprocessed pills to keep Johnson locked up for life, with local, state, and federal charges. After he came clean, he said he didn't know where the final destination distribution center was located. They believed him because he was scared to death. His drop off location was in the back of a Shell station near Charlotte Avenue in East Nashville, near Exit 211 off of I-65 N," Mark continued.

"As his drop off took place, they picked him up in less than two minutes, before anyone else arrived. They removed some of the pills and placed the pills in a secured signed off evidence bag, enough to secure a felony, possession with intent to sell. They hopped in his car, followed by the team in their cars. They brought him to the unacknowledged Homeland Security detention building in Nashville. After securing Mr. Johnson, the technician team programmed the drone immediately to hover over the pickup site behind the Shell station. When the Chevy pickup truck went behind the building, about ten minutes later, the drone followed it home. The last stop was in the 5000 block of Charlotte Avenue in East Nashville. The nondescript building is a rather large warehouse, set back about one hundred and fifty feet from the main road.

"After explaining to Mr. Johnson, back at the detention center, that he could be arrested on a state charge for possessing raw meth pills, unsalable in their present state, and with accessory to federal murder one in the first degree, with a death sentence hanging over his head, he decided to cooperate. He hadn't even changed vehicles.

"We caught him in his 2005 Ford Bronco, the same one spotted by the drone the other day. He wrote out his statement that he was a mid-level delivery person in a complex delivery chain. He didn't know who picked up the pills but he did know that it was a green Chevy pickup truck, probably late 1990s. He said it looked like a farm truck and even had hay sticking out of the back. He had a partial plate number but it didn't help at the time."

"Do you know how many late 1990 pickup trucks there are in the state of Tennessee? A lot." Mark then went on to tell Joe that the drone flew over the building all night taking pictures of anyone moving in and out of the building. "The drone took photos of twelve vehicles parked in and around the building. The cars and trucks were identified by license plate and owner registration.

"Your plan found some very bad people with very bad records, Joe. Not just meth related. There were a few individuals who'd been arrested for attempted murder, manslaughter, possession with intent, and a multitude of other crimes too numerous to mention. We're going to the Homeland Security set up, now, to meet with all the team members at 8:00 p.m. The drone has stopped flying. The pictures have been processed and enlarged and are hanging at the center for review. We'll need several teams for the takedown tomorrow night, and I mean fully armed. This is a bad group of people."

Joe sighed. "It will be for naught, as far as I'm concerned, if the Banks brothers aren't there, especially that murdering son of a bitch, Jefferson."

"We'll put your request on my mother's prayer hotline," Mark said. "I'm not kidding you. It's worked before and I'm sure it will work again. I have to call her tonight, anyway. You'll be bunking with me tonight, sweetie." He grinned. "You made the Evergreen Motel the most popular hotel in East Nashville. All our FBI team members are now staying there—those who came in from out of town for the big event. You should see the specialized assault weapons sitting back on the beds at the motel. Two agents are standing guard as we speak. Ten agents will be working with us tomorrow night. They all look like badass dudes, not including the badass dudes from the TBI team. The only non-bad asses are you and me. If the murder doesn't give them incentive, the takedown of the largest meth distributor on the east coast surely will."

"I only care about Tom and Lacey's murder, right now," Joe said. That's all I can think about. Other than the terrific time I had this weekend. Did I tell you what a terrific time I had?"

"Need I ask? Okay, I'll ask. Did you get laid, Joe? Is that why you can't stop grinning from ear to ear?"

"The answer is a lot. A lot, Mark." Joe was still smiling.

"I hope it continues. You're a lot nicer now, Joe. A lot nicer. Oh, by the way, I didn't tell you. The meth distribution center on Charlotte is less than three miles from the airport that we were using for the drone. We may eventually find that they probably flew some meth right out of that airport since it was so close. So we'd better check planes and dates and see what meshes with any delivery schedules that we'll hopefully find on computers in the center. Also, worth noting, Lacey's burnt out car was found less than a mile and a half from the

Charlotte Street address. I'll bet that Jefferson Banks dropped the car and burned it where he did because he knew that he could walk to where his brother was working at the distribution center. In fact, our motel is only three miles down the road at Exit 211 off I-65. We didn't plan any of this, but they certainly seemed to have done so. These aren't stupid people, Joe. We'd better be very careful tomorrow night. I'd like to make it home and attend an upcoming wedding."

"Me, too," Joe said.

ఌఌఌ

On the way to the meeting at the Homeland Security center in downtown Nashville, Joe called Frank to find out what he'd discovered at the Dunkin' Donuts in Orlando. Mark had filled Frank in but Joe has asked Frank to sit on it until they both got back to Orlando, after the takedown tomorrow night.

"Hi, Frank, it's Joe. How are you?"

"Good, Joe. I just got back to our Port Canaveral Station. I was going over everything we found at the Dunkin' Donuts. Jack got back to us and, I'll tell you, I'm quite impressed with his findings. I don't know if we could have gotten any more than we did from anyone else."

"Jack is the best in the business and has been doing this for a long time," Joe said. "What did he find out? Or for that matter, let's start with what you found and go from there."

"Right after I got the call that you were heading to Albany and that Mark was going to Nashville to fill in, I gathered my guys here at Port Canaveral and made a complete list of what we wanted to find out. I then called Jack to let him know that we were heading over to Orlando the next morning and that we'd be shuffling him videos, pictures, and whatever we could get from the store. We showed up early, flashed our Homeland Security credentials, and scared the crap out of the day manager. We told him we wanted the video from the day Tom was murdered and, specifically, at 8:02 p.m. when Apple downloaded software updates to Tom's computer through the Dunkin' Donuts's WiFi network. We were lucky that Tom's computer didn't have password protection. You know, I don't have it on my own computer at home either and I should. All our phones and iPads are fully protected."

"I know, mine wasn't protected either, but we have encrypted iPhones and IPads as well. So, what did you find?" Joe asked.

"We got the videos for the exact time and it produced pictures and video of all the employees for that night and of three customers who were sitting in the store drinking coffee and looking at their computers. Two of the three didn't seem to be someone we'd be looking for. The first was a college student doing his homework. The second was a grandmother type, around sixty years old. The third seemed to be the perfect fit. It was a guy with a ponytail, about thirty to forty-years old with a lot of tattoos. We got jpegs made of all the employees and the three customers. Jack ran the pictures against the facial recognition software and Florida driver's license pictures. Nothing came up for the college kid on any police records and none for the grandmother either. The picture did match the kid's driver's license and the car in the lot was registered to him as well. The grandmother didn't drive so he couldn't match her picture.

"We went back to speak to the night crew after we got hold of the pictures and the employees did recognize the older woman because she lived down the street," Frank continued. "They didn't know who the kid was. The employees all turned out okay. We can go visit both the kid and the grand-mother, if need be, probably more as a witness to identify the third customer. The employees, as you could guess, had various conflicts with the police but nothing serious. The jobs at Dunkin's are min-imum wage, low level positions, except for the night manager, so you would suspect that there might be some issues."

"While this is all very interesting, Frank, please get to the point."

"Sure, Joe. The jpeg pictures came back and the ponytailed guy was identified in several ways. First, the facial recognition software identified him as William Hammond, better known as Wild Bill Hammond, age 34, a member in good standing of the Warlocks biker gang. As a matter of fact, the clubhouse for the gang is exactly six tenths of a mile from the Dunkin' Donuts here in northwest Orlando. Mr. Hammond has several felonies for drug possession and sale of a controlled substance. He had two felonies and one more could send him away for a long time. His driver's license picture matched the facial recognition of the jpeg and the motorcycle was registered to him with a home address of the Warlocks clubhouse, over on Fourth Street, at the end of the dead-end road."

"So far so good. What else did you get?" Joe asked.

"Besides the inside pictures, we got the video from the outside cameras. We saw Wild Bill's motorcycle parked right by the front door. The other car in the lot belonged to the kid. It was a Junker and we matched the ownership to him. The grandmother lived down the block and didn't own a car. What was interesting was a video of Wild Bill receiving an Apple computer from an unknown individual. He was directly in front of the camera by the front door. The hands in the picture, giving Bill the computer, were those of a man. In fact, the man had a watch on his left wrist, probably meaning he was right handed. Now, the watch was very interesting. It was a very expensive *Tourneau* brand watch. Jack was able to hone in on the picture and he then went to the Tourneau website and looked for the identical watch. Obviously, online were the 2014 models but the watch on the wrist looked almost identical to the $1,500.00 model. It's a TNY 40 mm Aviator GMT in stainless steel."

Frank paused for a breath. "Jack forwarded the advertisement with the picture of the watch. It stated that 'the Aviator model, as pictured, featured key design principles of the classic pilot's watch: large case, oversized Arabic numerals, large crown, and signature triangular marker at 12 o'clock with dots on each side—allowing the wearer to recognize that the watch is properly oriented at a moment's glance. This 40 mm Aviator GMT with its leather strap, bold black dial, and automatic movement gives this piece its sporty yet refined elegance. This watch features a dual time complication, showing home time on a 24 hour display and local time on an independent 12-hour display—giving the wearer the ability to keep track of home time while traveling across time zones. Recalling the heritage of a pilot watch combined with its outstanding value, the TNY 40 mm Aviator GMT is a statement-making timepiece that will last for generations to come.'"

"How does that help us?" Joe sort of knew but wanted to see if Frank was on the same page.

"Well, first, I'll bite, Joe. You're testing me, right? Don't answer. Here's what I'd do at this point. Mr. Wild Bill Hammond has been caught red handed with Tom's computer. We don't even need to find the computer if he's gotten rid of it. Eyewitnesses in the Dunkin' Donuts at the precise time Apple downloaded the software into Tom's computer will be enough. The pictures of him receiving the computer outside the store is enough to get him for receiving stolen goods, but we can grill him and tell him that he's an accessory in a federal murder investigation and could be given the same death penalty as the murderer. I'll bet we get a written statement from him, identifying the man who handed him the computer. Then when we find that individual, he would never suspect that his watch would star in a Homeland Security video that would send him to death row. How's that for a straight line to the murderer?"

"That's great, Frank. That's exactly what I was thinking as soon as you mentioned the watch and the man's hands. Obviously, Mr. Hammond knows who he is. He can't bullshit us on that. He would never take a computer from someone he didn't know, unless he was forced to, I'd imagine. There's something about that watch but I can't put my finger on it. I might have seen it before, maybe not the same model, but a lot like it. I hope it comes to me before we get back to Orlando."

Joe took a breath then continued. "Tomorrow night, around midnight, we'll pull our full on assault on the meth distribution center. I don't want you to go anywhere near Jim Butler because he's a suspect and, in fact, probably involved in the murder. You don't need to follow up with Wild Bill Hammond yet, but someone should keep a close eye on him without notifying the Orlando police department," he said. "You can get a team from the local FBI office to follow him around until we get back. Then, and only then, should we pick him up and read him the riot act. If Butler's involved, notifying the police that we're watching the Warlocks might screw up the operation and send Hammond on the run."

"I understand."

"Thanks for everything you've done, Frank. I apologize for grilling you so hard."

Frank laughed. "I didn't expect any less. Your reputation has already preceded you."

Joe laughed as well. "It's hard to let go but I'm working on it. We'll be back no later than Wednesday."

CHAPTER 21

As soon as Joe ended the call with Frank, he called Rear Admiral Barnes in Miami and caught him just before he left his office for the night. It was 7:45 p.m. Joe filled him in on everything that had happened. He also thanked him for giving him the time to go home and be with his father. Joe also thanked him for suggesting the trip to New York City. "I got engaged over the weekend," he said.

"Congratulations, am I going to be invited to the wedding?"

Joe got flustered, for the first time in a long time. "Of course." Then, it was back to business. "Mark and the team found the distribution center in Nashville and they're getting a warrant for the raid for Monday night."

"Do thermal imaging of the premises and the facility, before going in," the rear admiral reminded him.

"We'll be discussing the takedown at 8:00 p.m., right after this call."

Joe made a mental note to himself to mention

that. It was easy to forget in the planning, but it was critical to know beforehand where everyone was inside and outside the building.

"Thermal imaging can't see through walls but it gives off enough heat from individuals so you'll know where everyone is, hopefully," the rear admiral said.

"I'll call Jack Forest and ask him to get the architectural building plans to see where rooms are located. Jack can get the plans to me almost immediately, well before the chain of command can figure out where to go. The thermal imaging would also be useful after the takedown to find any secret hiding places in the building or even in the cars and on the perimeter. Within the building walls, there should be substantial differences in areas that aren't insulated and spots that could be jammed with drugs and cash." Joe also told the rear admiral, in detail, why he believed that Jim Butler was dirty. "We got lucky and found Tom's computer being downloaded at a Dunkin' Donuts and got pictures of the individual. We will pursue that after the meth distribution center is shut down and, hopefully, at least the one murderer that we know of, Jefferson Banks, will be apprehended."

"It looks like things are well organized, Joe," Barnes said. "It's good that you are on the cutting edge of technology because I don't have a clue about this new environment. It's a whole new investigative world that is now passing me by and

I'm glad that we have people like you, Jack, Mark, and even Frank, who can understand this new world of technology."

Joe chuckled. "I wish that we had a few smaller drones that could be hooked up with thermal imaging to make it easier and more undetectable, but we'll manage without it. I just saw a story on ESPN, *Outside the Lines*, where the UCLA, Division 1 football team is now utilizing smaller drones, less than fifty pounds, to watch both the offensive and defensive units practice their drills from above. It gives a whole new perspective and shows holes on both sides of the ball that need to be plugged, which were never seen before. The head coach at UCLA said that as soon as they stopped running the drones into the goalposts, the drones were a major breakthrough in coaching." He chuckled. "I'll call you as soon as the takedown is over."

"You'd better."

Joe immediately called Jack. "Can you get the architectural plans for the building?" He gave him the address.

Jack gave him the GPS coordinates that he'd gotten from the drone. While on the phone, he went directly to the Nashville planning department with the exact GPS coordinates for the Charlotte Avenue address. This gave him the exact parcel information, #381700 80.58-1-2/5000, which he needed to get the schematics. The building was fairly new, by normal standards, being built in 1998. From there, it would be easy to get the digitized architectural plan downloaded, put into a zip file, and sent to Joe for the meeting. "Give me a few minutes and I'll have the file," he told Joe.

∽∾∽∾

The Nashville Homeland Security Center was not publicized for many reasons. Meetings held there were on a "need-to-know" basis and not everyone in the Nashville Police Department or other Tennessee law enforcement agencies needed to know.

Attending Joe's meeting was the assistant director of the TBI, who Joe had originally contacted when he first arrived in Nashville. Others included the meth task force team and the violent crime response team. The local FBI agents were in attendance, as well as the FBI agents from out of town, now staying at the Evergreen Motel, waiting to participate in the takedown. The two members of the drug investigation division were also there, in addition to the highway patrol, who'd be controlling traffic.

Everyone wanted to know how Joe's father was and how he came through the operation. Joe told everyone that he was doing well and that he would be coming home in a week or two at the latest. He also told them that he got engaged over the weekend, in New York City.

"New York City, what the hell did you do that for?" one of the guys said.

And they all laughed.

The female members of the various teams told him that it was very romantic, which made him blush. The women wanted to know all about his new fiancée, and he told them who she was and that she was a writer. Two of the women knew exactly who Julie Chapman was and they were very impressed.

I'll never get through this meeting. Why the hell did I say anything? I guess I'm just happier than I've ever been before. Now back to reality.

The meth building was now fully under surveillance. The drone wouldn't make any difference at this point. Everyone thought having the thermal imaging going right down until the time of the takedown would be important. They had the warrant in their hands for tomorrow night. Just then, Joe's phone buzzed. It was Jack and attached to his email were the building plans. Joe forwarded it to the computer at the conference table and produced the schematic within seconds. He then had the picture placed on the large screen on the wall. The architectural rendering was perfect. The TBI guys turned their heads and looked at each other, probably thinking about *Star Wars* in the new millennium.

Joe smiled. "Hop on board. This is the twenty-first century. Get used to it," he told them.

The building was open to the roof except for the backside, which had both upstairs and downstairs offices with a metal stairway leading to the second floor. The offices jutted out about thirty feet into the main warehouse space, which was two stories tall. "This is probably where the computer and records are kept," Joe said, pointing to a spot on the diagram. "The second wave team is to secure the building after the takedown and head immediately to the offices to prevent destruction of records."

The assistant director suggested that they get permission from several of the building owners surrounding the facility to perform thermal imaging from their rooftops and, if not, from windows directly facing all four sides of the building.

"By the time we go in, we'll have a pattern of people going in and out of the building," the assistant director said. "By 11:30 p.m. Monday night, we will stop anyone leaving the facility, after they've traveled a few blocks beyond the building, so as not to alert anyone of our presence. Anyone turning into the building will be allowed to do so and, if still in the vehicles by midnight, they'll be among the first people to be taken out. Dart guns are to be used on anyone guarding the outside of the building. This is to keep noise to a minimum."

They all thought it would be a good idea, as long as the people using the dart guns knew exactly what they were doing. The FBI team used the darts regularly. The thermal images taken would determine where the first assaults would start.

"The first teams will use stun grenades, also known as a flash grenade or flash-bang," Joe said. He knew that most everyone had used flash-bangs before but he wanted to make sure that everyone on the first team going in was familiar with the capabilities. "Stun grenades are a non-lethal explosive device used to temporarily disorient the senses. They are designed to produce a blinding flash of light and loud noise without causing permanent injury. They were first developed by the British Army's SAS in the 1960s. The flash that's produced momentarily activates all photoreceptor cells in the eye, making vision impossible for approximately five seconds, until the eye restores itself to its normal, un-stimulated state. The loud blast is meant to cause temporary loss of hearing and also disturbs the fluid in the ear, causing loss of balance. We'll have to be careful because the concussive blast of the detonation can still injure, and the heat created could ignite flammable materials such as fuel."

Joe hesitated. "I don't know what chemicals, if any, are used in the stamping process that puts the 'TN' on the pills, so we'll have to be careful there, too."

The assistant director nodded. "The second wave of officers will be in charge of securing the facility, and they'll immediately disperse to prevent any destruction of computers or records. We will need the records to make the distribution case and not just the possession case."

"My main priority is to get a murderer off the streets," Joe reminded the teams.

On the wall, there were pictures, taken by the drone, of people and vehicles. The vehicles were then connected to the drivers' picture IDs. Those IDs, with each person's criminal record, were pasted below the pictures, which had been blown up. Of the twelve vehicles, almost all of them were owned by known criminals.

Joe pointed out the pictures of both Jefferson and Buddy Banks. "Please make sure that they are taken first. Anyone running out of the building will be taken down by the third wave of officers stationed outside the doors, in a tactical position. They aren't to shoot any unarmed individuals, but they are to use extreme force, other than that, to take them into custody. This is a one-time opportunity to close down the biggest meth distribution center on the east coast," he reminded them. "Are there any procedural questions?"

"Who's in charge, specifically," one team member asked.

Joe explained the pecking order. "I'm the lead investigator. All decisions will go through me. Mark Silva is next in my absence. This is a federal case both for the meth operation and the murder. The immediate take down will be led by the FBI. They'll be followed by the TBI officers on the various teams. Once the building is secured, the TBI will take charge of the meth investigation. The TBI will use thermal imaging throughout the facility to determine if there are any hidden drugs in the walls or other spaces. They can file state or federal charges, depending on what they find and the resources they require. Obviously, the more resources needed point to federal charges."

Joe grinned at them. "You'll get all the credit for the drug seizures." That made them happy. "Any money found will be distributed by the feds to cover the costs of all their operations. The two murders are under federal jurisdiction and I will lead that task force. Both Buddy and Jefferson Banks will be shackled and taken back to this Homeland Security facility, if we find them at the premises. From there, because it's a federal murder case, they'll be transported to the much more secure Homeland Security lockup in Miami. This is a shared responsibility, and everyone participating will receive enough credit to last a lifetime," Joe said to all of them.

They all clapped and Joe ended the meeting. They'd be back at the facility by 10:00 a.m. the next day, and earlier if any problems came up. The meeting broke up, but Joe stayed to coordinate the administration with the assistant directors of the TBI and the local FBI. Joe wanted no confusion on any of these issues. The assistant director had already selected two teams for the thermal imaging that would start as soon as they got there. He would personally go visit the other property owners to place his people all day Monday, leading up to midnight.

Joe felt good about this operation. Both the FBI local director and the TBI head told him that if he ever wanted out of the Coast Guard to please call them and he'd be working the following day.

That feels good.

He told Mark and that made him feel good as well. Joe knew praise for one was praise for both. Joe would never leave him behind and vice versa.

CHAPTER 22

At 10:00 a.m. everyone arrived at the Homeland Security facility. The thermal imaging had started last night, right after the meeting, but it would be more effective when they got to the key spots in the surrounding buildings. The assistant director had gone very cautiously to each of the proposed buildings, early that morning, and had spoken to the person in charge of the building where he wanted to maintain a thermal imaging camera and staff.

He was smart enough not to go alone. He had the senior FBI special agent from Nashville at his side. It seemed to help. Flashing that badge said everything to the owner. Last night had proved very fruitful, even without the additional spots, but with the strategic positions, they'd know as much as they could before going in at midnight.

The team running the thermal imaging cameras noticed that at 9:30 p.m., right after last night's meeting, when everything was set up, there were limited vehicles, only three, in the parking lot. From the thermal imaging cameras aimed at the building, when they first set up, there appeared to be two heat sources in the office on the second floor and three heat sources in the main part of the warehouse. There was one heat source at only one door but that heat source moved and another heat source showed up at the other doors, at fifteen-minute intervals. So it was suspected that one guard covered all three doors.

Just as before—when the drone had found the building and identified twelve vehicles on the first night—at 11:00 p.m. more vehicles started to show up. At midnight, there were ten vehicles parked in the lot, and eighteen heat sources were identified inside and outside the building. There continued to be two heat sources on the second floor, and two new heat sources in the first floor office. There was a heat source at each of three doors. That must have meant that there was more activity, requiring a guard at each door.

The team wasn't sure if it was just to keep people out or to keep people in, as well. There were eight separate heat sources in the middle of the main warehouse, meaning there was a full crew working in the stamping operation. Three individuals showed up in the thermal imaging camera, guarding the outside perimeter. The thermal imaging camera could see the individuals who appeared to be carrying guns, patrolling the outside. The surveillance teams also had night-vision goggles and, when the suspects were walking around the building, they saw them clear as day. The suspects were armed.

                                         ↄ꙰ↄ

During the day, Joe was antsy, along with everyone else. The clock ticked slowly up to 10:30 p.m. when they started to head out. Joe used the time during the day, to call the rear admiral one more time. He took a long nap in one of the rooms set aside with cots for Homeland Security agents staying over during other investigations. He and Mark and a few of the guys ordered in for lunch and a light dinner. Mark called in to his station in Dania Beach. It had been a while. He just hadn't had time until now. He called his wife and spoke at length. Louise told Mark to tell Joe to be careful, now that he was engaged.

Joe called Joan and clued her in. They talked for a while and, of course, she wanted to know all about the wedding plans. Julie had already called her and asked if Joan's daughter Lucy could be a bridesmaid. Lucy was an up-and-coming cross-country star who now ranked nationally and Julie was Lucy's coach. Lucy had two years left of high school and would probably wind up with a track scholarship to college. She was thrilled, as were Joan and Julie.

God, she's moving quickly, Joe told himself, trying not to panic. *We need to rein this in before it gets away from us. We don't even know where or when we will be getting married. Or does she know already and just hasn't told me yet. It's only been a few days, for God's sake.*

Joe called Claire at the Hollywood Studios in Walt Disney World. "I can't tell you much at this point but the entire case will come to a full conclusion by Monday, if not sooner."

"Thanks, Joe. I'm pleased that you are on top of it, as well as Mark and Frank. I'm still getting over the fact that Dad's deceased and probably caused it himself. The final memorial service will be in a few months," she told him. "I secured a plot at the Florida National Cemetery and I plan to have everyone show up."

After he hung up with Clair, Joe called Frank.

"We're following Wild Bill Hammond around town and he hasn't suspected anything," Frank told Joe. "We followed him back to the Warlocks' clubhouse where he remains every evening. Evidently, he doesn't get out much,"

Joe laughed. "I know the feeling."

He finally called Tillie. "Julie and I had a great weekend and we'll both probably be home within two weeks at the latest. My father is doing well. I just called and spoke to my brother this afternoon."

"Julie called me right after she got home from dropping you off at JFK," Tillie said. "I'm thrilled to death for both of you. Julie already asked me to give her away, since I'm both a mother and a father to her." Tillie hesitated. "I offered Julie my own wedding ring that I've kept locked up in my drawer since Julie's grandfather died so many years ago. I don't want to interfere. If you both want to pick out a new ring, or incorporate my ring into the new, that would be great. Do whatever you want. I just wanted to offer it to Julie as a keepsake."

"Thanks, Tillie. We both appreciate it."

Joe called Julie around 7:00 p.m., knowing that's when she normally came back to her apartment after eating dinner at the small Italian restaurant around the corner.

"Hi, Julie, it's Joe."

She laughed. "I believe I know your voice by now."

"I hope you never forget it. You'll be hearing it a lot within the next few weeks."

"How's the investigation going?"

"That's why I wanted to call you. It's going down around midnight tonight. Everything is in place and everyone has his or her own individual job to do. If it goes well, there will be a very large dent in the meth trade around here and elsewhere. Better yet, we'll get a murderer off the street. That's my main goal," he said. "Dad's doing fine. Pete and Tanya have visited him every day at Albany Medical Center. I'm really starting to love that girl. I just got off the phone with Pete a little while ago. I told him that he and Tanya should make plans to come down to Key Largo before the winter sets in and he said he would ask her. Pete's never been any place. This would be good for him."

"Tell Pete that would be fine with me and tell him that I was asking about my new father-in-law." She paused. "Joe, please be very careful and tell Mark the same thing. I've never been engaged before and I want this wedding to happen. Please don't get hurt."

"I'm very careful when it comes to these operations and I'll be especially careful now, Mrs. Traynor," he said then chuckled. "Mrs. Traynor, wow. I don't believe I've ever heard that before except for my own mother."

"Unless Pete beats you to the aisle, I'll be the next Mrs. Traynor. Julie Traynor, or Julie Chapman Traynor has an even better ring to. If I become rich and famous, as the author of *Conch Town Girl*, I'd like to be introduced as 'Julie Chapman Traynor.' Let's hear a loud round of applause, ta da."

"I actually like Julie Chapman Traynor or just keep the name, Julie Chapman. It's your decision not mine. I'm not marrying your name. I'm marrying you."

"You're no fun," she told him. "I love you, so please be careful."

"I love you, too. I'll call you in the morning," he said. "I'll be very busy up until then."

It was now 10:30 p.m. and all the teams were ready to go. The FBI, TBI, and the others would meet two blocks away in a school parking lot and walk to the site. There were three separate teams of ten officers each. The first team was the FBI takedown specialists, with three agents, utilizing dart guns, to take out the outside guards. Then three teams of two special agents would take each door.

Joe and Mark would immediately follow the first team after the doors were broken down and the flash-bangs were set off. Two individuals from the second team would be used for each door. They had battering rams to take down the doors, so six of the ten officers would immediately follow the first wave. The remaining four, on the second team, would head toward the offices to secure the computers and records, if any. The third team would guard the perimeter and the doors from the outside, in case anyone tried to escape. They'd go in and search the premises after everything was secured.

Other officers from the highway patrol units, not on the three teams, would stop traffic during the assault period on Charlotte Road for two blocks on each side of the building and on all the side streets within a two-block radius. The FBI and TBI cars would have additional drivers who'd show up after receiving the call from the TBI assistant director on site.

∽∾∽∾

Everyone got to the school parking lot at 11:00

p.m. There were ten FBI special agents, twenty TBI officers, and drivers for ten police cars. Six highway patrol vehicles would monitor traffic after midnight and block the roads until the operation was completed. Already at the site were six teams, manning the thermal imaging cameras. As soon as the assault teams were ready for the take down, the camera crews would be pulled back and meet at the school parking lot for assignments later. They'd go into the building and do thermal imaging on all the walls and potential hiding spots that could house drugs, guns, and cash, as well as anyone trying to hide.

The three assault teams went in separate directions, coming in from three different sides, so they wouldn't be seen. The FBI team had the three special agents, armed with dart guns, head up the line. They got into position first.

Just like clockwork, they took out the guards walking the perimeter, with limited noise. There was also one guy in his truck ready to leave. He was immediately taken down and cuffed. They taped his mouth shut and dragged him behind the wall of the building in the rear. The rest of the first team had their flash-bangs ready. Each had one grenade and a gun in their shooting hand. The six members of the second team had synchronized their watches and, at precisely midnight, they counted on their fingers "One, two, three," then they hit each door with the battering ram. It caught the inside guards by surprise with the first team grabbing the guards and pushing them out the door to be picked up by the second team.

Within seconds, the flash-bangs went off in the middle of the warehouse. The people on the stamping machines began to moan. They had their hands over their ears and were completely disoriented. Most of the workers were young women. They looked like Mexicans but, at the moment, no one could tell. The rest of the second team came in, went to the offices—one upstairs and one downstairs—and grabbed the four people holding their heads after two flash-bangs went off.

Joe and Mark were right at the front door when the battering rams hit. As soon as the flash-bangs went off, both of them—wearing protective headgear and noise reduction flaps, along with their protective vests—started looking around for Buddy and Jefferson Banks. There were clouds of dust and smoke but Joe saw both men, heading to the rear door, near the south end of the building.

Joe took off after them. Mark was right behind him. Buddy opened the door and was shocked to see two officers there with guns pointed directly at him. Jefferson Banks saw the door close quickly and started to open it. He wasn't sure what was outside. He had a gun and turned around to shoot at both Joe and Mark, who were heading in his direction.

Joe didn't hesitate and shot Banks in the shoulder. He didn't want to kill him, unless he had to. Banks was thrown into the door and started to head out into the darkness. Joe went through the door and saw Banks running toward the back lot. Joe stopped, aimed, and shot him in the rump. He hoped that would be enough to slow him down. Mark ran around Joe and came toward Banks from the right. Joe, being left-handed stayed on the left, his best side, of Banks.

Banks was lying on the ground with one hand on his shoulder and one on his rear. Mark went over to him and pointed his gun at his head. Banks had dropped his gun as he ran out the door. It was about ten feet from him, lying on the ground. He looked for it but Mark had kicked it away. Joe went over, slapped plastic cuffs on Banks, and dragged him back into the building. He "accidentally" slammed Banks's head into the door as they were going into the building. "Sorry," he said.

The scene in the warehouse was chaotic at best. Joe dropped Banks on the floor next to Buddy, who was brought in by the third team, handcuffed, and guarded. Joe immediately got hold of the FBI assault team officers and told them to take the Banks brothers to the Homeland Security Center in Nashville and lock them up.

"Don't even worry about their rights. One's a double-murderer and the other's going down for accessory after the fact, plus twenty other felony charges." Then Joe shouted at the top of his lungs.

"Everyone meet in the center of the warehouse with prisoners in tow."

There were sixteen individuals rounded up, outside of the Banks brothers and the one guy sitting in the truck—nineteen in total. The six Mexican ladies didn't speak English and were brought over to the side by themselves. Joe spoke to them in his Mexican infused Spanish dialect and they understood every word. Mark was there as well with his Mexican face. They were scared to death.

Joe and Mark both asked them in Spanish if they were all right.

"Yes," they replied.

They were shaking, of course. They really didn't know what was going on. They knew they were doing a job and were paid in cash. Not a hell of lot, considering the problems they now had. Mark would take their statements, after calling INS to process them for deportation. Putting these women in jail wouldn't stop crime. They should go home to their families. How they wound up in Nashville was a question for another day.

"Don't come back to Nashville because you'll be prosecuted for several felonies if you do," Joe said in Spanish.

They nodded their heads in agreement. They weren't coming back. The guards inside and outside were locked in the back of the police cars that had just arrived.

The other six, who ran the show, were a different matter. Two were in charge of the stamping operation. They both had long felony records. The four in the office were the brains of the operation. The second team picked up the computers immediately and put all documents into large, black plastic garbage bags. They found $25,000.00 in cash and that was bagged and tagged. The third team and the camera crewmembers went through the facility with a fine-tooth comb. They had sledgehammers, special saws, crowbars, and enough power tools to knock the building down.

Sitting at the stamping station were over two hundred pounds of meth pills, already stamped, along with those that were ready to be stamped. In the walls, using the cameras, they found two suitcases full of money, all in one-hundred-dollar bills. These were specially made cases to hold cash. Joe knew how much a Halliburton aluminum carrying case held because each case was especially made to hold one million dollars in hundreds.

The large briefcases were waterproof, hermetically sealed, and cost over $1,000.00 each. Joe took the money and gave it to the FBI special agent in charge. All the units of the task force would receive a special monetary thank you, once the cost of the operation was calculated and reimbursement made. Joe had plans for the $25,000.00 after everything was resolved. He wanted it to go to Casey Bradford to finish her degree in nursing. Losing her sister was bad enough. Having her turn out the same way was not acceptable to Joe. He would ask the rear admiral to set up a scholarship for her. She was alone and broke. And she needed a second chance.

In the walls were cases of the "TN" meth pills, all ready for distribution. The meth pills found on the premises were probably worth close to five million dollars. This was only one week's worth of production. Multiplying that by at least fifty weeks of production would have a street value of over two hundred and fifty million dollars.

The pills would be destroyed after the trials were held. They were too tempting to allow everyday local law enforcement staff to sit on them until then. All the money and drugs would be sent by armored car, in an FBI-controlled environment, to the large multi-unit Homeland Security facility in Miami. The TBI could prosecute the six real criminals who were strictly tied to the meth operation. The guards and the poor sap in the truck would receive enough time to keep them off the streets for the next decade. The others would now be lifers in either state or federal prisons.

Joe went to all the people involved in the takedown and shook each of their hands. Both men and women had participated and each would receive a citation from Homeland Security for a job well done. Joe got the heads of the various operations together quickly and told them that the take down would have to be kept under wraps for as long as possible. He still had arrests to make in Orlando and, if the criminals found out about the bust, those arrests would be in jeopardy, especially if the media got wind of the operation. "All you can say at this point is that arrests were made for the sale of meth and it's an ongoing investigation."

They all agreed.

Joe called the rear admiral's office and left a message that the operation was successful and that he and Mark would be headed to Orlando. Someone needed to pick up their car in Nashville and deliver it back to Miami. They were flying back to save time.

Evidently, the rear admiral had someone waiting all night for the call as he immediately called Joe back. "You can use the navy plane that you took to Nashville and Albany at the beginning of the week. Please convey the same message to Mark that it was a job well done."

"When we arrest Jim Butler, then the job will be done and not until," Joe argued.

The rear admiral concurred.

Joe would call the next day and meet the navy jet at the Nashville Air National Guard facility. He and Mark were heading back to the Evergreen Motel along with the rest of the FBI agents. They'd have a few beers before hitting the sack but they'd been up for over twenty-four hours with only a two-hour nap in the afternoon.

Back at the motel, Joe made all his calls, telling everyone that the takedown was successful and no lives were lost. He didn't tell anyone that he shot Banks in the ass.

CHAPTER 23

At 8:00 a.m. the following morning, Joe and Mark met the FBI agents in the parking lot of the Evergreen Motel. They were all headed to the Homeland Security facility in Nashville. Joe would be part of the interrogation team that would speak to the Banks brothers. They'd been separated in adjoining rooms at the facility.

Mark would be part of the team interrogating Buddy Banks. They wanted him to turn on his brother and serve as a witness against him for the murders of Tom Jones and Lacey Bradford. They were sure Jefferson had said something to his brother when he got back to Nashville. They'd been together at the meth distribution center ever since Jefferson burned Lacey's car and walked through the woods to the facility only a mile and a half away.

Joe would be part of the team that read Jefferson his Miranda Rights. After the interview, Jefferson would be escorted to the Miami Homeland Security facility where he would be held on federal first degree murder charges for the intentional, premeditated murder of Tom Jones and Lacey Bradford. He would also be charged with the federal crime of meth distribution across state lines and, as the murders were in connection with this crime, they'd ask for the death penalty. They'd also hold the death penalty over the head of Buddy Banks if he didn't cooperate and become a witness against his brother. He would serve a long time for the other federal charges, in any case, but at least the death penalty and first-degree murder would be taken off the table—if he cooperated.

They arrived around 8:45 a.m. after Joe stopped at the Dunkin' Donuts on their way. He needed his large-regular-coffee-and-two-donut fix, especially this morning. He'd missed it most of the previous week. He smiled to himself. He had to admit, the previous weekend more than made up for missing his donut fix.

After arriving at the facility, Joe spoke first to the FBI interrogation team before going in to talk to Jefferson. This was not an interrogation but a simple reading of rights after being arrested. The brother was a different story and Mark would handle that with the other team.

Joe was sitting at the table along with three other FBI agents as Jefferson was led in to the room, shackled at the waist, with chains on both his arms and legs. He had to be guided into the room by the two guards who had brought him from the holding cell. He'd been treated very well since he was brought to the facility in the early morning hours of Tuesday morning. The only visible bruise was the knot on his head over his left eye where he accidently fell into the door after being captured and brought back into the meth warehouse. They'd taken him to the hospital for the gunshot wounds to the shoulder and rear end. The wounds required a few stitches. So he was patched up and sent to the Homeland Security facility holding cell, guarded by the FBI agents. They weren't going to let him stay in the hospital once he was cleared by the doctor, in the emergency room. They had too much riding on this arrest.

Joe spoke first. "Are you Jefferson Banks?" he asked. At first, Banks didn't answer but only sneered at Joe and the other agents sitting at the table. "Are you Jefferson Banks?" Joe asked one more time.

"Yeah, I am," he finally said.

"We're here to read you your Miranda Rights, sir. 'You've the right to remain silent. Anything you say can, and will, be used against you in a court of law. You've the right to an attorney. If you can't afford an attorney, one will be provided for you.' Do you understand the rights I've just read to you? With these rights in mind, do you wish to speak to me?"

"I don't have to speak to you. I want my attorney."

"That's fine. The special agents, attending this

meeting, will sign an affidavit that you've been read your Miranda Rights. This conversation is also being recorded," Joe said. "Jefferson Banks, you're being charged with a federal double count of first degree murder for the premeditated murders of both Thomas Jones and Lacey Bradford." He read off the additional charges that went with the murders, including all the charges for the sale and distribution of meth across state lines. "We've asked the federal prosecutor to seek the death penalty as prescribed. You will be held at the Nashville facility until you speak to your attorney. Then you will be immediately transferred to the Miami Homeland Security facility to be held over for trial."

Jefferson looked at Joe with disgust. Joe looked right back at him and smiled. He turned to the others in the room. "Please make sure Mr. Banks is made comfortable for the rest of the time he has here—while he's still alive."

While Joe was reading Jefferson his rights, Mark was in the other room with three other FBI special agents, reading Buddy the same rights. When Mark was done, Buddy's eyes went very wide. "I didn't murder anyone. I don't know what the hell you're talking about. I was not in charge of anything. I was there packing pills when you nabbed me."

Mark looked Buddy in the eye. "Conspiracy after the fact for a first-degree murder charge, and murder in the commission of another crime, is the same as if you'd murdered both Thomas Jones and Lacey Bradford."

"I know Lacey. I've no idea who Thomas Jones is," Buddy said.

"It doesn't matter," Mark said. "All that matters is that you were part of this meth distribution chain from here to Orlando and back. You're just as responsible for anything that happened as if you'd murdered them yourself. You can probably help yourself and not be put to death for the two federal murder charges, but only if you give us a written and oral statement of what your brother told you, exactly, and only if it leads to a conviction on the first-degree murder charges against him."

"What happens to me if I testify?"

"You'll still have to go away for all the federal meth distribution charges but the murder charges against you will be dropped. Your brother will receive the death penalty. You will, too, if you don't turn against him."

"I'll sign," Buddy said.

Mark turned to the other agents in the room. "Blood is only thicker than water if it doesn't include a death penalty charge."

Buddy gave an oral confession, while being videotaped. He told them exactly what his brother said to him when he got back to Nashville. "My brother told me that he killed Tom Jones because he got too nosey and was in the way. Jeff told me that he killed Lacey for the same reason. He said he thought that she was the only witness against him and, if she were gone, he would be in the clear."

The confession and transcript took about a half an hour. By 10:00 a.m., the Banks boys were well on their way to the federal lockup, just waiting for Jefferson's attorney to arrive. Mark and Joe could leave at any time, after they did their own write-ups. The FBI was now in charge from here on out.

Joe met Mark in the hallway. "We have to write up our participation in this entire investigation and forward it to the rear admiral, to the Tennessee Bureau of Investigation, and to the local Nashville FBI office."

He called the rear admiral's office and spoke to Barnes's assistant. Joe told him they were wrapping up this part of the investigation and needed to get back to Orlando. They were told to board the navy jet by 4:00 p.m. at the Nashville Air National Guard facility. Joe said they also needed someone to bring their car back to Orlando.

One of the FBI agents said he would drop it off on his way back to Miami and leave it at the Embassy Suites Hotel, in Orlando, with the keys under the mat. Joe called Frank, who'd meet them at the Nashville airport at 6:00 p.m. that night. He said he would stay over and booked a room at the Embassy Suites as well.

On their way out, carry-on bags in hand, Joe and Mark were congratulated by the entire office. They were given a round of applause as they left the building. They hopped into their car. They'd a few hours to kill before going to the airport so they decided to go into town and see the sites before heading out. Neither one thought they'd ever be back, but you never knew.

It was crazy that somehow two Coast Guard chief warrant officers had wound up in charge of a federal murder case leading to the takedown of a major meth distribution center. It would also cause a major problem to those small meth labs in Nashville who, without the national "TN" trademark, now had to compete with each other in the meth trade in the local Nashville area. It would expose them even further to arrest since they'd have a smaller market and more interest from the local Nashville police.

Joe was very surprised that he'd received such a hard time from the local officer in charge of the West Nashville Precinct.

After lunch in downtown, they drove around and saw the Grand Ole Opry and other points of interest. Joe wanted to see The Basement on Eighth Avenue in South Nashville, where a number of emerging recording artists had appeared before hitting the big time. One of Joe's favorites was Noah Guthrie, a bluesy-pop singer-songwriter who was only twenty-years old. He was a big YouTube star and teamed up with Christina Grimmie, who came in third in the 2014 *The Voice* program, making his song "Somebody That I Used to Know" a big hit.

He'd performed at The Basement when he was only in his teens.

Joe and Mark managed to kill a few hours before heading over to the airport. They left the car there to be picked up by the FBI agent heading to Miami later in the day. They walked into the national guard facility and presented their credentials. Dressed in jeans and T-shirts they didn't make a huge impression on the staff until the navy jet landed and pulled up for them to hop on. Joe and Mark chuckled, still thinking about judging a book by its cover. Their speaking to each other in Spanish for the entire time didn't help matters much either.

❧❧

They landed in Orlando right on schedule. Mark had told Frank to pick them up at the Disney Magical Express Terminal, main terminal, B-side, Level 1, right outside, where the Walt Disney World buses took families to their resort hotels. There was a parking spot for the police, and it was right outside the door. Joe and Mark got to the first floor, B side, and jumped into the car which was idling, all by itself, at the curb.

"Welcome back," Frank said.

They decided to get dinner first and went to downtown Orlando to the barbeque restaurant that Joe liked and had eaten at when he first arrived. It was right around the corner from the Embassy

Suites, so they parked the car first, went in, and checked into the hotel. The desk clerk welcomed them back and gave them the same room that they'd shared before. Frank was right down the hall for the foreseeable future. At dinner, Joe and Mark gave Frank the overview of what had happened in Nashville. Frank congratulated Joe on his engagement. Frank had been married for fifteen years and had three children, ages twelve, ten, and nine—two girls and a boy.

"I know what a big step you're taking, especially if you're to continue to be in the Coast Guard as a career," Frank said. "My wife has a good job, working as a customer service specialist with a government contractor in Cape Canaveral. The pay for a chief warrant officer won't cover the cost of a college education for our kids. Alana's putting money away for that purpose."

"I'm facing the same situation with my two kids, Mark said. "I know it will cost a lot. I hope we've the money to put them through college. I didn't get that opportunity. But I can't complain about the Coast Guard. They saved my life."

After eating, and having a few beers, the conversation came back to what they'd have to do in Orlando to finalize the investigation. They hadn't picked up Wild Bill Hammond yet, but they were watching his every move. Joe decided that they'd pick him up the following day after he was well away from the Warlock's clubhouse. They'd probably have to bring him to Port Canaveral, where they had a secure lockup facility that served as a temporary site for Homeland Security.

They'd have the local FBI agents involved so there would be no confusion as to chain-of-custody issues. Joe didn't want to bring him the fifty miles to Port Canaveral, so he was hoping that the FBI could supply them with an interrogation office far from the prying eyes of the Orlando police. At this point, they would not involve the Orlando Police Department until Joe and Mark met with the chief of police, after getting a written statement from Wild Bill. They weren't sure of his connection to Jim Butler but they believed there was one.

"If Butler was in on Tom's murder, he had to be the one who handed the computer to Wild Bill in the parking lot of the Dunkin' Donuts," Joe said. "How Butler knows Wild Bill, I can only imagine."

They would not be sure until they met with him and asked. At that point, they'd try and meet with the chief.

They were all tired and decided to walk back to the hotel, make their calls, and go to bed. Tomorrow would be the culmination of a very trying investigation. They just hoped that Wild Bill Hammond would be the key that would unlock this Orlando end of the investigation.

CHAPTER 24

Joe, Mark, and Frank met for breakfast downstairs at the Embassy Suites dining room at 7:00 a.m. Embassy Suites had a free, cooked-to-order breakfast for guests. Frank's FBI team, following Mr. Hammond, was already in place and had been there all night. As soon as he left the Warlocks' clubhouse, the team would follow him and pick him up when he was alone. They didn't want to alert any of the other Warlock members if they could help it. The main interest was in getting Hammond to talk about the murders and then finding out where the meth was delivered in Orlando. But that was secondary to making sure that whoever was responsible for Tom Jones's death would be brought to justice.

As they were finishing their breakfast, Frank got the call from his team. "Mr. Hammond's on the move," he said. It was now 7:45 a.m. "He's alone and just pulled into the Dunkin' Donuts, the same one where he got Tom's computer." Joe and Mark just smiled.

"I'm hooked on Dunkin' Donuts," Joe said.

"But in Hammond's case, it could prove fatal for him."

"Hammond got off his bike," Frank continued, "went into the store, and is drinking his coffee and eating a breakfast sandwich."

The team waited for him to leave the building, then three FBI special agents grabbed him two blocks south of the store and away from the club-house. They took his motorcycle keys and one of the agents hopped on his bike. They put flex-cuffs on Hammond's wrists, with his hands behind his back, and placed him in the back of the FBI car. They were headed to the FBI satellite office at 850 Trafalgar, Suite 400, in Maitland, about eight miles south of their hotel. Joe, Mark, and Frank could be there in less than fifteen minutes as traffic wasn't as heavy heading toward Disney World and down-town Orlando.

When they got there, Hammond was already in the interrogation room. Joe, Mark, Frank, and two other agents decided that they'd team up in ques-tioning Mr. Hammond. Frank took the lead since he'd been on top of this since Joe left to go home and Mark went to Nashville. He'd been patiently waiting for their return so they could take Mr. Hammond into custody. That time had finally come. The five of them walked in together.

Frank started the conversation. "Mr. Hammond, I'm going to read you your Miranda Rights. 'You've the right to remain silent. Anything you say can, and will, be used against you in a court of law. You've the right to an attorney. If you can't afford an attorney, one will be provided for you.' Do you understand the rights I've just read to you? With these rights in mind, do you wish to speak to me?"

"Why am I here? I didn't do nothing," Mr. Hammond said eloquently.

"Mr. Hammond, you're being charged with the federal crime of premeditated murder in the first degree. That carries the death penalty. You're being charged with the federal crime of sale and distribution of a controlled substance across state lines. You're being charged with receiving stolen goods that were stolen during a federal crime that ended in first-degree murder. Do you understand these charges?"

"I've got no idea what you're talking about."

"Mr. Hammond, you're entitled to speak to an attorney and I'd advise you to do so but before you take me up on that, you should understand exactly what you're up against. We've traced Mr. Tom Jones's computer to the Dunkin' Donuts that you frequent. As a matter of fact, you were just there. At 8:02 p.m. on the night Tom Jones was murdered, you received the computer from an individual right outside the store. You then ordered a coffee and were seen on tape in the store looking at the computer. We know it was Mr. Jones's computer because, unbeknownst to you, that computer had software downloaded at exactly 8:02 p.m. that night, using the Dunkin' Donuts's network. There were only two other individuals in the store at the time and they witnessed you in the corner looking at an Apple computer. Mr. Jones was murdered earlier in the day. His computer was stolen and handed to you before you entered the store. Do you understand what I'm saying to you?"

"What's a computer got to do with me murdering anyone?" Hammond asked.

"You don't have to be the murderer to be convicted of murder if you were part of a conspiracy to commit murder. You get the same death penalty sentence as the person who killed Mr. Jones. By the way, that person killed another young lady on their way to Nashville. He's been captured and will also be tried under the death penalty statute. Now if you would like to start talking now about where you fit in to this, we could actually wind up only charging you with receiving stolen goods, a Florida state charge, and a charge of intent to sell a controlled substance, another Florida state charge. You would be out in less than ten years, more likely five years, for good behavior. Would you trade that for a death penalty charge? I'd start talking now, if I were you. You've five minutes and then you'll be sent to the Miami Homeland Security facility where you'll never see the light of day again."

"I didn't kill anybody and I'm not going down on a murder charge. I'll tell you everything. I received the computer from a cop, just like you said, outside the Dunkin' Donuts. I've been the cop's snitch for a couple of years. I give him stuff and he helps us. We paid him a hell of a lot more than I got as an informant," Hammond said. "After he gave it to me, I brought it into the store to play with it. I didn't know what was on it. There wasn't much and I got rid of it. I threw it in a dumpster in downtown late one night. A cop handed that Apple computer to me, and I didn't steal it from anybody. We've been dealing with him for a year or two now. He would tell us what they were investigating and then he would push any drug sales that they were investigating toward the Outlaws and not us. He was involved with a meth dealer who got his stuff from up north. He brokered the meth with us and took a cut every week, about four or five grand a week, or so I was told. I didn't handle that. I gave the drugs to another guy at the club and he pushed it throughout Orlando. It was stamped 'TN' which meant that it carried a premium price because it was the real thing. I didn't kill anybody. I don't know anything else."

"Who was the cop," Joe asked.

"His name is Jim Butler. He's a detective in the violent crime section in the Orlando Police Department."

"You'll sit here and write out your entire statement. This session has been taped. If, and only if, Mr. Butler is arrested, charged, and then prosecuted successfully for the murder of Tom Jones, will your charges be reduced to that of receiving stolen goods and intent to sell meth. This is your lucky day, Mr. Hammond," Joe said. "By the way, was it Mr. Butler who handed you the computer in the parking lot?"

"Yes, it was," Hammond said.

"Did he wear a watch on his left wrist?" Joe asked.

"As a matter of fact, one day, he showed me the watch. He said it was a gift from his wife for their twentieth anniversary. He was very proud of that watch. He said it was a Tourneau Aviator watch and it cost around $1,500.00. I don't know why he still wears it now. He was just recently separated from his wife."

ᏨᎦᏨᎦ

It was getting late in the afternoon. Joe, Mark, and Frank had to make up their minds on what they wanted to do next. They could simply go to Jim Butler's house and arrest him, if he was there. They could make a big deal about it and wait for him to arrive at police headquarters the next day. Neither option would help them in the long run. They could very easily piss off all the cops and further alienate the feds from the local police department. There was always enough animosity to go around in that area.

Joe thought it would be a better idea to get the chief's home address and stop by his house. No one would suspect them of going there for a discussion about a dirty cop.

❧❧❧

Cal Roberts had been the chief for the last ten years and appeared to be well respected. Joe'd liked him immediately when he'd seen him on the first day he barged into his office to complain about Jim Butler.

Chief Roberts handled the situation with wisdom and grace and told the detective that he would be out on his ass if he didn't cooperate. Joe had made peace with the detective but had had an uneasy feeling about him from the beginning.

Joe told the chief that he believed Jim Butler may have turned a corner and was providing the help they needed to find Tom Jones's killer. He felt embarrassed that he now had to tell the chief that he had a dirty cop on the payroll, and it was Jim Butler.

Joe called Jack up in Virginia. If he needed something quick, Jack was the man to call. "I need the home address of Chief Cal Roberts, his phone number, wife's name, any children living at home, and anything else that will help ease the tension when the team and I press his doorbell in an hour or two. I know that all Orlando employees have to live within the city limits, if that narrows your search."

"Hold on, Joe. This won't take long."

Jack went into the Orlando police personnel files and came up with the address of 9600 Bay Pine Lane, a gated lakefront community, several miles from downtown, near the Orlando International Airport, still within the city limits. The house had 2,400 square feet and sat on a small lakeside lot with four bedrooms, two baths, a large deck, and access to a pool, tennis courts, and other various recreation facilities. The house was appraised at $450,000.00. The chief had been married for twenty-two years to his wife, Estelle, who was the same age as the chief. They had three children: one girl, nineteen, in college locally and two children still in high school, a girl, age seventeen, and a boy, age fifteen, both still living at home. Jack gave Joe the phone number and the chief's cell number as well.

Joe thanked him. "This investigation is almost over and you should head down to Florida for a week when you get a chance. He paused. "I can't remember if I told you that I was engaged."

"Yes, you told me last week and that's great." Jack was a confirmed bachelor at this point but he was seeing someone up in Virginia on a regular bases. She was a schoolteacher and that was all that Jack would tell anyone. He was really holding close to the vest in his job and in his personal life.

Jack fed the GPS the address and all three, Joe, Mark, and Frank, headed to see the chief at his house. It was nearing 6:30 p.m. so they hoped that he would be home. Joe called the chief's number on the way, and the dispatcher told him that the chief had left for the day. He asked if Joe wanted to leave a message and Joe told him no.

In about twenty minutes, Joe pulled up to the gatehouse, manned by a rent-a-cop. Joe showed the guard his Homeland Security ID and told him they were meeting the chief. The guard wanted to call the chief first to confirm and Joe told him that it wouldn't be a good idea. Mark and Frank showed him the same IDs.

Joe pulled through the gate and wondered what the guard was thinking at the moment. *Maybe that we're here to arrest him*, Joe speculated and smiled. He pulled up to the house and parked in the front to the left of the driveway. He told Mark and Frank to stay in the car as he wanted to see what the chief's reaction would be before there was a big scene that could be avoided. Joe pressed the doorbell twice and waited.

Mrs. Roberts looked through the glass and opened the door with the safety chain still attached. "May I help you," she said.

"Yes, I'm Joe Traynor with the Coast Guard, as are the other two gentlemen in the car. We're working on a case with the chief and it's imperative that we speak to him now."

"He's in the back grilling our dinner. I'll go get him. If you don't mind waiting for him right where you are?"

"Not at all ma'am. Please take your time. We appreciate it."

About five minutes later, the chief came to the front door and opened it wide. He smiled. "Hi, Joe. How can I help you? You can invite the others in as well. I won't bite."

"Chief, we wouldn't bother you if it wasn't of the utmost importance. We need to make an additional arrest in the murder of Tom Jones. We need to speak to you privately because it will affect you and we want to keep that as quiet as we can for the moment."

"Estelle, honey, these gentlemen are going to go with me to the backyard. Please go ahead and eat and I'll eat later. Gentlemen, did you eat yet? We've plenty and I can put more on the grill."

"Thanks for your hospitality, Chief, and to your wife as well," Joe said. "But I don't think this is going to be one of those occasions when we should stay any longer than necessary."

They went out to the back picnic table and the chief's wife brought them out a pitcher of iced tea. They thanked her and she went inside, closing the sliding door.

Joe went on to tell the chief everything that had happened since he first got the call from Claire that her father had been murdered. He brought him up to date on what went down in Nashville. As an aside, he told him about his father and his engagement all at the same time. He then went in to specifics about how they had sufficient evidence that Jim Butler was involved in Tom's murder.

Joe started with the first day that he'd met Butler and how he thought he was very unprofessional, but he had changed his mind as Butler's cooperation had come full tilt after the chief's reprimand. "We found Butler's fingerprint in Tom's living room on an end table, but dismissed it as non-incidental. My suspicions about him arose after he ingratiated himself by attending both memorial services, and after he asked a lot of questions that didn't seem pertinent. He also told me that the Outlaws sold the most meth in the area. I ordered a full investigation of Butler through the head of clandestine operations in Virginia. Our investigation proved that Butler has sent $234,000.00 in cash to the Cayman Islands to his own personal account within the last eighteen months. It was right about the time his wife left him. The money was wired every fifth week after he deposited $1,000.00 each week into each of four separate savings accounts set up for that purpose. This went on for eighteen straight months. His personal checking account, where his police pay is deposited, was pristine and has been so forever.

"I also had the Coast Guard Jacksonville-Gang-ID team look into the claim that the Outlaws motorcycle gang was the biker gang moving the most meth in the Orlando area. It wasn't. It's the Warlocks. This was the first lie after the cash discovery. Then we got really lucky and found that Tom's computer received software updates through the Dunkin' Donuts's WiFi network at their location, less than a mile from the Warlock's clubhouse."

Frank took over at this point and told the chief about the videos and what they found. "We busted Wild Bill Hammond, yesterday, and he was taken to the local FBI office, where he was interrogated at length. When presented with the choice of a small state drug charge and receiving stolen goods versus a federal charge of first-degree murder with a death sentence, Wild Bill caved and gave up Jim Butler."

Frank also told him about the pictures of the expensive watch on the left arm of the man handing the computer to Mr. Hammond. "I have testimony from both the patrons and the staff working that night that it was Wild Bill Hammond looking at the Apple computer with the obvious Apple logo.

"With Tom's new Apple version, all software was automatically downloaded as soon as the computer was turned on at 8:02 p.m. at the Dunkin' Donuts store. Also, Hammond told us that he was an informant for Jim Butler and had been so for some time. The tradeoff was the money to Butler and Butler's pointing the finger at the Outlaws instead of the Warlocks. The money, the full

$234,000.00, is being transferred out of Butler's Cayman Island account and sent to the Islamorada Coast Guard office account."

Joe chuckled. "I have to raise a few hundred thousand dollars every year to keep my home office happy and me still employed there."

Mark and Frank got a kick out of that as well.

The chief sat at the picnic table, stunned. "I don't suppose you and your friends would consider working as detectives for the Orlando Police Department. It looks like I have an immediate opening and one of you could start tomorrow." He smiled at Joe. "I've never seen such a remarkable investigation tied up in one bow like this. I can only imagine what you had to do to bring down the largest meth distribution operation on the east coast." He sighed when they all shook their heads. "How do you want to handle this," he asked Joe.

"You'll more than likely want to shut down the Warlocks meth ring, Chief, and that could happen when we take Jim Butler into federal custody tomorrow and then immediately send him to the Miami Homeland Security Center, to await trial."

The chief agreed.

"We'd like you to call a special meeting of your top brass tomorrow morning for 8:00 a.m. in your office conference room," Joe said. "I want you to have Butler attend under the guise of updating your brass on what they're doing in Orlando as far as finding the meth operation. You can also ask him to bring them up to date on the murder investigation. Mark, Frank, and I will attend and we'll be armed. We'll need to receive clearance all the way around the front area and not have to go through all the checkpoints. I believe Butler will also be armed, so we need to immediately take him down and put him in handcuffs after I tell him he's being arrested on several federal charges, including first-degree murder."

"I agree with everything you're proposing, Joe," the chief said. "Thank you for bringing this to me this way. It's appreciated."

Joe didn't care if he got an explanation from Butler. The man was going to jail. "We'll come back to testify on all the Warlocks' state charges involving their meth connection. I would keep this under wraps until we get the Warlocks under lock and key. It will be up to you, Chief, to make the announcement, and you can word it anyway you want that Butler is headed for federal lockup. But all questions regarding him should probably be addressed by the local FBI and Homeland Security in Miami."

"Thanks for you discretion," the chief said. "I won't forget you kindness. None of the three of you act like FBI special agents." He chuckled. "And that's a good thing."

Joe, Mark, and Frank headed out to dinner and then back to the hotel to make calls and hit the sack.

It had been a very long day, and tomorrow would be even longer.

CHAPTER 25

Joe, Mark, and Frank arrived at the Orlando Police Department Headquarters at twenty minutes to eight in the morning. They showed their credentials at the front door and were allowed to bypass security. They went directly to the chief's conference room. The chief was already there with three deputy chiefs who were in charge of investigative services—special operations, community policing, and patrol services division for the West Patrol Division, where the Warlocks clubhouse and the Dunkin' Donuts were located.

Chief Roberts introduced everyone. "The three detectives from the violent crimes team will be here in a minute, including Jim Butler. It's already been set up so that you, Joe, Mark, and Frank will be opposite Butler, and the two detectives will be on the left and right side of him, when you all sit down."

The three deputy chiefs were scattered around the table. Nothing was said but the chief nodded to Joe and hit the intercom button to ask the three detectives to enter the room.

As planned, Butler sat down between the other

two detectives, facing Joe, Mark, and Frank.

The chief began the meeting with introductions and gave a quick overview of why they were there. "Joe please bring us up to date on what transpired since you arrived in Orlando upon the notification of the death of Tom Jones by his daughter, Claire Murphy. The deputy chiefs aren't fully aware of what happened."

The three detectives appeared attentive.

Joe began the update by explaining who he was and why he was in charge of the investigation on the federal level. He explained who Mark and Frank were as well. He told them that all three of them, at any particular time, represented the Coast Guard, the FBI, and Homeland Security. Most of the officers didn't realize that the Coast Guard was under the umbrella of Homeland Security, nor did they realize that the FBI reported to Homeland Security. Joe passed around his three IDs, one for each entity.

He went through a timeline, culminating with the takedown of the largest meth distributor on the eastern seaboard and the arrest of both Jefferson and Buddy Banks, who were now in Miami in the Homeland Security facility. "Buddy Banks will turn on his brother and his life will be spared. We're now back here in Orlando to complete the investigation, which would end the distribution of meth into the Orlando area from the major Nashville distributor. Over two hundred and fifty million dollars in meth came from that center annually, with a big chunk landing in Orlando. The cooperating agencies will receive a piece of the two million dollars in cash secured from the distribution center to cover part of their expenses for this investigation." He paused for a breath. "The murder trial, especially one with a death penalty attached, will run well over a million dollars, all by itself. The rest of the money will cover the costs of the drone and the manpower costs at the Nashville and Orlando investigations."

All eyes were now on Joe. He then turned directly to Butler. Joe wasn't sure what the chief had told his deputies before the meeting, just that the two detectives were told to keep an eye on Butler and if he made any overt moves, they were to jump on him and cuff him without warning. "Mr. James Butler, I'm here to inform you that you're under arrest on the federal charge of premeditated first-degree murder of Mr. Thomas Jones, in partnership with Mr. Jefferson Banks. 'You've the right to remain silent. Anything you say can, and will, be used against you in a court of law. You've the right to an attorney. If you can't afford an attorney, one will be provided for you.' Do you understand the rights I've just read to you? With these rights in mind, do you wish to speak to me?"

Immediately, the two detectives jumped up, removed Butler's holstered weapon, and placed handcuffs on him.

"What the hell is this?" he demanded.

"You know exactly what this is," Joe said. "Outside this police station, there are three armed Homeland Security officers, who'll be taking you directly to Miami to the Homeland Security facility there," Joe said. "And, by the way, your $234,000.00, that was sitting in your account at the Cayman National Bank, has been transferred to the United States Coast Guard, Islamorada facility's account."

Butler's eyes went wide. He didn't know what to say. It was over. His life was over. He thought he'd gotten one over on Joe, but he never thought that Joe would ever catch on to what he'd done. As Butler stood up, Joe looked at his left arm. Sitting on his left wrist was a beautiful Tourneau Aviator watch. It looked like it was a few years old but it was obviously expensive.

"Your watch and left wrist will be starring in a Homeland Security video that's being placed into evidence," Joe said. "Along with the picture, is a signed eyewitness statement that places you in the Dunkin' Donuts' parking lot, handing off Tom Jones's computer, after he'd died. Your informant, Wild Bill Hammond, is now a witness against you."

They took Butler, in handcuffs, out the front door of the station. The deputy chiefs were shocked to say the least.

After Butler was removed, Joe gave a full description of what they had in evidence against him. "The evidence is overwhelming. Coupled with the eyewitness accounts and Wild Bill Hammond's written statement, outlining everything that transpired, there's more than sufficient evidence for Butler to be handed over to Homeland Security. Each charge is federal in nature."

Joe finished up the explanation about a half an hour later and, as he rose from his seat, each of the officers in the room shook his hand and then went to Mark and Frank and did then same. They were very grateful that the men were keeping this low key.

Joe handed off the Orlando meth investigation to Chief Roberts. "If needed, we and the local FBI will be part of the takedown of the Warlocks clubhouse. I doubt that there's much of anything there that will be of any substance. I guess that they got weekly shipments from Nashville through Jefferson Banks to Jim Butler and then to their clubhouse. I doubt that there will be more than $100,000.00 in pills in their possession. However, there could be that much cash and you can keep the money. You can get title to the clubhouse, too, if it's owned free and clear by the Warlocks," Joe said. "That will be determined after the bust."

He handed them a federal warrant for the pending Warlocks bust, but if they wanted the money, they needed to get state warrants in place and that might take a day. Joe let them keep the federal warrant to show the local judge that it was a courtesy to the local police agency. "If necessary Mark, Frank, I, Homeland Security agents, and local FBI agents will also be available to testify at trial. We'll need advance notice or we'll have to send in a notarized deposition."

"Joe, can I see you see after this meeting is over?" the chief asked.

Joe went to the chief's office and the chief closed the door. "What happened should never have happened under my watch. I feel betrayed and personally responsible for this. All three deputy chiefs, who attended the meeting, apologized to me just a few minutes ago. After the takedown, I'll hold a press conference and tell everyone on air that it was my fault and I will offer my resignation to the mayor."

"You're a very honorable man but this is unnecessary," Joe said. "And I'll tell the mayor exactly that."

"Thank you for that, Joe, but I'll tell him anyway. It's the right thing to do, regardless of the consequences. I'll be all right one way or the other. I told Estelle what happened right after you left our house. She agrees. She thinks you're a good guy and said thanks, too."

❧❦❧

Joe and Mark headed back to the Embassy

Suites to check out. They said their goodbyes to Frank and thanked him for everything he'd done. Frank headed back to Port Canaveral. Joe would personally tell the rear admiral about Frank's competence. He figured the rear admiral already knew about Frank and that was why he'd assigned him to Joe.

Both Mark and Joe felt great relief. They'd drive down to Fort Lauderdale from Orlando after a nice lunch. Joe would stay overnight and meet the rear admiral in the morning, before heading back to Key Largo. Julie was getting home in two days and Joe wanted to be there to meet her. After his New York City trip, he missed her even more.

He'd called Claire right after the meeting.

"I'll join you for lunch," she said.

He wanted to let her know what Tom meant to him and Mark and, evidently, to the Coast Guard. He didn't believe that they'd have spent hundreds of thousands of dollars for drones, technicians, and investigators, if Tom hadn't meant anything to the rear admiral, or to all those young guys that Tom had turned into men. Joe'd also tell her that he and Julie and Mark and Louise would attend the final memorial service. She could feel good about setting a date now because all of this was behind her. Her father did a foolish thing that got him killed but, overall, when the ledger was added up, Tom Jones was a damn good man, who deserved a proper memorial service.

A third service is a little much but what the hell? He laughed and told Mark his thoughts.

Mark laughed too. "When my time is up, Joe, one service will be more than enough. Just make sure the drinks are on you."

"Cheers," Joe said.

CHAPTER 26

After lunch, Joe and Mark headed to Fort Lauderdale. They took the Florida Turnpike to I-95 S to West Palm Beach and then on to Fort Lauderdale and Dania Beach. The total trip took about three and a half hours with a stop about halfway. It was two hundred and twenty miles door to door. They got in around four-thirty.

Mark had worn his regular Coast Guard work clothes for the last two weeks. He didn't need his full uniform for either Nashville or Orlando. Joe had left his uniforms at the Embassy Suites to be cleaned and he'd picked both up when he got back. He needed to wash the rest of his clothes at Mark's house. He was out of everything and didn't feel like himself, especially for the meeting with the rear admiral. Mark didn't have to attend because he was way behind in his own investigations out of his Dania Beach facility. And Joe had to drive by Miami anyway, on his way back to Islamorada.

Once back at Mark's house, they both felt like a weight had been lifted from their shoulders. Louise took the night off from the Hard Rock Café, switching for Saturday night. She wanted to catch up with Joe about the wedding, anyway, and she'd hardly seen Mark over the last few weeks. The kids were there and jumped into both Mark's and Joe's arms.

Joe was Jennifer's godfather, but he was as close to Mark's son, MJ, as he was to Jennifer. Louise ordered pizzas, enough to choke a horse, and already had a twelve-pack of Sam Adam's Oktoberfest beer on ice. Joe loved Louise.

He immediately stripped, took a shower, put on a T-shirt and shorts, and threw the rest of his clothes in the washer. Louise helped him separate the colors, the same problem he'd had since he was eighteen. He didn't want to do two loads but Louise's look was enough to tell him to hush up. She put the laundered clothes in the dryer and, when they were done, she folded everything and put it into the spare room with his overnight bag.

If this is marriage, I could get used to it in a hurry.

Louise and Julie were very good friends, very close, but a decade apart—meaning almost a generation apart.

Joe and Mark polished off half the twelve-pack with dinner and started to fade. Joe had to be at the rear admiral's office by 8:30 a.m. in the morning. The Miami office was a good forty-five minute drive down I-95 S. He would have to leave by 7:00 a.m. to make sure he got there on time and have a few minutes for coffee and to compose himself, before the meeting to close up the investigation.

Joe hugged the kids and Louise and said goodnight to Mark. Hopefully, after tomorrow, he would be back to normal, working out of Islamorada. He and Julie could take their time and plan their wedding without a lot of hassle.

⌒⌒⌒

Joe got to the District Commander, Rear Admiral, Jake Barnes's office around 7:30 a.m. The seventh district headquarters was located in the Brickell Plaza Federal Building, in Miami. It was about forty miles, give or take, from Mark and Louise's house. Joe parked in the Coast Guard's visitor lot. He had a Coast Guard vehicle and placard for the front window. He didn't know how long this meeting would take so he decided to park where there wouldn't be a problem. Many times, he'd rushed into the building for a meeting and had to leave the car by the curb. He took a lot of heat those times.

Around the corner was a Dunkin' Donuts. He got his regular large coffee and two donuts and ate standing up by the counter. After going through security, he went on into the building right around 8:00 a.m. and hit the head. He combed his hair, washed his face, and looked into the mirror. He guessed he was presentable. His uniform was pressed and cleaned and it was the first time in weeks that he actually looked like a chief warrant officer.

Joe went up to the rear admiral's office and ran into his assistant.

"Joe, go right into the office and take a seat at his desk. He said he would be right in."

Joe walked in and looked around. The rear admiral was a thirty-year man and you could teach a history lesson just from the pictures on the wall. There were mayors, congressmen, senators, Washington Coast Guard brass, and one with President Bush, right after Hurricane Katrina. He and his staff had received a special citation for doing an outstanding job of rescuing citizens trapped in New Orleans. Joe was well aware of what he and his fellow Coasties went through during that time period.

That was not the main reason Joe left the service. The reason he left was that he didn't believe the leadership of the country did enough to support its own citizens during this most trying time. Racism abounded and Joe wanted to move on and make a difference back home in Troy, New York.

Well, this has certainly come full circle. He was back in the Coast Guard and seemed to be making a difference, now.

The rear admiral walked in the door " Lieutenant Traynor, how are you?"

Joe just stared. *Lieutenant, huh*? He then had a big smile on his face.

"You're not the only smart ass in the Coast

Guard, Joe," the rear admiral said. "Congratulations, the promotion is well earned. I also want you to know that Mark Silva, your partner, will also receive the same promotion back at his Dania Beach facility. One of my staff is driving up this morning to meet with him. It will be a complete surprise to him as well. I know he's a lot older than you, and your promotion says a lot about you, at your age. However, I know who was in charge of the operation from the beginning and who lobbied for a full investigation. You did, Joe. I respect what you stand for and the work you did. It was outstanding. Frank Cortez will keep his grade level but with a bump in pay. However, he didn't have to put his life on the line like you and Mark. He'll receive a citation as well."

"Thank you, sir, very much," Joe said.

As soon as Joe shook the rear admiral's hand, the rest of his officers came into the conference room that they'd just entered. These were the same officers who met with Joe at the very beginning when he asked to look into Tom Jones's death.

The rear admiral spoke to his team. "Joe has just received a promotion and Mark Silva will as well. Both are now lieutenants. Joe, please make the presentation outlining the entire case from beginning to end."

Joe spoke for one hour and fifteen minutes. They handed him a few bottles of water to get through the presentation. In his mind, the investigation was linear. In other words, he took them step-by-step, day-by-day, on how he'd planned the investigation and how he worked with his own team and officers from several local and state police agencies.

They marveled as he told them how they programmed the drone to sniff out the manufacturing of meth, chemical by chemical. He told them how they used technology to trace Tom's iPhone and computer, and how they used facial recognition and other pertinent software. He didn't mention the pizza boxes.

He didn't tell them how they broke into various state and local agencies to get online information, pictures of the meth warehouse, and personnel files on various individuals, including the Orlando Chief of Police. He would keep that for another time. He would tell the rear admiral all about it, after this meeting, because Joe felt that he should be the only one who knew, in case anything happened to Mark, Joe, or even Frank. At the end of the meeting, there were several questions that Joe deferred to the rear admiral. Those questions involved some of his clandestine efforts involving Jack Forest. Other than the rear admiral, they didn't need to know any of that.

After the meeting, everyone congratulated Joe on his promotion and on a job well done. Joe turned to the rear admiral. "Sir, can I see you alone for a few minutes?"

"Are you asking me to be in the wedding, Joe?"

Joe was embarrassed and just nodded.

"Cat got your tongue, Joe. No words?"

"No, sir, but I need to see you for a few minutes to discuss some efforts you should know about and how we determined to split the money we uncovered."

They went back into his office and Joe closed the door. Joe told him everything that he'd done so the rear admiral wouldn't be hit with any surprises.

The rear admiral stared at him. "I guess it's easier to ask for forgiveness than permission?"

"Tom Jones was clean but caused his own death through sheer stupidity," Joe said. "He should have never been involved in solving a case because, regardless of what he thought, he didn't have a clue what he was doing. It caused his death."

That was between Joe, Mark, and the rear admiral. In addition, Joe told him how the money flowed into their coffers. First, Joe asked the rear admiral if they could set up a $25,000.00 trust fund for Casey Bradford, the sister of Lacey Bradford who was murdered by Jefferson Banks. "She's heading down the same path and needs to get a degree to get away from the crushing blows of poverty. She's started to study nursing but dropped out because she couldn't support herself and pay for college at the same time. This would make a difference."

"Yes, go ahead and set up the fund. It's nice

when good things come out of bad," the rear admiral told Joe.

"The $234,000.00 that Jack and Mark found in Jim Butler's account at the Cayman National Bank was transferred out and placed into the Coast Guard's Islamorada office account. It will keep them happy about me running around doing other investigations."

The rear admiral laughed. "Brownnoser. Never get on the bad side of Joan Talbot, I hear."

"Great lady. She needs a promotion though. Just saying, sir," Joe said.

He also mentioned that there was two million dollars in cash in two Halliburton briefcases sent to lockup at the Miami Homeland Security office. Joe felt that the Tennessee Bureau of Investigation and the highway patrol should be reimbursed for their time helping Joe close down the meth center and catching a murderer.

The Nashville Police would get as much as they put in, which was nothing.

Joe also wanted some money to go to the Orlando Police Department for shutting down the Warlocks meth sales in Orlando. He felt they'd get about $100,000.00 from the raid and could use the same amount as a match.

"Joe, when did you have time to think about all this?" the rear admiral asked.

"I keep a daily log every day of my life. I couldn't possibly remember everything but my notes jog my memory and everything comes floating back."

"Is this your photographic memory that I keep hearing about?"

"That's an over exaggeration. It's not photographic per se, but I remember everything I did or what was told to me, every day. That's good and bad, sir, because I remember all of it equally, the good and the bad. I write down everything in short form and it does the rest."

"Well, you've convinced me that it works, Joe. No question there. All you've asked for doesn't include anything for yourself. Everything you've asked for will be approved. However, I'm backdating your promotion to the day you started this investigation and I'm giving you a $15,000.00 bonus for finding the Coast Guard several million dollars in funds. It's to pay for your wedding, Joe. We all thank you," the rear admiral said. "I also want to present you with an opportunity. There's no position open, but I'd like you to work directly under me at least for a few days a week so that I can better understand how you think. It's not the standard that we're used to around here, unfortunately. I believe in getting the best available athlete, regardless of position. Would you mind coming here and helping me?"

"I'd be honored, sir," Joe said. "Can I still stay at Islamorada in my current duties, especially now that Julie will be home in a few days, and we will be getting married in the near future?"

"That would be fine. Please take the rest of this week and go back to your job at Islamorada. Can we plan on you meeting me two weeks from Monday, here in Miami? I'll get you set up with an office, and a parking spot, and I'll have new gear sent to you, reflecting your new rank."

"Thank you for everything, sir. Especially, thank you for allowing me the opportunity to clear Tom's name. It was honor to do so," Joe said. "By the way, can I call Mark and congratulate him on his promotion and at least congratulate Frank for his citation?"

The rear admiral nodded. "Go ahead but wait until after noon. It should be done by then."

With that, Joe left the building and walked around for a few minutes at the Bayside Marketplace, the huge outdoor mall in downtown Miami. He would take care of the wedding and reception. If it was up to the bride's side, Tillie had done enough for Julie and him to last a lifetime. Joe smiled. By the time the wedding happened, Julie might even be rich from the potential movie rights for her book, *Conch Town Girl*. It had certainly been well received by the public in general, and young girls and their mothers, in particular. After his stroll, and a stop for a Cuban sandwich and a beer at Bayside, he'd head home, first to see Tillie in Key Largo, and then to his officer's quarters in Islamorada.

CHAPTER 27

Joe made several calls before heading south. He called Joan at Islamorada to tell her that the Islamorada Coast Guard account would have a $234,000.00 increase in its balance with a wire transfer from the Cayman National Bank. "I'll explain the circumstances to you when I arrive."

He then called Tillie. She'd just gotten home after working the morning shift at the Waffle House in Key Largo. Joe hadn't seen her since his early arrival at the restaurant on his way to see the rear admiral in Miami.

"I'll call Julie and let her know that you're on your way home and everyone's safe," Tillie said.

Since it was now after noon, Joe called Mark on his cell phone. "Yes, I'm looking for Lieutenant Mark Silva. May I speak to him, please?"

"Lieutenant Mark Silva speaking. May I ask who's calling?"

"Yes, this is Lieutenant Joseph Traynor, calling from the seventh district headquarters of the United States Coast Guard, located in the Brickell Plaza Federal Building, at 909 South East First Avenue, in Miami."

"Sounds weird, doesn't it, Joe? Congratulations to you as well. I know we shouldn't think it, but it's well deserved. Breaking up a quarter-billion-dollar meth enterprise, while paying for the entire operation in cash, seems to have put us over the top. What do you think?"

"Actually, I think that bringing Tom's killers to justice was probably just as important to the rear admiral. It took the Coast Guard out of the limelight and turned Tom into a victim instead of a cold-hearted drug dealer."

"That too," Mark said with a chuckle. "You have to ruin everything don't you, Joe? Huh?"

"Yes. I'm wrapped a little tight right now, Mark. You didn't have to spend two hours with the brass, explaining everything from A to Z. They drove up to see you to present your lieutenant bars. Whoopee. Did you call Louise yet?"

"I just got off the phone. Trust me, she was proud but the first thing she wanted to know if we got a raise. I didn't know. Do we?"

"Yes, about $8,000.00 per year. Does that help? Based on your fourteen years and my ten years, I'll get a few thousand less, but I'll take it."

"You know it," Mark said. "I'll take it, too. And, Joe, I know you had a lot to do with this. I couldn't have handled the pressure of being in charge of this major investigation like you were. For that I'm grateful."

"I just wanted to let you know that the rear admiral wants me to report directly to him in Miami for a few days a week and keep my position in charge of investigations out of Islamorada," Joe said. "He didn't say it but I think I may be the only one fluent in Spanish and Russian. He wants me to do strategic planning with him. He was aware of my RPI MBA and, after finding out how it helped with the meth operation and uncovering Tom's murderers, he's fully bought into building a solid strategic plan for the seventh district in Miami."

"Wow."

"Got to go. I'll call you in a few days. Say hi to the kids and Louise. Again, congratulations, Mark. You deserve it. You always have my back."

With that Joe hopped in his car and headed to Key Largo. It was around sixty miles from the Brickell Building to Key Largo and Tillie's new apartment. He got back on the I-95 S ramp and headed to US-1 S.

He bypassed all of downtown, made it to the Florida Turnpike, and picked up US-1 once again after getting out of Miami. From there it was clear sailing for another twenty-five miles. Joe didn't mind this trip.

It was only an hour and fifteen minutes, without speeding. Going into Miami in the morning, once he was on board at headquarters, reporting to the rear admiral? That was another story.

☙☙☙

Joe pulled up to Tillie's new garden apartment, right off of Overseas Highway, a block from Saint Justin Martyr Catholic Church. It was centrally located, only a few blocks from the Waffle House and the elementary school where Julie was assigned as a teacher's aide. Joe parked and met Tillie at the front door.

She gave him a big hug. "Congratulations on your engagement to Julie. I couldn't be happier for both of you." Since she'd raised Julie from an early age, she was like her own daughter, not her granddaughter.

"Thank you for that, Tillie. I'm happy to be part of your family. Not that I wasn't before."

"You have been and will always be part of our family, Joe," Tillie agreed. "If Julie ever throws you out, you can always come live with your grandmother," she said laughing.

"Grandmother? I thought it was just Tillie."

"I stand corrected."

Joe went in and looked around. He'd only been there a few times since she moved in after selling her family home in Key Largo. Since the house was free and clear, what she'd netted from the sale, coupled with her social security, would keep her afloat for quite a while. She was still on Julie's medical plan at the school district and would remain so until she hit sixty-five and could switch over to Medicare. Her current plan would then kick in as a supplemental plan for as long as Julie stayed with the district and continued to receive benefits.

The apartment complex was a combined Section 8 senior apartment and regular apartment building. As more and more seniors, like Tillie, sold their homes, more Section 8 housing units were opened. The benefit was that, regardless of how much money they made, the tenants only had to pay a maximum of 25% of their annual income toward the rent, heat, and electricity. It was a great deal for older residents who wanted to stay in the Keys but could no longer afford the upkeep on their homes. These Conch residents—lifers if you will, for multiple generations—were considered house poor. They couldn't afford to stay, nor could their extended family afford the upkeep and growing taxes required for an increasing population that included lots of kids.

The school districts had to keep increasing taxes to offset the increase in the number of students served. It was a vicious cycle that seemed to hurt the low-income families the most. Tillie and Julie had been low income for most of their lives. All they had was each other until Joe arrived as a fresh-faced Coastie, coming into their lives at nineteen years old, that fateful day that he met Julie at her grade school career day.

Julie was actually coming home tomorrow, flying into the Miami International Airport at 6:00 p.m. She normally flew into Fort Lauderdale with Southwest but she didn't have anyone to pick her up since Mark and Louise and their kids were going away for a few days. She had been going to fly out of Tampa to the Key West Airport but it would cost three times as much as landing in Miami. There were hourly flights out of JFK to Miami. Hell, half of New Yorkers had family in Miami so the planes were always filled.

"Tillie, call Julie and tell her that I'll pick her up tomorrow night at the airport."

"Will do."

Tillie gave him a copy of the flight number and gate so he would park in the short term lot and head out from there. He wanted to treat Julie so he would look up a nice hotel in Key Biscayne for the evening and make reservations at a classy restaurant in downtown. They could walk the beach after dinner and be close to their hotel.

Joe said goodbye to Tillie and headed to Islamorada.

෧෨෧෨

He reached Islamorada, right down the Overseas Highway, in about a half an hour, and pulled up to his parking spot outside the office. He was wondering if it would still be there or if they'd forget about him completely. He hoped the extra cash helped them remember him. Joe walked through the front door and was immediately greeted by Joan. Jacob Cramer, the chief warrant officer of the facility, stuck his head out of his office door and waved.

"Joan, can I meet with you two for a few minutes after I put his stuff in my office?" Joe asked.

"Let me ask, Joe," she said. She went down to Jacob's office, said a few words, turned to Joe, and gave him the okay sign.

Joe went down the hall in the opposite direction to his cubby that was formed from a broom closet when he first arrived back in Islamorada, a few short months earlier. He dropped his bag on the floor, looked around, and brushed off the picture of him and Julie, standing outside the facility.

He smiled. "Welcome home," he said to himself.

⁂

They met in the small conference room outside Jacob's office. Jacob grabbed Joe's hand. "Welcome back. You were truly missed."

They were sitting on five cases, the same five cases that Joe was working on when he left.

"Our Coast Guard account is now flush with a few hundred thousand dollars to use, as we need," Joe told him.

Jacob simply shook his head and laughed. "Is this a yearly contribution, Joe?"

When Tillie had turned in the $300,000.00 cash

drug money that was found in her attic, the Coast Guard netted $225,000.00 and St. Justin Martyr Catholic Church got $75,000.00 for their food bank and second hand store.

Joe laughed. "Don't expect it every year, guys."

"Every other year?" Joan said, smiling.

"Maybe, if you're nice to me. Were you both informed about my promotion?"

They both nodded. Evidently, the rear admiral had called them around noon today, right after Joe left, and told them both on a conference call, that Joe would be splitting his time between headquarters in Miami and Islamorada.

"I don't want to hear about that. I want to know when the wedding is going to happen. Julie already called me to ask if Lucy could be in it." That appeared to be Joan's only interest at the moment.

He told them about his father's operation, about his trip to New York City—not all about the trip, of course, only about him asking her to marry him on the steps of St. Patrick's Cathedral.

"How romantic, Joe. I didn't know you had it in you," Joan said, laughing.

"Neither did I, Joan."

Jacob was very much like Joe, all business. Now that Joe was a lieutenant and Jacob, as the head of the facility, was a chief warrant officer, he wanted to know who reported to whom.

"It will remain the same at Islamorada," Joe said. "My new promotion will only stand out in

Miami where rank is clearly important."

It was obvious that it was clearly important to Jacob. When they were both chief warrant officers, it hadn't mattered, since they both reported to someone else. Joe had a dotted line to Jacob and it would remain so. He didn't say it, but if that wasn't good enough for Jacob, it would be his problem, not Joe's.

Joe told them the entire story, from beginning to end about the investigation into the murder of Tom Jones, the eventual takedown of the Nashville meth distribution center, and the shutting down of the Warlocks' headquarters in Orlando, culminating with the arrest of the Orlando Police Detective, Jim Butler.

In a way, after the conversation, Joan was well aware that Joe and Jacob weren't equal in any respect. She was absolutely amazed at how Joe, whom she'd known since he was eighteen years old, had grown as a person.

She thought that he was finally getting the recognition he was due. She knew why he left the Coast Guard in the first place. Now she knew that since he came back, he was a much different person. He seemed to be on a mission.

Julie had only enhanced his personal attributes, since they'd become a couple. Joan was very pleased when Joe told them about the trust fund set up for Lacey's sister, Casey, and how it would pay her college tuition so she would not wind up like

Lacey. That explained Joe's personality to Joan, better than anything else. He had great compassion for people and didn't let anything get in the way. That's why he'd solved Tom's murder, not just for Tom's sake, but for Claire and her family's sake as well.

❧❧❧

Joe opened the door to his small officer's quarters. He'd been gone close to a month and the air was stale and muggy. He opened the windows to air it out, put his bag on the bed, and hung up his two uniforms on hangers in the closet. He looked in his refrigerator and found a six-pack of Sam Adams Oktoberfest beer, ice cold, and waiting. He didn't remember having any. Then he smiled.

Joan must have filled his refrigerator. There was a nice chunk of cheese and a stick of pepperoni in the refrigerator and a new unopened box of crackers on the cupboard shelf. He was getting hungry. Joan left a note and told him, if he wanted to, he could join her family for dinner. She was only two doors down. It was pizza night and to be there at 6:00 p.m.

He showered, changed his clothes, and put everything away. He put on shorts and a Coast Guard T-shirt and walked out the door to walk around the place he'd missed. He was a Coastie first, and now a lieutenant. Life was good.

CHAPTER 28

Julie had called Tillie to let her know that she'd be flying into Miami International Airport at 6:00 p.m. on Friday night. Tillie wrote everything down, not trusting her sixty-year-old memory. Julie was taking a non-stop direct flight, #1417, out of JFK, at 2:30 p.m. The flight was three hours and thirty minutes in duration, arriving at 6:00 p.m. in Miami.

Joe knew it took a little over an hour and fifteen minutes to travel the fifty-eight miles to the airport from downtown Key Largo. He would park in the short-term lot near the American Airlines Terminal, Concourse D, and Gate 16. It was still amazing to him, after all these years, that you could fly non-stop from JFK to Miami Florida, 1,092 miles door to door, for $196.00 one way. Julie was on a Boing 757, sitting in economy class. First class wasn't worth the $1,000.00 more when you arrived at the same time as economy. It was also nice that her seat was preselected and waiting for her, unlike for Southwest Airlines, where it was first-come-first-served in getting your boarding pass. Joe had gone online on previous occasions, twenty-four hours ahead, and barely gotten a first-come-first-served "A" seating arrangement. If you wanted to pay $12.50 more, you could go online twenty-four hours ahead of schedule and still barely get an "A" seating plan.

Joe had taken the afternoon off so he could take his time getting there. The weather was fine and the flight was on schedule. Flying south was a lot less of a problem than heading back to the great Northeast. You never knew what you'd get weather wise, flying north, until the day of the flight. It was a crapshoot at best.

Joe was going to surprise her when he picked her up at the airport. The night was still young for Miami. Hell, nobody went to dinner before 9:00 p.m. It was the capital of the Latino world, and normally, Latinos always ate much later than everyone else. They never went clubbing before midnight, anyway. Getting home at 5:00 a.m. was a way of life.

Joe booked a room at the Ritz-Carlton Key Biscayne. It was only ten miles from the airport and less than three blocks to the downtown city center. At $369.00 per night, he hoped she'd enjoy the room. It was rated 4.7 out of 5 starts. Joe couldn't figure out, at those prices, what could be missing, but it couldn't be much. Their "guestroom" featured an ocean view. It had a beautiful balcony, marble bathroom, flat-screen TV, and of course, a fully stocked minibar. Joe could take or leave the WiFi hookup. Julie might have to get some emails, but he certainly hoped that she wouldn't have time.

He wanted this to be a night to remember. He booked dinner at the Capital Grill, arguably one of the finest restaurants in Miami. The restaurant was complete with a sophisticated atmosphere of art deco and other trendy nuances. The restaurant prided itself on its liveliness. It was as if the Capital Grill was a nightclub, a place to be seen, not just a restaurant. In terms of food, besides signature steaks, it offered lobster, which was Julie's favorite, and more than 5,000 different wines.

The online blurb stated that it was a great place to bring a date or to jump-start a Friday night out. Joe had learned about the hotel and restaurant from the rear admiral when Joe received his promotion the day before. The nice thing was its location on Brickell Avenue in Miami, only doors from the Coast Guard headquarters in Miami. He couldn't seem to get away from the Coast Guard, but Joe was grateful for the heads up. *It should be a wonderful time.*

He headed out of Islamorada around 4:00 p.m. It took fifteen minutes to get to Key Largo and then an hour and fifteen minutes from there. He headed up Overseas Highway and merged onto FL-821, the Florida Turnpike, to the airport. He kept left to merge onto the Don Shula Expressway toward FL-826, the Palmetto Expressway North. Exiting at

Flagler, he headed to the airport, about two miles from there. He pulled into the airport short-term parking lot right around 5:30 p.m.

He headed toward the American Airlines terminal, Concourse D, and waited right by the exit where passengers left their gates and headed to pick up their luggage. Joe looked at the flight board and saw that American Airlines Flight #1417 was right on schedule, arriving at Gate 16, at 6:00 p.m. It was now a few minutes after six and he was watching people coming through the terminal to the luggage area to meet their loved ones. With children in tow, parents greeted their extended families. Grandparents picked up their grandchildren with big hugs. It was the same in every airport in the world.

Joe turned his head back to watch the passengers coming out and saw Julie about five persons back. She smiled and waved at him. He did the same. As soon as she got to where he was standing, she put her arms around him, gave him a big kiss, and didn't let go.

Joe used to be self-conscious about public displays of affection, but at that moment, he could have cared less. He pulled her away to look at her and gave her another big kiss. Then he grabbed her by the elbow and they started to walk toward the luggage area to retrieve her two bags.

On the way, she turned to him. "I missed you, Joe. How is my fiancé doing?"

"Right this minute, it's the best I've ever felt."

"Good answer, Joe." She giggled. "That's sounds like a line from *Family Feud*, doesn't it?"

Joe laughed, gave her another kiss on the cheek, and took her hand. They went down the escalator and found the right luggage area. The bags from Flight #1417, by way of JFK, were coming out on the baggage carousel. After a few minutes, Joe grabbed her two bags. He'd helped her carry them to the airport on many occasions. They weighed a ton.

She told him that they were each barely under the fifty-pound limit by just two pounds each. She'd placed the bags on the bathroom scale back in her borrowed New York City apartment. She thought they were pretty close and she wasn't sure if a people scale worked the same as the baggage scale. She lucked out, but just barely. They rolled the bags, each carrying one, to Joe's car sitting in the lot.

Once there, they kissed again, "I hope you don't mind, but I've a surprise for you." Joe said.

"What is it? I don't know if I like surprises. The ones I had in my life growing up weren't of the good variety of surprises, you know?"

"I know," he said. "But I think you'll like this. I booked us a room at the Ritz-Carlton Key Biscayne for the night. We also have dinner reservations for 9:00 p.m. at the Capital Grill. We can head home at a leisurely pace tomorrow. I have the weekend off and I've a lot to tell you to bring you up to date."

"That sounds wonderful," she said with a coy smile. "We should hurry to the hotel because I've some plans of my own before we head out to dinner."

"Yes, ma'am. Your wish is my command."

With that, they headed quickly to the hotel and parked right by the front door. They each took a bag. Joe had his overnight bag along with his suit that he would wear to dinner. It was a gray pinstripe that he wore with his wingtip shoes, white shirt, and reddish paisley tie. He hadn't worn it in so long that he was worried that it might not fit. He was hopeful because he hadn't gained a pound since he came back into the service. His activities lately had more than allowed him to shed any fat that he'd accumulated while working back in Albany.

They checked in to room 1725, overlooking the ocean. Joe opened the sliding door to the balcony and felt that he'd entered another universe. Even for only one day and a night, he hoped that Julie would remember this. Sitting in a bucket of ice was a bottle of chilled champagne and a plate of cut fresh fruit, cheese, and chocolates. Julie didn't even ask what the occasion was. She already knew.

એસ્

About eight thirty, Joe and Julie left the hotel and walked the few blocks, hand in hand, to the

Capital Grill. It was a beautiful night in downtown Miami. Unlike most of the country, people in Miami got dressed up when they went out. It was the in place to be and they dressed accordingly. Julie had obviously learned a thing or two about dressing for success at both Brown University and in New York City. She was dressed elegantly in all black and was stunning.

He felt funny being in anything other than his every day Coast Guard clothes and even his officer's attire. The suit looked good on him. They looked like a dressed-for-success couple. No one would ever guess that Joe spent most of his day chasing criminals or that Julie had grown up as one of the poorest of the poor in Key Largo.

After dinner, they strolled down the promenade, along with all the others out for the evening. You could hear Spanish in the air. The clubs had both flavors of mainstream American and the Latin beat coming from all the buildings as they walked past. It was after 1:00 a.m. so they decided, since they were staying at the Ritz-Carlton, that they should have a drink at the bar before heading up to their room. When Julie walked into the bar, every male head turned to look at her.

Joe felt strange, not jealous—hardly jealous—but out of place, knowing how lucky he was to have someone like Julie in his life. He had a Sam Adams Oktoberfest. Some things never changed. Julie sipped an apple martini—appletini for short—

a cocktail containing vodka and one or more of apple juice, apple cider, apple liqueur, or apple brandy. Optionally, vermouth was included, as in a regular martini. Typically, the vodka was shaken or stirred with sweet and sour mix and then strained into a cocktail glass. Joe tried it and shook his head.

"I'll stick with my beer."

He paid the bill and tipped the bartender. Then they headed to their room. Joe knew that he wouldn't sleep much tonight. Julie simply smiled at him, kissed him, and they headed for bed. It was a very long but pleasant night.

⁓⁓⁓

They had a wake-up call for 10:00 a.m. They ordered breakfast in their room. Around 10:30 a.m. there was a knock on the door and Joe let the waiter in with his rolling cart of goodies. There was coffee, Danish, fresh croissants, bacon, eggs, and home fries. Joe was in his glory. They ate on the balcony, both in their Ritz-Carlton bathrobes. Julie wanted to take it home with her, so Joe called downstairs and added it to the bill.

She laughed. "Perhaps, there are other things in the room that I'd also like."

He put his hands up in the air. "*No mas.*"

They had a late checkout at 1:30 p.m. so they packed up leisurely and headed to the checkout counter. Joe and Julie's romantic evening cost Joe around $1,200.00 including dinner and the robe. He put it on his credit card, his own, not his Coast Guard Visa. Not only did he not want any financial repercussions, he didn't want anyone busting his chops about his romantic getaway. Just like the TV commercial, Joe thought the time spent was *priceless*.

They packed the trunk of Joe's car and left it in the parking garage. Everything was paid for, including his parking so they walked around downtown for a short time before leaving. Joe had never spent much time in Miami other than for meetings at the Brickell headquarters. It was nice. They walked hand in hand to the outdoor mall and went through a few shops.

Around 3:00 p.m., they went back to the car, pulled out of the garage, and headed home. Neither of them wanted to leave. Joe would be back to work on Monday. Julie had to attend several meetings the following week for her teacher aide duties at the elementary school and then had to go to the high school to check in for her new career counseling duties.

She hadn't been home in a while and it was bittersweet. She loved her life in Key Largo, but she loved New York City as well. Maybe they could arrange two weddings.

One small intimate wedding could take place at the St. Patrick's Cathedral for his New York State family and friends and one in Key Largo at Saint

Justin Martyr Catholic Church for all her and Joe's friends in the Keys.

CHAPTER 29

Joe pulled into Tillie's apartment complex right around 4:30 p.m. Julie was staying the night with Tillie and would then meet Joe in the morning and go to his place in Islamorada. She really didn't have a place of her own at this point. Tillie's apartment complex had mostly seniors but Tillie had already asked the owner of the apartment complex if Julie could stay with her until she got her own place. That had been non-negotiable for Tillie to move in. The owners had known Tillie for some time and ate at the Waffle House many times during the construction phase.

By the time the buildings were completed, Tillie had met practically every construction worker at the site. In fact, when the construction was going strong, Tillie had made a few lunch deliveries to the workers, using her manager's car.

They worked out the lunch schedule around the busy time at the restaurant so they could get the meals delivered. It worked out for everyone and, especially, for Tillie. She was one of the first new tenants in the complex after selling her home of over forty years to snowbirds from Atlanta.

Julie hadn't seen Tillie in sometime and, as soon as she walked through the door, they hugged each other like long lost sisters. Julie had only been away a few times since Tillie became her mother, not just her grandmother, those many years ago.

Joe walked in behind her rolling Julie's two large luggage bags behind him. He gave Tillie a big kiss as well.

"Can you stay for dinner?"

Tillie had made a pot roast, Julie's favorite, so he could hardly say no. He would head out after dinner to his office. He had a ton of work to make up since he'd been gone. He'd left five investigations with the rest of the team. They'd just about completed two of the five. The others needed Joe's Spanish and Russian translations before they could put together a plan. Joan had told him last night over pizza that he was drastically needed if they were to finish the other three investigations. He would meet with her and the facility's Chief Warrant Officer Cramer in the morning before he came back for Julie.

During dinner, Tillie let it slip that the Chief of Detectives, Mike Kenny, of the Monroe County Sheriff's Department had called her. "He wanted to know who the new owners were that bought my old house on Glendale Drive. I told him the name but I don't have the new owner's phone number. So I told him to call my real estate agent in town who sold the house to them because she had all the information." She paused. "I asked him why and he said that the house had been broken into and it was a disaster. He wanted to get in touch with the owners so they could come down and check the damage. He said our old neighbor across the street thought she saw a car pull out of the driveway a few nights earlier. It was a dark and she didn't see what the car was or who was in it. She told the deputies that she went across the street the next day to look into the window to see if anything was wrong. The owners didn't leave her a key because they were new, but they'd introduced themselves when they were there. She never wrote down their names. They had just completely remodeled the house so the neighbor wanted to check to see if everything was okay. It wasn't. She called the Monroe County Sheriff's Department. They stopped by and noticed the damage inside. Back at the station, the deputies were talking about it and Detective Kenny overheard them speaking. He knew that it was my old house and that's why he called me. I told him I couldn't understand why someone would ransack my old house."

However, Tillie did think she knew why but had kept it to herself. "My next door neighbor here, Marilyn, told me that two large men stopped by my apartment and looked into my window, while I was at work, early around 6:00 a.m. I still go in for the breakfast shift at the Waffle House every day. Marilyn said that they tried to turn the doorknob but it was locked," Tillie continued. "They went around the side and then back to their car. Marilyn thought they looked suspicious and when they were on their way back she took a picture of the two men and their car. As they were pulling away, she tried to take a picture of the license plate but it wasn't very clear. She did get a picture of the men's faces." Tillie turned to Joe. "Do you think this is starting all over again?"

"I won't lie to you, Tillie, but I really don't know. I do know that until this is cleared up, both here at your apartment and at the old house, I don't want you, or Julie, staying here."

He immediately called Joan and asked her if it was all right for Julie and Tillie to stay with him at his officer's quarters on campus at the Islamorada facility. He told her about the two incidents. Joan knew everything that had happened previously. She went in to see Cramer, who also knew about the previous situation. He said no problem.

"I want to put a plan together when I get there, Joe told her. "We'll be in Islamorada around 7:30 p.m."

They cleaned up after dinner and Tillie went to pack her bags. Joe put Julie's luggage right back into the car. They checked the faucets, the toilet, and made sure that the doors were double locked. When Tillie was done, they hopped into the car and headed out.

As they talked in the car, it was very clear that something was coming back to haunt them. Julie's father and Tillie's son-in-law had been presumed dead for over seventeen years, supposedly dying at sea, and Julie's mother was so distraught at the time that she died of a drug overdose two years later. Tillie had raised Julie from then on. Being poor, supporting a granddaughter on only a waitress's salary, Tillie had been closer to Julie than mother and daughter. Julie's book, *Conch Town Girl*, was based on their experiences together. It became Julie's thesis at Brown University for her Master's Degree in Fine Arts, and subsequently became a novel that was just recently published and was now moving up the best sellers list.

Julie's father had never died. He'd stolen a million dollars from the Russian Mafia the day his boat was lost at sea. His two friends had died but he'd gotten off before the ship sank and had one million dollars in cash he was supposed to use to buy cocaine from a ship from Columbia that they were meeting that day. The boat never came because of bad weather—the same bad weather that had killed Tom's friends.

Tom Chapman, Julie's father, had been running drugs for quite some time before this, unbeknownst to the family. That day, Chapman abandoned his wife and daughter, taking $700,000.00 in cash, and headed to Pensacola where he lived from that point on. As he passed through Key Largo, he'd stuffed the remaining $300,000.00 in cash in the attic of Tillie's home where they all lived. This was for a rainy day. The rainy day came seventeen years later. Tom Chapman ran out of money and came back to Key Largo to get the rest of the cash. He'd spied on Tillie and Julie for some time after he got back into town.

One day, Tillie saw him parked across the street from the Waffle House. She panicked and drove back home to tell Julie. She never got there. Chapman ran her car off the road, almost killing her, and putting her in a coma for a few weeks. Julie was left all alone, not knowing if Tillie would live or die.

She'd called Joe who was just coming off of a major case for Homeland Security in Albany where he'd helped take down the Mexican Mafia. To do that, he'd had to rejoin the Coast Guard, which gave him back his FBI and Homeland Security credentials.

He'd asked his superior officer to be transferred back to Islamorada while Tillie was in the hospital and Julie was alone. They'd granted his wish. They needed his investigative skills and Spanish linguistics as much as he needed to come back. As Joe and Julie were cleaning out Tillie's house, while she was still unconscious in the Mariner Hospital, they found the $300,000.00 in the attic all in Cyrillic money wrappers.

Joe and Julie had placed the money in a safe deposit box and Joe went to work to find out how the money got into Tillie's attic. He discovered that Julie's father was still alive, living as Ted Champion all those years. One evening Chapman broke into Tillie's house and was holding both Tillie and Julie at gunpoint. He wanted the money. Joe, putting two and two together, knew he was there. Joe snuck in through the back window and shot Chapman in the arm and leg. Chapman went to prison as Ted Champion rather than have it be found out that he was actually Tom Chapman. No one wanted the Russians to know about Tillie or Julie. However, when Champion went to Raiford State Prison in Florida, it housed many Russian criminals. Joe thought that maybe Champion had talked too much and they found out who he really was and killed him. Joe also felt that, if that was the case, no doubt, he'd told them that he still had a million dollars in Tillie's attic, trying to use the money for leverage.

The $300,000.00 that Joe and Julie found in the attic had been split, with $75,000.00 going to the Catholic Church in town and the remaining put into the Coast Guard account at Islamorada. Joan and Jacob graciously accepted the largess from Julie.

Now, Joe studied Julie and Tillie. "It looks like Ted Champion spilled the beans before he was killed in prison. The break-in at Tillie's old house, and the two men showing up at Tillie's apartment—that was no accident."

Joe needed a plan to end the Russian inquiry as soon as possible. The Russia Mafia was very revengeful and, if one person ripped them off, they'd make an example of the entire family, murdering every last one of them. That was why Joe had wanted Chapman to keep his mouth shut and keep his new Ted Champion identity. In either case, the man would have gone to jail where he belonged for trying to kill Tillie with the hit and run and then with a gun aimed at her head. True to his nature, Chapman was a bad guy to the end, and might well have caused the impending death of his own daughter.

That was not going to happen if Joe had anything to say about it.

CHAPTER 30

During Joe's reenlistment back into the Coast Guard, he was asked to become fluent in Russian, in addition to his fluency in Mexican infused Spanish. It wasn't just a matter of learning the language, both written and spoken. It was a complete submersion into the culture and history of the Russian people. Similar to English, there were different phrases that meant different things to the people you were conversing with.

Joe went to the Boston area and learned that "wicked good" was actually a compliment. The New York saying of "Let's just stay fat, dumb, and happy," meaning to go along with the crowd, was considered an insult of the highest order to some non-New Yorkers. It was the same in Spanish and Russian, depending on where the person came from. Joe had to know the differences when listening to chatter they intercepted. It could mean the difference between life and death.

To that end, Joe needed to fully immerse himself in the history of the people. He particularly needed to understand how the Russian Mafia came to be and where it was today. It was so prevalent in New York and Miami that it was a given that you would hear people speaking both Spanish and Russian on the streets on a daily basis.

When first asked to learn Russian, he had professors from the university come to Islamorada and teach him everything they could about the Russians. It was that important to the Coast Guard for drug investigations. They had no one with this ability or aptitude, other than Joe, in the entire Keys area. Joe's studies would prove most important in finding out who was involved in the break-in at Tillie's old house and the attempt at her apartment. He knew it was the Russians but he needed to get to the bottom of it quickly. He needed to find out, not who the flunkies were, but who was in charge, and he needed to make this go away in Key Largo as quickly as possible. Lives depended upon it.

∽∾∽

The Russian Mafia, or Bratva, was a term used to refer to the collective of various organized crime elements originating in the former Soviet Union, headquartered in Moscow. Although not a singular criminal organization, most of the individual groups shared similar goals and organizational structures that defined them as part of the loose overall association. After World War II, the death of Stalin, and the fall of the Soviet Union, more gangs emerged in a flourishing black market, exploiting the unstable governments of the former republics and, at its highest point, even controlling as much as two-thirds of the Russian economy.

A former director of the FBI had once said the Russian Mafia posed the greatest threat to US national security in the mid-1990s. Currently, there were as many as 6,000 different groups, with more than 200 of them having a global reach.

Criminals of these various groups were either former prison members, corrupt communist officials and business leaders, people with ethnic ties, or people from the same region with shared criminal experiences and leaders. During the 1970s and 1980s, the US expanded its immigration policies, allowing Russian citizens as well as criminals to enter the country, with most settling in a southern Brooklyn area known as Brighton Beach— sometimes referred to as Little Odessa. Here was where Russian organized crime began in the United States.

At the time that Joe was studying Russian, his professor said, "When the USSR collapsed in the 1990s and a free market economy emerged, organized criminal groups took over Russia's economy, and many ex-KGB soldiers and veterans of the Afghan war offered their skills to the crime bosses. There were so many mafia-related murders in Moscow that the bosses sent their members to Brighton Beach in 1992, allegedly because they were killing too many people in Russia. Now, they also wanted to take control of organized crime in North America. Within a year, they'd built an international operation that included, but was not limited to, narcotics, money laundering, and prostitution. They had ties with the American Mafia and Colombian drug cartels, eventually extending to Miami, Los Angeles, and Boston. Those who went against them were usually killed. As of 2010, Russian Mafia groups had been said to reach over 50 countries and have up to 300,000 members."

"Wow, I'd have never guessed that in a million years," Joe said.

℘℘℘

The first call Joe made, when he got to the Islamorada facility, was to Jack, the keeper of all things clandestine. Before leaving the apartment complex, Tillie's neighbor Marilyn, emailed Joe the pictures from her phone that included the car, the blurred license plate, and the clear images of the two men, who clearly looked Eastern European or Russian. Joe immediately sent the pictures to Jack, who never left the office before 8:00 p.m. He now had a girlfriend but they never went out before 9:00 p.m., anyway. He only needed five hours sleep a night. Joe didn't know how he did it. He was only four years older than Joe, graduating from college at twenty-two years old as compared to Joe dropping out of MIT at eighteen. Joe thought if time was catching up with him, it had to be catching up with Jack, now thirty-seven and with a ton of responsibility.

After sending him the pictures, Joe called him as well and told him all about closing down the meth distribution center and catching Tom Jones's murderers. He also updated him on his engagement. "I'd like you to be in the wedding, Jack. There might actually be two weddings, one in New York City and one in Key Largo."

"Of course," Jack said. "I'll be in the wedding as long as I don't get the garter."

"You can bring a date, too, Jack."

"Don't start, Joe. I'm not getting married anytime soon." Jack chuckled then sobered. "I know that this Russian issue is weighing heavily on you and I'll get back to you as soon as possible."

Joe told Julie and Tillie that they'd know what they were dealing with in a matter of hours.

Jack called back. "The car is a 2010 Mercedes-Benz E-Class E350 4matic, four-door. It sells for about $30,000.00. I redid the photo of the license plate and got most but not all of the numbers and letters. I'm missing three of the nine letters and numbers on a Florida plate. It doesn't matter much because I went into the Florida Motor Vehicles Department records and picked up every 2010 Mercedes-Benz E-350 in the state and then went through the license plate numbers and matched the first four—M149—missed the next two, picked up the next one—L—and missed the last three. The only license plate that matched the six of nine in the bunch is registered to DA Industries, Inc. of Miami, Florida. So the car's registered to a corporation that's wholly owned by Dmitry Assinoff, a billionaire Russian, living in Miami."

Jack gave Joe the company address and the personal home address as well. He also ran credit reports and corporation papers for DA Industries, Inc. "It's interesting, because sitting on his board of directors is a Miami City Commissioner, which is the same as a city councilman. His name is Emmanuel Blackwood. Mr. Blackwood is of African American descent, age 51, a commissioner for only three years, and self-employed. There is no known criminal record but I'll dig deeper. In addition, the two gentlemen knocking on Tillie's door were indeed Russian immigrants. The first, Nestor Bykov, age 45, is not a citizen but has a green card and has been arrested twice for misdemeanors. Mr. Marco Zotov, age 48, has a criminal record and is about to be deported but they can't find him."

Joe thanked Jack and asked him to do more searches. "Can you check Mr. Assinoff's bank records, credit cards, and see where he spends his time and money. I want to know who his friends are, high and low. Is he married? Does he have a girlfriend etc.? Whatever you can get will be helpful, Jack."

Joe knew, at this point, that this problem was not going away and he needed some help. Mr. Assinoff was big time but he was not a citizen yet, either. Assinoff was being sponsored for citizenship by Mr. Blackwood. Joe would have to see if he could put a monkey wrench in that.

"If I get any information at all, I'll call you immediately," Jack said.

Armed with what he had, Joe went in to see Joan and the Chief Warrant Officer, Jacob Cramer.

After Tillie and Julie got settled in his little quarters, Joe walked down to see the two of Joan and Jacob. "Hi, Joan. Hi, Jacob. How are you two?"

"Good," both said at the same time.

Joe then immediately went into what was happening. He went through what Jack Forest had given him already. They obviously knew what had happened a while ago since they were the recipient of the $225,000.00 from the $300,000.00 found by Joe and Julie in Tillie's attic.

After much discussion, Joe told them that he was going to see the rear admiral the following day and lay out everything that had happened to date. He told them, if approved, he would confront Mr. Assinoff in Miami. He would tell him that he really shouldn't be involved in Key Largo any longer or there would be severe ramifications.

If Mr. Assinoff didn't agree to Joe's terms, then Joe would pull in a lot of favors from everyone he knew to get rid of Mr. Assinoff, at least get him out of the US. Joe not only worked with and for the FBI and Homeland Security, but on a number of occasions, he worked very closely in the rendition of drug runners from Columbia and elsewhere. In Albany, he was instrumental in getting Mr. Jorge Hernandez, the general for the Mexican Mafia, while still in prison, sent to Romania under the United States Patriot Act. Mr. Assinoff, although powerful, was a foreign national, providing one of the bases for deportation and removal by force from the US. The meeting with the rear admiral would determine Joe's future and that of Julie and Tillie.

Chapter 31

Joe had called the rear admiral's office, early in the morning, and gotten his assistant.

"I'd like to meet with the rear admiral as soon as possible, concerning a very important matter," Joe said.

Being protective of the rear admiral, the assistant wanted to know what the topic was and what was so important.

"I can only divulge this information directly to the rear admiral," Joe argued.

That didn't sit well with the assistant who gave him attitude and told him that he would get back to him after he spoke to the rear admiral.

After Joe hung up, extremely pissed off, Jack called him and brightened up his day. He had more information on Mr. Assinoff. Jack had gone through all his financial transactions both for the corporation and personally. On the corporation level, Jack gave Joe the list of the board of directors in addition to Mr. Blackwood. "Each board member gets $100,000.00 per year as a board member."

Not bad, thought Joe.

"Mr. Assinoff set up a political super pact for Mr. Blackwood and got all the board members and key corporate officers to contribute thousands of dollars into his campaign coffers," Jack told him.

Joe guessed that Mr. Blackwood was bought and paid for. The company had been opened for several years and was a big time real estate developer with numerous sub-corporations, using sub-contractors to renovate older buildings and start up new ones. Most of the contractors who worked for DA Industries, Inc. had dubious pasts at best. None of them would show up on the Better Business Bureau's list of honest contractors.

Jack went farther into Mr. Assinoff's personal life. "He's 53 years old and was born in Moscow in 1961. He arrived in Miami seven years ago, directly from New York City. To be specific, he arrived in the United States and lived only for a few months in Brighton Beach, before leaving for Miami. He hit the ground running and made many friends in local government, especially Mr. Blackwood, who'd served as his entry into Miami's cultural life."

From transactions Jack had found, Assinoff had spent a fortune in the first two years, meeting and greeting the Miami bluebloods—Anglo, Cuban, and African American. He was nondiscriminatory in his invitations.

"Something stuck, because he is now considered a patron of the arts and a guest on the "A" list for every major invitation in the city of Miami," Jack went on. "How no one picked up that he's the head of the Miami Russian Mafia is beyond comprehension."

Jack had also gone through Mr. Assinoff's American Express purchases. "I noticed that for the last four months, he and three others have attended the Sunday champagne brunch at the Biltmore Hotel in Coral Gables. It runs from 10:00 a.m. to 4:00 p.m. every Sunday, seated at the outside terrace in good weather. It costs $85.00 per person for the best brunch in the United States. The American Express card was signed around 3:00 p.m. every Sunday for four individuals, plus tip. The meal came to about $370.00, including tax, with a $130.00 tip, making his weekly lunch around $500.00. It isn't bad if you can afford it. It assures that Mr. Assinoff gets the seating arrangement that he wants every Sunday."

Joe was impressed. Jack was truly amazing.

"I got the video for last's Sunday's brunch and came up with a picture of Mr. Assinoff and his girlfriend at one table right near the walkway with another table for the two obviously Russian guards, with bulges in their coat pockets. With Mr. Assinoff was Vera Bokay, a thirty-year-old gorgeous Russian immigrant, who'd been in the United States since 2012. Guarding Mr. Assinoff and Ms. Bokay were Victor Yerzov, age twenty-nine, and Maxim Galkin, age twenty-six. Neither gentleman has records in the United States, as opposed to the two Russians who tried Tillie's door. It looks like Mr. Assinoff is recruiting younger and younger Russians for his Miami enterprise. I matched the Biltmore pictures to immigration pictures that showed when Yerzov and Galkin arrived in the United States. They were sponsored by Mr. Assinoff and arrived on the same day." Jack said.

If Joe was ever going to confront Mr. Assinoff, there couldn't be a better setting than the Sunday Biltmore champagne brunch, out in the open, with a clear shot for what he had in mind. He needed the rear admiral's permission, of course. He would also need a few highly trained technicians like the ones who came to Nashville from Dallas to fly the drone for a week. That worked well and, if planned right, this would work well also.

He called Mark and told him what was happening and what he had found out to date. "I'm going to the rear admiral's and ask for permission for what I need to do. If I don't get it, it will be a little more difficult, but I'll move forward anyway."

"I'm in, regardless," Mark told him.

Neither Mark nor Joe would allow Julie or Tillie's lives to be put in jeopardy, regardless of the consequences. Joe would do the same for Louise and the kids, at any time, anywhere.

Joe also made a call to a friend at the CIA. He was the same friend who managed to pluck Jorge Hernandez from the California prison and send him to Romania. After meeting with the rear admiral, Joe would hop over, meet his friend, and have a nice discussion about placing another individual into the program. Mark said he would meet with him as well, since he knew him, and the CIA contact knew that Mark was Joe's partner.

About an hour later, the rear admiral's assistant called. "Joe, you can meet with the rear admiral at 4:00 p.m. in his office, today."

Joe called back his CIA contact and set up a meeting for 6:00 p.m. at the Argentinian Steak House in the Bayside Marketplace's outdoor mall around the corner.

In the meantime, Joe asked Joan and Jacob if he could use the facility cameras to place near Tillie's old house and her new apartment. If anyone came back to either place, the cameras would be used as evidence to get the men deported. Hopefully, they'd be the same individuals as before. They'd then contact the Monroe County Sheriff's Department and have an APB put out to stop the car and arrest the two gentlemen. Since one was already wanted, Joe didn't think there would be a problem.

As he explained it to Tillie and Julie, no one knew why these two criminals targeted them. They'd lived here all their lives and would certainly be believed as pillars of the community. Julie smirked and Tillie smiled slightly as if to tell Joe that his Irish bullshit didn't work on everybody.

Joe smiled too. "Oh well," he said.

CAN'T SING OR DANCE

ℰↄℰↄ

Joe barely made it to the Brickell Federal Building by 4:00 p.m. He pulled in front, double-parked his car, and put a Coast Guard placard in the windshield. He went through security and up the stairs to the rear admiral's office. The assistant told Joe to go into his office and that he would be right in after another meeting. The assistant seemed to have resigned himself to the fact that Joe would be around for a while and he probably should get used to it.

As Joe was sitting down in one of the two mate chairs in front of his desk, the rear admiral walked in. "Hi, Joe, what's up? I know something must be bothering you or you wouldn't be here. Is it business or personal?"

"A little of both," Joe said. He then went on to explain from the very beginning about Julie and Tillie's encounter with her long lost father, his murder in prison, and what appeared to be happening now in retribution for her father's million-dollar heist from the Russians. Even if it was seventeen years earlier, the Russian Mafia never forgave or forgot and anyone related to the situation suffered the consequences.

"That's one hell of a story, Joe. If I didn't know you or Mark, I probably wouldn't have believed it. I'm not sure I'd have handled it the same way that you did but I'm a lot older than you and I've a hell of a lot more clout. At least the Coast Guard benefited from the largesse given it by Julie. How much was it, $225,000.00? I was listening, Joe. really I was," he said.

"I guess I deserve that after the pizza box speech, huh, sir?"

"Yes, you do. So how do you want to handle this?"

Joe went on to explain that he needed two smaller drones for next Sunday, manned by technician drone specialists. "The first will hover over the Biltmore Hotel during the champagne brunch with a laser pointed directly at Mr. Assinoff. I would prefer it if it was armed. The second drone will be programmed to sweep in at the last second and pick up the state-of-the-art Coast Guard IED that I will place between myself and Mr. Assinoff to get his attention. Mark will be nearby in case of a problem. In addition, Mr. Assinoff's driver will be arrested and taken away from the scene before I even get into the brunch to meet Mr. Assinoff. So there will be no chase scene, if it comes down to that," he said.

"The team will have to practice at the Biltmore all week so if you could run interference so we can have staff sitting at the tables and practicing the confrontation."

"I've been to the brunch there many times," the rear admiral said. "And I know the manager of the facility. It won't be a problem. I would never tell the manager the real reason for the assistance, just that we'll be testing a new method to intercept kidnappers in a hotel restaurant setting," he told Joe. "I'm not as good at bullshit as you but I'll be effective enough."

Joe smiled and gave him his undying gratitude. The mini-drones would be available for Joe in two days. That was more than enough practice time before Sunday's brunch.

Joe had about a half an hour to make it to the steak house at the Bayside Marketplace at 6:00 p.m. The meeting with the rear admiral took a little longer than expected. Joe walked into the restaurant bar and ordered a beer. He waited a few minutes and Mike Hanley walked in. Mike was his connection to the Central Intelligence Agency, working out of the Miami area and covering all of the Caribbean in search of terrorists. He'd worked with Joe on many an occasion when the Coast Guard was intercepting drug runners. Joe had also helped him out of a few binds when he needed translations of documents in Russian or Spanish, especially coming out of Cuba.

"Hi, Mike, how have you been?" Joe said.

"Good, Joe. Let's get a table. I'm starving."

"Me, too."

During dinner, Mike asked, "What's on your mind, Joe?"

Joe told him the entire story about Julie's father, where they now stood, and the problem that could continue. He also told him the entire story about Tom Jones and the takedown of the meth distribution center in Nashville. He told him how they shut down the pipeline for the entire eastern seaboard, right down to Orlando.

Mike was duly impressed and said so. Joe told him of his promotion to lieutenant and Mark's promotion as well. Mike knew Mark since he was always with Joe when the CIA was involved. Mark's gang background gave the CIA a leg up when dealing with gang activity outside the US that was directed *at* the US. Both Joe and Mark were close to experts in dealing with the Patriot Act and helped the CIA in that regard. Mike asked Joe what he wanted the CIA to do. Joe told him that he believed that the Russian Mafia, if they were smart, would drop their interest in Key Largo, specifically an interest in Tillie Carpenter and Julie Chapman. He told Mike that he and Julie were officially engaged so this was now a family issue.

Mike understood that completely. "The children should have to never pay for the mistakes—or in this case, the crimes—of the parents," he said. "We'll fix this, Joe. Don't worry about it. My end will be covered."

"If Dmitry Assinoff doesn't cooperate, I want the CIA to send him and his guards to wherever you decide is in the best interest of the US," Joe said. "Having Mr. Assinoff in charge of a growing Russian Mafia in Miami and the Keys is not in the best interest of the US. The fact that Mr. Assinoff is being supported for citizenship by Commissioner

Emmanuel Blackwood of Miami means that if he continues to pursue Tillie and Julie, we'll have to act immediately before he becomes a citizen in good standing. It's clear that with the money that he's been floating around Miami, he'd be considered a model citizen."

Joe had already lined up Mark, a few Coast Guard friends, and Joan's husband, Jeff Talbot, who was in charge of the marina at Islamorada for the Coast Guard. Jeff had a go-fast boat all ready to go whenever they needed it. Jeff Talbot was a boating expert and pilot and would serve that purpose. The CIA couldn't work within the confines of the US. However, Joe could certainly meet a CIA ship just past the 12-nautical-mile or 13.8-mile territorial waters of the US. Joe had it set up that if the Biltmore persuasion attempt didn't work, the rendition would. They'd done this plenty of times before. It was dangerous, but it wasn't their first rodeo.

After dinner, Joe headed home to meet with his team and get the plans in order.

CHAPTER 32

T he cameras, installed by Joan at Tillie's place, showed the same Mercedes-Benz drive by slowly the day after the installation. There were the same two men in the car. They didn't stop.

Julie had her car back at Joe's officer's quarters and drove it back and forth to school. Tillie hadn't replaced her car, as of yet, because she simply didn't need one and the insurance and upkeep was too much of a burden. She could walk to the Waffle House in the morning and to mass down the street on Sunday. The apartment complex had a senior bus go by once a week to the grocery store so she was set for transportation. Now, she was at Joe's and didn't need anything, anyway. She made herself busy outside his quarters by volunteering at the facility to help out with whatever they needed. She'd taken a short leave from the Waffle House until this problem was solved. The manager, a lifelong friend, never asked why and she never told him. She didn't need to tell him.

Joe found out that the men had cruised by, but

he didn't want to pick them up until after his Sunday confrontation with Assinoff. If they showed up after that, it meant a new level of drastic measures would kick in and then Joe would have them arrested. He told Marilyn, the neighbor, not to take pictures or anything else because they had things under control. Her nosiness had paid off the first time, but she could get hurt the second time. And she knew that he was someone who could take care of them.

ℰ𝒮ℰ𝒮

The mini-drones came in the next night. There were two of the flying miracles. They landed at the Islamorada facility and the truck with the technicians came right behind them. Joe was waiting for them. They, too, came from Dallas, and the two technicians, who'd helped Joe in Nashville, arrived as well. The first mini-drone weighed twice as much as the second because it was equipped with cameras and a laser. But it was also armed.

The second drone was the package retriever, very much like the one shown on *60 Minutes* that Amazon was considering for delivering packages in very large urban areas. Miami and Coral Gables very much qualified for the test. The first drone was programmed to fly over the Biltmore and hold its position for a minimum of twenty minutes and a maximum of one hour. That would be more than enough time for a discussion at the outdoor table.

The armed mini-drone would be programmed to lock onto one individual and have a laser pointed at the person's chest from a distance of 400 feet above the earth. The other drone would land on the top of the Biltmore roof and the technician would send it directly to the table by exact GPS coordinates. The mini-drone would pick up the IED package and take off. Mark and two of his Dania Beach staff would handle the driver, parked in the lot. He would be delivered to the FBI who'd grill him for several hours and, hopefully, he too would be deported. There was nothing but Russians surrounding Mr. Assinoff.

Joe received the IED from Jack the following day. It was armed but only Joe could unlock it in order to make it explode. It was the very best that the Coast Guard had. Four inches square and two inches thick, it weighed about two pounds. Joe could turn on the flashing light with a switch as a wake-up call for Mr. Assinoff but that's not what would send it off. Only Joe could do that. He'd made arrangements for the technicians to stay at his station for the night, and they'd move out to the Biltmore early the next day. They'd practice around peak hours, early in the morning and later at night, so they wouldn't interfere with the restaurant's business.

ഐരെ

It was now Sunday and, after practicing for the most of the week, they were prepared for the day. Joe took Julie and Tillie to mass at Saint Justin Martyr's Church in Key Largo for the 9:00 a.m. mass. He would bring them back to Islamorada, have a quick breakfast, and head out to the Biltmore with the men. He'd take his own car and leave it several blocks from the hotel just to be safe. He would meet Mark in the Biltmore employees' lot several blocks away and then go to work.

Julie gave Joe a big kiss. "Please be careful. I know you're doing this for Tillie and me and I'm grateful. However, I love you, Joe, and I don't want to see anything happen to you. It was my father who caused this problem and I know he must have given us up while in prison. You're right. We can't wait until something happens."

Joe needed to confront this now, for the people he loved, and stop it, or it would never end until they died.

They all headed out around 11:00 a.m. It was Sunday so the drive up to Coral Gables took about an hour. Joe was just guessing that Assinoff, his girlfriend, and the guards would show up at 1:00 p.m. If the man left at 3:00 p.m. every Sunday, he surely would give himself at least two hours to eat, drink, and relax.

So Joe would have the armed drone move in a little early and, as soon as it spotted the people sitting at the GPS location table, it would notify the crew, who'd give Joe the signal to move in.

The other drone could simply sit on the top of the Biltmore until it was ordered to swoop down and grab the IED from the table fifteen minutes after Joe had left.

Joe received the signal from the technicians and started to move down the sidewalk to the brunch seating area. He knew what all four individuals looked like. The two guards would only be ten feet away so Joe needed to convey that a laser was pointed at Assinoff chest, as soon as he could, and that Ms. Vera Bokay should join the two guards at the other table.

"Mr. Assinoff, May I have a few minutes of your time?" Joe asked as he approached the man's table.

"Who are you? Can't you see that I'm having my lunch?" As Assinoff said this, he turned beckoned to the guards, who placed their napkins on the table and started to stand up.

"Mr. Assinoff, before your guards can reach me, you'll be dead," Joe declared. "Please look down at your chest. There's a laser pointed at you. If I move my right hand one inch, you're a dead man. Do I make myself perfectly clear?"

As Joe said it, Assinoff looked down and saw the white dot on his chest. When he moved, the dot went with him in the exact location where it was before. He turned to his guards and told them in Russian to sit down.

"What do you want," he asked.

Joe turned to Ms. Bokay and, in Russian, asked her politely to go sit with the guards. Assinoff nodded. Joe continued to speak to him in Russian, without a flaw. That surprised Assinoff because Joe was clearly not an ethnic Russian. At this point, Mr. Assinoff was very attentive.

"Whatever business you have in Key Largo is now permanently ended," Joe told him. "Chasing a grandmother and trashing homes in that town is not acceptable. Whatever was told to you was untrue. And killing a man in prison won't get to the truth. There was no money. The man who was murdered in prison spent most of it over the seventeen years he was in hiding from your predecessors. The rest was given to charity and there's none left. If you decide on retribution for retribution's sake, you will be handled severely."

"Who are you?" Assinoff asked once again.

"I'm probably your worst nightmare," Joe said. "If you pursue this situation any farther, the penalty will be severe. For so little money, you should think twice about starting something that won't end well for you."

"I could say the same for you," Assinoff said with anger in his eyes. "Do you think I scare that easily? Within ten minutes after you leave, you'll be dead."

With that, Joe pulled out the IED and pushed the button that made the light flash. He placed it on the table. "Mr. Assinoff, do you know what this is? It's a state-of-the-art IED that will blow you to kingdom come. Perhaps I didn't make myself clear. You don't want to screw with this. I'll take out you and your Russian Mafia friends before you ever know what hit you. Mr. Blackwood and your associates won't be able to protect you, wherever you go. If you think *I* scare easily, you really don't have a clue. I can take you out at any time I want to without impunity. This isn't Moscow. You're now on my turf, asshole. And don't you forget it."

And with that, Joe rose. "I'm now leaving. The IED will stay right there for fifteen minutes and if you move a muscle, you'll be dead. Your bodyguards and girlfriend will probably need a ride."

As he got up, the guards started to move and Assinoff raised his hand to stop them, pointing at the IED. They sat down very nervously. Joe told them in Russian that they had to wait fifteen minutes and the IED would deactivate.

To the second, fifteen minutes later, the other mini-drone left the top of the Biltmore Hotel and swooped down to Mr. Assinoff's table. It landed right on top of the IED, placed its mechanical arms around the package, and immediately flew off. It was gone within seconds.

Assinoff signaled to his guards and girlfriend and headed quickly to his car. It was not there and neither was his driver. He called Emmanuel Blackwood. "We need a ride and information. Get here as soon as possible."

Blackwood showed up a half hour later and Assinoff was furious. He handed him his girlfriend's camera. She'd taken a picture of Joe right when he showed up. Assinoff told Blackwood that he wanted to know who this guy was immediately, because he was a dead man.

Assinoff called his two employees, who were driving around Key Largo, and told them to pump up the surveillance and to pick up Tillie this time. Whoever it was, who had showed up at his brunch, would pay the price and anyone associated with him was dead. Tom Chapman or Ted Champion, Assinoff didn't care. The man stole a million dollars from the organization and the family would pay the price. No one stole from the Russian Mafia and got away with it. No one. By the time Dmitry Assinoff was done, everyone would have paid for this crime against them. It was a given.

ᘒᘓᘒᘓ

After the confrontation, Joe met with Mark, his crew, and the mini-drone technicians in the employees' parking lot. He'd gotten to his car that was parked on the street and then drove the back way into the parking lot. He assumed that Mr. Assinoff would be long gone.

He thanked the technicians and told them that he might still need them for a few days depending

363

on what happened after he left Mr. Assinoff.

"I don't think that Mr. Assinoff will ever back off from his plans of dealing with Tillie and Julie in Key Largo," Joe said.

"I don't think so either, Joe," Mark agreed.

Joe called Joan from the parking lot. He asked her if some of the men at the Islamorada Coast Guard Station could stake out Tillie's apartment for at least a night or two. He didn't believe that Assinoff would wait for revenge. He would do something immediately to show who was in charge. Joe knew he'd pissed him off and he'd done that to make him back off or else escalate the situation so Joe could finally end the problem.

"Six men will alternate shifts, watching the apartment," Joan said. "If the two Russians in the Mercedes-Benz come back, they'll immediately notify Detective Kenny, the Chief of Detectives for the Monroe County Sheriff's Department. Each team will have a federal warrant for the Russians' arrest."

Joe got the warrants from the rear admiral's close friend, a federal judge in Miami. This had been outlined when Joe had met with the rear admiral to discuss the situation. Joe had already known that the one Russian was a fugitive.

"Joan, please make sure that the Monroe County Sheriff's Department handles it and keep them at arm's length. If they pick the Russians up, we'll need to be in on the interrogation since I'm the only one who speaks fluent Russian."

"Got it, Joe. Stay in touch. Things are moving fast but we'll cover this end. No problem."

On the way back to Islamorada, Joe called Mike Hanley, who was waiting for the call. "I'll let you know if the confrontation solved the problem. But I don't believe it did, Mike, so it's on to Plan B. If Mr. Assinoff is taken out, it's on him. His pride and sense of entitlement and power won't let him back off. We'll be ready to hit as soon as I see an escalation on his part."

In place, ready to move, were the fast-go boat and pilot, and the CIA ship to be met outside the US territorial waters. Jeff Talbot would be docked at the Port of Miami for the next several days, on call to move in seconds. Mark and his team were also ready, fully armed with weapons, night-vision goggles, flash-bang grenades, vests, laser dart guns, and the armed mini-drone, which could take out Assinoff's car, anywhere, and at any time. The mini-drone would follow Joe and the teams and then be programmed to follow Assinoff's limousine at will. If Assinoff was moving around in downtown Miami, it would only be a few minutes to take out the car, hit the men with darts, to make them unconscious, drive to the Port of Miami, and place them on the go-fast boat.

But Joe sincerely hoped that all this would not be needed and the problem would just go away.

CHAPTER 33

The next day, word got back to Joe that Mr. Emmanuel Blackwood was flashing a picture around to the chief of police and others, wanting to know who the person was in the picture. As soon as inquiries went to the FBI for confirmation, it was rejected by the system since Joe was under the jurisdiction of all three entities, including the FBI. At Joe's request, two FBI agents showed up at Mr. Blackwood's house and asked him about the inquiry.

Mr. Blackwood was clearly nervous and stepped around the agents' questions, trying to evade.

They asked for the picture and he handed one to them. They asked how many he had and he said he'd made five of them. The first went to the chief of police in Miami and the second to the Monroe County Sheriff's Department. Mr. Blackwood still had three other pictures and the agents wanted them as part of an ongoing investigation. When the picture went to the sheriff of Monroe County, he passed it on to the Chief of Detectives, Mike Kenny. Kenny held the inquiry up, thinking that it was very suspicious, especially after the break in at Tillie Carpenter's old house and the attempt at her new apartment. He called Joe and told him about the inquiry. Joe, once again, let him know that it might be in the nation's best interests if Kenny sank the inquiry.

"I'm involved in an investigation that includes the break-in," Joe told Detective Kenny. "And Homeland Security and the FBI are aware of the situation. Mr. Blackwood was informed that interference in an ongoing FBI investigation was a felony and he could be charged, if he continued. He was also told that if he mentioned anything about the FBI's visit, it would constitute continued involvement. They didn't have to tell Mr. Blackwood that his buddy and benefactor, Dmitry Assinoff, was under continued surveillance. Blackwood told the agents that he'd be going on an extended vacation until further notice."

❧❧❧

As expected, Nestor Bykov, and Marco Zotov, again drove by Tillie's apartment at 1:30 a.m. The undercover Coast Guard crew was waiting at the corner, hidden behind the bushes. They knew that the car was a Mercedes-Benz and they had the full license plate number now, which was found when Jack did his research on the six of nine numbers and letters he'd managed to bring out on the blurred photo from Marilyn's cell phone.

The Coast Guard crew immediately called the Monroe County Sheriff's Department, and the dispatcher, who was waiting for the call, notified two patrol cars on duty. He also called Detective Kenny and Joe. It looked like they'd have a very long night when the two Russians were apprehended.

The Coasties got into their car, pulled out, and followed the Mercedes, staying a block or two behind it. They were in constant contact with the two patrol cars at this point. There was no traffic that late at night in Key Largo, so they didn't want to be discovered following the car. The Russians were driving along the Overseas Highway, about a half-mile north of town, when the two sheriff's patrol cars hit their sirens. The first car pulled in front of the Mercedes as the second made an announcement for the car to pull over. From the look on the two Russians' faces, it was clear that they were very surprised. They were told to step out of the vehicle with their hands in the air, spread their legs, and put their hands on the roof of the car.

One of the two men asked what was going on in broken English. The deputy in the first car told them that they were under arrest and read them their rights in English. They both said they didn't understand the deputy. However, they did understand the four guns aimed at them. They then complied and put their hands behind their backs to be handcuffed. The two men were put into the backseat of the patrol car and taken to the sheriff's substation in Islamorada, very near the Coast Guard facility.

Joe and Detective Kenny showed up as the two men were being taken into the interrogation room. It was a very small substation because it was only a storefront, with a small holding pen and two other rooms beside the front desk area. Joe and Detective Kenny went into the room and looked at the two men, who were still in handcuffs. Detective Kenny spoke in English and the men said they didn't understand him. He asked for their names and they didn't know what he was talking about. After a few minutes of charades, they finally gave the detective two phony names and phony driver's licenses, with a Miami address. By this time, Detective Kenny was getting frustrated. The two Russians had smirks on their faces.

Joe smirked back at them. "There's an easy way or a hard way and it's up to you," he said in Russian. He then told them their names, ages, employment, and where they really lived. Joe read them their rights in English, Russian, and Spanish just to show off a little. Detective Kenny was duly impressed.

"Mr. Bykov, your green card has been officially pulled, Your previous misdemeanors, coupled with the break-in and attempt, will send you to federal prison, not state prison, for a very long time," Joe told him. He then turned to Marco Zotov, who had a criminal record and was already about to be deported when he vanished. "You are not a citizen of the United States, either. I really don't care if you cooperate because you will be given a life sentence in federal prison under the Patriot Act, to join some others under the rendition program. It's up to you."

"What do you want to know?" they both asked at the same time.

"Why are you were back in Key Largo after the break-in?" Joe immediately asked them in Russian. "I thought you'd be long gone by now."

"We received orders directly from Mr. Assinoff at 10:00 p.m. Sunday night to go to Key Largo and grab Tillie Carpenter. We were told not to come back without her and her granddaughter."

That was enough for Joe. He was taking Assinoff out of the country tomorrow night. Joe translated everything for Detective Kenny and made the men write out their statements in Russian. Joe translated it back into English, counter-signing both copies. INS had already been notified and the FBI would be picking the Russians up in an hour at the station. At least Joe didn't have to worry about *them* anymore.

As Detective Kenny and Joe were walking out of the station, the detective said, "Joe, I know we had our differences in the past about Tillie's investigation and treatment, but I always felt that there was more to Ted Champion than any of you ever let on."

"You're right. It wasn't just about the break-in and sending Champion to jail. He stole from the Russian Mafia a long time ago and he was a danger to Tillie and Julie. His murder in prison was not a fluke. The Russians were involved, but that's all I can say for now. It's a federal matter."

"Well, thank you for that. I really don't know how to tell you how impressed I am at your skills, Joe. You have fluency in Russian and Spanish. No wonder the Coast Guard wanted you back."

"Just so you know," Joe said. "I'm affiliated with the Coast Guard, now a lieutenant, and I have official credentials with Homeland Security and the FBI."

"I think we keep forgetting that. But I'm still impressed. Thanks for helping solve this break-in and the attempt at Tillie's apartment. I know *I* feel better about the safety of our residents now. The only problem that still exists is the trashing of Tillie's old house. I hope they had insurance to cover it," Detective Kenny said.

Joe smiled. "If they don't, let me know. I picked up a few dollars on our last investigation and I may be able to squeeze some funds out to help. Keep that to yourself, though, until further notice."

"I will and thanks."

CHAPTER 34

Joe had known that Assinoff wouldn't back off, and now he was fully prepared to take him out of the country. It might not end the Russian Mafia problem, but if Joe took that cause up in his new position in Miami, working under the rear admiral, he could probably put a damper on it. If the Russians had to run around protecting their assets and themselves, they would most likely forget about the small potatoes in Key Largo. And they might just change their minds about revenge for revenge's sake.

At least with Assinoff out of Miami, whomever he reported to in either New York City or Moscow would have a tough time replacing him and building up the rapport that Assinoff seemed to have enjoyed with Miami's elite. Sooner or later, Blackwood would either resign from office or run out of money without Assinoff's super-pact funding. Blackwood would be persona non grata on the board of DA Industries, Inc. losing his $100,000.00 a year fee. At fifty-one years old, he might have a hard time starting over. He'd never been tight with the African-American community because of his Russian ties. And, in the long run, that would hinder his getting back into the ballgame.

めめめ

Joe was on the phone all day. Since Tillie and Julie resided in his officer's quarters for the time being, they'd be safe. Joan and Cramer were on board, especially since the rear admiral called them personally and told them that he blessed Joe's activities.

Hell, the main problem the Coast Guard had was the drug running out of Miami and the Florida Keys. This could be a major step in slowing down the Russian-Cuban drug distribution programs. Joe had already put a large dent in it on the Eastern Seaboard by shutting down the Nashville center. This takedown might not be as clean as they wanted it, but this was not the RICO Act. The Patriot Act covered these situations. The rear admiral checked out the plan with the FBI and Homeland Security lawyers. He liked Joe, but he'd never have approved this action if it hadn't met all requirements under the law. It did.

Rear Admiral Jake Barnes had read the entire investigation report when Joe had taken down the Mexican Mafia's infiltration of non-profits and national foundations. Both investigations were similar, the only exception being Joe's personal involvement with Tillie and Julie. He'd assured the rear admiral that he would walk away and remove both of them from the scene if it became an issue.

Joe made all his calls. The armed drone was flying tonight. It would simply point a laser at the front of Assinoff's limousine and take out the engine. When Assinoff and the bodyguards got out of the car to see what happened, they'd be hit by darts and put to sleep for a few hours. The driver would be picked up and shuffled off to the Homeland Security site. They were hoping that Ms. Bokay wouldn't be in the car yet and, perhaps, they'd be on their way to pick her up. She was his girlfriend and he'd placed her in her own condo in a towers complex in downtown.

He stayed at his own place for business reasons—he didn't want her to overhear anything that was said. He made that mistake before with a previous girlfriend, who had to be sent back to Moscow. Her whereabouts were unknown.

Jeff Talbot was waiting at the Port of Miami in a designated CIA spot. Just because they couldn't operate within the continental US didn't mean they didn't have safe houses, facilities, docks, and other clandestine support ready and waiting. While they couldn't be involved in the pickup, they could meet Joe outside the restricted area.

Joe headed up to Miami around 4:00 p.m. He was to meet up with Mark and his crew at 5:30 p.m. near Coast Guard headquarters in downtown

Miami. It was not far from Assinoff's condo. The drone technicians were scheduled to launch the drone from the Broward County Airport at 320 Terminal Drive in Fort Lauderdale. Mark had set it up a long time ago. They'd started flying drones to catch drug runners several years ago, when drones were in their infancy. In the Keys, they used the Key West Airport when flying south of Key West.

The drone would take off at 6:30 p.m. and hover over downtown Miami, near Coast Guard head-quarters. When Assinoff came out of his building, Joe would give the technicians the GPS coordi-nates, and the drone would lock on to them for the duration. It had to stay ahead of the car in order to aim its weapon at the engine. It could take the car from either of the front side panels as well.

Like clockwork, Assinoff's limousine came out of the subterranean parking garage and headed down Brickell. As soon as Joe saw the vehicle, he latched onto the GPS coordinates and fed them to the technicians up in Fort Lauderdale. The drone locked onto the vehicle and would remain so until notified to hit the engine with a laser. As they went down the street toward a secluded section, Joe gave the signal and, in an instant, there was a relatively large bang from the laser hitting the engine com-partment. The front end of the vehicle caught on fire.

The driver stopped immediately. Assinoff and his two guards got out and looked around, wondering what the hell had happened. The engine was smoking so they concentrated on that.

Mark had stopped his vehicle in front of Assinoff's as soon as it started smoking. Joe pulled up to the rear. Mark's team hit all three with the darts as soon as they could. Assinoff got hit in the neck and the two larger guards got hit with several to ensure they went down. The driver, who was standing outside the vehicle, looked around and had his hands in the air. The tow truck that Joe had ordered, at the last minute, was a godsend. Joe hadn't been sure if they'd need it but, looking at the vehicle now, he knew it wasn't going anywhere on its own. The Coast Guard tow truck operator hooked up the limousine, which was never to be seen again.

The driver went into Mark's car. Assinoff, the two guards, and Mark went into Joe's vehicle. The driver was taken to the Homeland Security facility. Joe would drive to the Port of Miami. Mark's team would later pick up Joe's car and take it back to Fort Lauderdale. Joe planned to leave the keys in it.

As soon as the drone hit the limousine, it had flown back to Fort Lauderdale and landed. The technicians had packed up everything, cleaned the area, and left for Dallas, Texas.

Joe and Mark made it to the Port of Miami in ten minutes. The boat was waiting, its engines running. Jeff Talbot waved to them, giving them the on-board signal. In the parking lot, they put plastic ties on their prisoners' hands and feet and taped their mouths shut. The men would be out of it for some time. Joe and his team used a hand truck, which they'd brought in the trunk, to carry each man on board, one at a time. The bodyguards were enormous and it took some time to get them on board. Assinoff was a lightweight by comparison and Joe simply threw the man over his shoulder and dropped him onto the deck. They turned off the car and left the keys in it, knowing that the other team would pick it up in less than fifteen minutes. Some chances had to be taken. Then they took off to meet the CIA ship past the legal limits.

A typical go-fast, or cigarette boat, was built of fiberglass, with a deep V offshore racing hull, usually from thirty to fifty feet long, narrow in beam, and equipped with two or more powerful engines, often with more than 1,000 combined horsepower. The boats could typically travel at speeds of over eighty knots, or almost ninety miles per hour, in calm waters; over fifty knots, or sixty miles per hour, in choppy waters; and maintain twenty-five knots in the average five-to-seven-foot Caribbean seas. They're heavy enough to cut through higher waves, although at a slower pace. They made it to the CIA ship in less than half an hour, pulling up alongside of the vessel.

Joe and Mark, with Mike Hanley's help, along with two other CIA agents, pulled the still-unconscious men out of the go-fast boat and placed them on the deck of the ship. In addition to the agents, the boat was well equipped with supplies for a longer trip and had ten sailors on board. Joe thought they could have been navy but he wasn't sure and didn't want to ask.

Before leaving, they put smelling salts under the three men's noses and, as they began to wake up, they each started choking. Mike gave each of them a bottle of water. As they looked around, they were clearly confused. The last thing they probably remembered was their vehicle stopping in the middle of the road with the engine smoking.

Assinoff's head began to clear and he looked right at Joe. "You again?" he said. "Where am I? What've you done to us? Release us now. You're in a world of hurt, asshole. You're a dead man and everyone else here."

"Mr. Assinoff, you're being held, along with your two bodyguards, under the United States Patriot Act," Joe said. "Neither you nor these men are US citizens and you've been identified as terrorists under this enactment. You're being taken for questioning and you'll be interrogated shortly. You'll never step foot in the United States again. I hope that's clear. Now for your men, who probably don't speak English, I'll repeat what I just said in Russian. There are no Miranda Rights required for known terrorists. Mr. Assinoff, I asked you to let your little Key Largo problem go away. You didn't. You couldn't, or wouldn't. In any case, that problem is now moot at best."

"You can't do this," Assinoff said defiantly. "I'm up for citizenship and sponsored by a Miami commissioner. I own property in Miami. I'm a well know philanthropist and patron of the arts. I'll be missed. They'll come looking for me."

"Where you're going, Mr. Assinoff, you won't ever be found. You'll be forgotten. If the reasons do ever get out—that you jeopardized the Russian Mafia's entire Miami empire for revenge on a dinky little grandmother who had no money and lived in senior housing, they'd probably kill you on the spot as an example of pure stupidity."

The officers on board grabbed Assinoff by the shoulders and threw him into a locked cabin. They moved the other two into similar quarters.

Joe thanked Mike Hanley and the crew. "Whenever you need translation services or investigations done," he said to Mike, "we will gladly oblige."

They all shook hands. Joe and his team hopped on the go-fast boat and headed for Islamorada. Jeff turned to Mark and Joe and gave both of them the thumbs up. Joe couldn't thank him and Joan enough. They'd both put their lives on the line for him and he was grateful.

When they got back, about an hour later—because Islamorada was fifty miles south of Miami—they were exhausted but also greatly relieved. Jeff blew his horn, coming into the dock, and a whole crew of men, women, and children gave them a mighty cheer and a round of applause. As they docked, everyone asked how things went and the three of them said it went well. Nothing more.

No one needed to know more than they did. After hugs and kisses all around, Joe excused himself and went to his office. He called the rear admiral who had deliberately stayed late to hear the news.

"I'm elated," Barnes said. "You got the job done and no one was hurt."

Joe was relieved. He called the drone technicians on their way home and thanked them again for all they'd done. After all his calls, he went to the yard and popped an ice-cold beer—sitting in the cooler, just for the occasion—and saluted everyone there. He hoped that it was now over. He needed to see the rear admiral in the morning as a formality. There wouldn't be much of a write-up on this operation, if any. The longer it lay dormant, the better.

Perhaps with time, it would finally go away. He still wanted to close down the Russians in Miami. To this day, it was still a shock to everyone how fast they had moved and how much power they yielded in less than twenty short years. Their organization seemed to go on, in spite of losing men over and over again. Their numbers seemed to increase every year and the US Government had a hard time keeping up with them. It was also evident, that without the Patriot Act, foreign criminals would swarm the country like locust. The US form of prosecution for the most heinous crimes seemed like a picnic in the park for someone raised under the threat of the Gulag.

CHAPTER 35

Joe headed out to meet Rear Admiral Barnes for lunch at noon. When the call came in from his assistant, Joe was asked to bring Julie with him. He thought that was rather interesting, but he certainly couldn't refuse the request. Julie was understandably shocked as well. She'd never met Barnes but she wanted to thank him personally for allowing Joe to protect both her and Tillie from what amounted to certain death at the hands of the Russians if left unabated.

They left a little after 10:00 a.m. Joe was dressed in his officer's uniform with the new lieutenant insignias. Julie wore her black dress, appropriate for all occasions, with a small string of natural pearls taken from Key Largo waters, around her neck. She wore her best heels and matching pocketbook.

Joe had to go with Julie in her car since his vehicle was now in Fort Lauderdale after being picked up at the Port of Miami dock. They pulled into the Coast Guard headquarters around 11:20 a.m., parking in Joe's assigned spot. They went in the front door and passed through security. Joe felt a little awkward, as everyone's eyes were on him and Julie. She excused herself and headed to the ladies' room to freshen up. Joe hit the men's room, washed his face, combed his hair, and went out the door to wait for Julie. He knew she'd take her time and come out without a blemish. He'd no idea how women did that.

Hand in hand, Joe and Julie walked into the rear admiral's office and were greeted by the assistant. This time, he couldn't have been nicer. Evidently, he'd picked up a vibe that he should be more cooperative.

That was fine with Joe.

As soon as they went into the rear admiral's office, Barnes got up immediately and went around his desk to greet Julie. "Hello, I'm Jake Barnes. It's a pleasure to meet you, Julie," he said. "I've heard nothing but great things about you, and not just from Joe. I'm certainly glad that everything seems to have worked out in Key Largo. How is your grandmother doing? I hear that she's one hell of a woman. I'd like to meet her someday as well."

"Thank you for inviting me today, and thank you for your concern for both me and my grandmother. It's appreciated."

"Congratulations on your engagement to Lieutenant Traynor, Julie. When is the wedding taking place?" With that, he winked at Joe who smiled broadly.

Joe chuckled. "I think he's hinting at an invitation to the wedding."

"Damn straight, Joe. Someone has to keep an eye on you and make sure you show up without causing trouble for someone. Julie, did he tell you about the pizza boxes?"

"Pizza boxes?" she asked.

"Get the story from Joe on the way home," the rear admiral told her. "Is he always like this, breaking the chops of everyone in his wake, regardless of rank?"

She smiled. "That's the way he's been since I met him when I was ten years old."

The rear admiral was impressed with Julie and wanted to hear all about her book and her assignment at the Monroe County School District. Then they went to lunch at the rear admiral's favorite Italian restaurant, Cafe Abbracci, steps away from headquarters. It seemed everything was right around the corner from Coast Guard headquarters.

Joe laughed to himself. Dmitry Assinoff wouldn't be right around the corner anymore. He'd be half way around the world when he landed.

When Julie excused herself at the restaurant, Joe knew it was for him to speak to the rear admiral.

"You're a very lucky man, Joe, and I certainly can see why you wanted Julie Chapman protected at all costs," Barnes said. "I was very reluctant to approve what you wanted done, but now I understand it was the only way that made sense. You have to cut out the cancer to save the patient. Waiting for it to get better was not a valid argument. After watching you under adverse pressure and conditions, I definitely want you in the office on a regular basis. I want more contact with Mark, as well, since you feed off each other."

He asked Joe bluntly what needed to be changed in the Coast Guard and Joe only mentioned one thing, for now.

"Older officers have the experience but little or no technical background. The younger officers have plenty of technology training and could solve more crimes quicker but their lack of experience could also get them killed. Experience is key and I want more younger and older officers teamed together like a mentor program. If Tom Jones hadn't placed me and Mark together, all those years ago, I wouldn't be where I am today."

The rear admiral thought that was a great idea and he wanted to pursue it further. At that point, Julie came back to the table. They left the restaurant shortly after, as Joe and Julie wanted to head out. They still had to pick up Joe's car at Mark's office in Dania Beach and then head home from there. They were tired of living out of suitcases, both of them. Again, they thanked the rear admiral.

"You, sir, have saved our lives," Julie told the rear admiral, "and we will forever be grateful."

"I'm glad to be of service to you and your grandmother, Julie," the rear admiral said.

Joe and Julie got to Mark's office in about a half an hour. Joe went in and got his keys. Mark was at his main office in Miami today for a meeting. Joe told the guys in the office that he would call Mark when they got home. Two of the men in the office were Mark's crewmembers who had helped out with the takedown. They were still on a high.

Joe shook their hands and, again, said, "Thanks."

He got into his car and waved to Julie. He pulled around her and she followed him all the way home to Key Largo. They'd stay at Tillie's tonight so Joe stopped at the convenience store and sub shop to load up on beer, wraps, and subs.

Soon after dinner, Joe and Julie fell asleep on the couch. Joe stayed on the couch, in deference to Tillie. It was her house. Julie moved into the spare room that had all her furniture and stuff from when she was a child. Tillie insisted on moving everything here when she moved in after selling the house. It was Julie's place whenever she wanted it. There was no pressure. They each knew how to roll with the punches after all these years.

༄༅

Several weeks later, Julie had started up once

again at her school. She was in charge of the $100,000.00 technology grant that had been won from the Florida State Education Department. Maddie Malone, her friend from Brown University, had been down to help pick out the equipment and embed the lesson plans into the curriculum to raise student achievement. Everyone in the fifth grade got an iPad to take home to do their homework. It would be rolled out to the entire school once the bugs were out of the program and the students met their first set of deliverable objectives. Julie also had to work at the high school for several afternoons, serving as a career counselor for the juniors and seniors. She also wanted to continue assistant coaching the fall cross-country team. So she was very busy.

Joe was back to being fully involved in the remaining three investigations that had sat while he was away. He also had to commute two to three times a week to Miami to meet with the rear admiral and develop strategies for the new Coast Guard, including the mentor program for officers.

Julie was with Joe, living at his officer's quarters. It was a little before five o'clock and she'd just gotten back from cross-country practice. Their first meet was Saturday and it was Lucy Talbot's year to prove how good she was. She was All-Florida last year and, on graduation, she was expected to be first in the state and be granted several college scholarship opportunities. She was hoping for a scholarship from the University of Miami in Coral Gables. It was a nationally ranked program, a major university, and not that far from the Keys. Their retired coach had seen her run last year and made a recommendation to the current women's varsity cross-country coach to give her a full scholarship.

Coral Gables also had the weather that Lucy loved and had grown up in, and it would mean a very large break for her parents, financially. She was pumped and so was Julie. Julie had been all state when she attended high school, but certainly not of Lucy's caliber,

Julie's cell phone rang as she walked in the door at home. "Hello? May I help you?" she asked. She wondered who had her number because she didn't recognize the caller.

"Hi, my name is Marshall Tillman. I'm the president of Hollywood Studios at Walt Disney World in Orlando. How are you?"

"How may I help you," she asked.

"Perhaps, I should start from the beginning. Claire Murphy—a friend of yours, I believe—is my administrative assistant here at Hollywood Studios. She gave me a copy of your book, *Conch Town Girl*, which I read and I loved it. I know it's not aimed at me, but trust me, I've three young daughter, ages ten, thirteen, and fifteen. I didn't know if it was appropriate for the two youngest, but my oldest daughter Meg loved it. She said that it should be a Disney movie or a television series. There, that was a mouthful," he said.

"Well, I don't know what to say. Thank you. I appreciate your call," she said.

"This is more than just a call. I forwarded your book and my comments to Walt Disney Studios Motion Pictures in Burbank and they're passing your book around as we speak. I told them not to be cheap, to buy a hundred copies and pass the book out. I told them that they wouldn't regret it. I don't know if you know this, but my theme park, here in Orlando was where the original Mickey Mouse Club was filmed. We really don't film very many projects here anymore but I was entertaining the idea of working on bringing *Conch Town Girl* to the screen, right where the Mickey Mouse Club came to life. What do you think?"

"I don't know what to say," she repeated.

"Well can you at least say 'yes' to a meeting here in Orlando? If you accept, I'll personally fly a number of media executives into my Hollywood Studios to meet with you at your convenience. I know this sounds unreal, but please do me a favor and call Claire after you hang up." He gave Julie his office number, Claire's number at home and at her office, and both of their cell phone numbers. Julie thanked him for the call and told him that, after speaking to her attorney and to Claire, she'd get back to him as soon as she could.

She called Claire at home, who immediately

picked up the phone. "Claire, it's Julie Chapman, Joe's fiancée," she said.

"Julie, I believe you're more than Joe's fiancée. I think that in addition to being a published author and rising star, you may also soon be in the movie business, if I'm guessing correctly. Did Marshall call you?"

"I just got off the phone. Claire, how did this all happen.?" Julie asked.

"Joe told me that you wrote a book and I remembered reading about *Conch Town Girl* and how it's already affected the lives of so many young girls, not just in the Keys. My kids are small, but as a mother, if I loved it and saw the value, I thought that Marshall would as well. I also recommended it to a few other PTA members and they all came back with positive responses. So I sent those responses with the book to Marshall, and that was that."

"Wow. That's all I can say. Wow."

"Are you going to meet with him and the others?"

"I have to work on my schedule. I'm into my second book already and I'm back at school as a teacher's aide and career counselor at the high school. Perhaps we can make it for a Saturday into Sunday and then take you out to dinner for being so nice. I'm sure Joe will come as well."

"I wouldn't normally say this, Julie, but both you and Joe are very lucky to have each other. I know how you've been for years but both of you deserve happiness. I know about Joe's background and, from your book, I can only imagine what you went through growing up. As far as Joe is concerned, I can never thank him enough for clearing my father's name and putting the wrongs he did to rest. I know that you and Joe are coming to the memorial in a few weeks at the Sarasota Veterans Cemetery. I'll catch up with you then."

"Thanks, Claire. I appreciate your friendship and support."

With that, Julie hung up, smiling from ear to ear. Joe had just walked into the living room, finished for the day. When she told him about the phone call, he pulled her into his arms and hung on for dear life. This is what she'd been waiting for. To be a success after all that tragedy.

He hoped that the current problems were behind them and she could move on to greater things. Julie called her grandmother and told her the news. She also called her attorney, Jane Swanson, in Miami. She was a friend of Dan Simmons in Albany and had done a remarkable job with Tillie's home and with Julie's first professional writing contract with the New York City publisher.

Julie called her agent as well. After dinner, she pulled out her first contract. It was for one year only, as recommended by Jane, and the publisher had the English hardcover, paperback, and eBook rights. They could negotiate the audio if necessary.

The good news was that, thanks to Jane Swanson, Julie owned the foreign language and television and movie rights for the first and all subsequent books.

Both she and Joe thought they'd turned the corner in their relationship, now that they were engaged. They were looking forward to their wedding day, maybe in two places, and each had a new and exciting career for the future. They promised each other that they'd never let anything ever come between them, regardless of where they were in their lives.

Julie asked Joe to come with her to the meeting at Hollywood Studios and she asked Jane Swanson to be there as well. Jane was thrilled for her and said she wouldn't miss it. Julie called Mr. Tillman back and got a few dates. She'd clear it with her school, but it couldn't be on any Saturday that had a cross-country meet scheduled. That was a given.

It looked like everything was starting to fall into place, for the first time in a long time. The wedding would be the culmination of everything Julie wanted. She loved Joe and he loved her. That should carry the day.

"Joe, you forgot to tell me about the pizza boxes," she said suddenly.

The End

About the Author

Daniel J. Barrett was born in Rutland, Vermont and has lived his entire life in Troy, New York, ten miles north of Albany. He is a graduate of both Siena College in Loudonville, N.Y. with a BS in Finance, and from Rensselaer Polytechnic Institute in Troy, N.Y, with an MBA in Management. He has had a varied career, first as a commercial banker, then as the chief accountant and manager of financial and strategic planning for a large division of a major international corporation. He has extensive international experience, traveling worldwide.

Barrett has also served as the first executive director for economic development for a county in New York State, and as the first lay director for a Catholic shrine in Massachusetts. For the last twenty years, he has served as a financial, strategic planning, and educational consultant to corporations, non-profit organizations, colleges and universities, and government agencies.

Currently, he serves as a grant writing and development and strategic planning consultant for a major non-profit organization in the Capital Region of New York State. Barrett continues to live in Troy and has been married to his wife, Sandy, for 45 years. They have three children, Sean, Eileen, and Ryan, and four grandchildren, Shannon, Caden, Megan, and Declan.

An avid reader, and inspired by numerous authors, Barrett has read over 1,600 books in the last six years in preparation to write his first novel, *Conch Town Girl*. He continues to work, as a consultant, serving those most at risk in the Capital Region, and is now working on his fifth novel.

www.ingramcontent.com/pod-product-compliance
Lightning Source LLC
Chambersburg PA
CBHW071642260626
47170CB00001B/205